It's una...
Susan Grant's book

YOUR PLANET OR MINE?

"One of the best books of the year!"
—*New York Times* bestselling author
MaryJanice Davidson

"I absolutely love this book.
It is heartwarming and funny."
—*ParaNormal Romance Reviews*

"Wow! This book just has everything and I found
myself laughing out loud sometimes. [Susan Grant
has] a real gift for comedy at the right time."
—Lindsay McKenna,
USA TODAY bestselling author of *Unforgiven*

"A cute, quirky otherworldly romance
that's totally delightful to read."
—*Fresh Fiction*

"It's been a long time since I've read a story as
charming.... This multi-award-winning author has
incorporated military savvy, imaginative, action-
packed storylines, and great dashes of sly humour
into all her stories.... Do yourself a favour and pick
up a copy of *Your Planet or Mine?*—it's a keeper."
—*BookLoons*

"I love Susan Grant's books and this one was simply
incredible. I loved the characters, the story and the
whole premise behind this fabulous book!"
—*The Best Reviews*

SUSAN GRANT

My Favorite
EARTHLING

HQN™

ISBN-13: 978-0-373-77192-9
ISBN-10:   0-373-77192-4

MY FAVORITE EARTHLING

To Carolyn Curtice, aka "mommie." Here's to plastic trash bag dresses, the Go-Gos and Danish fighter pilots. May the next twenty-five years of friendship be as wonderful as the first.

My Favorite
EARTHLING

PROLOGUE

CALIFORNIA POLITICIAN AND ALIEN LOVER SAVE THE WORLD

Reuters—one hour ago

WASHINGTON, D.C. (Reuters)—After spending much of the night in emergency meetings, a visibly emotional President Laurel Ramos announced that the alien invasion force threatening Earth has been turned away. "Today we have two new heroes—California State Senator Jana Jasper and her extraordinary extraterrestrial friend, Cavin of Far Star. It is not an exaggeration to say that the two of them have saved the world. I hereby rescind the state of emergency and declare this day a national holiday. Senator Jasper, Major Far Star, today we celebrate your courage and vision as one world newly united by a common cause. A very grateful world indeed."

Over the weekend, Jasper, thirty-two, and Far Star, thirty-four (est.) were taken by officials to an undisclosed location in the western United States, where the pair were successful in deterring the invasion. Because of possible monitoring of Earth communications by the aliens, full details on the operation will not be revealed. At the news, celebrations broke out all over the world.

The tale of terror and daring had a romantic beginning. Jasper, the youngest child of U.S. congressman John Jasper and former Soviet ballet dancer Larisa Porizkova, met Far Star in the late 1980s when they were children. Far Star's father, a scientist, traveled to Earth to determine its suitability for alien habitation, a fact not known by Far Star at the time. Sources close to the couple say that after landing in the invisible spacecraft on the Jasper family ranch, young Far Star sneaked away to explore on his own and encountered the girl. "It was love at first sight," enthuses Evie Holloway, thirty-five, Jasper's sister.

Despite the brevity of their initial meeting and the passage of over two decades, the pair never forgot each other. According to sources close to the couple, Far Star abandoned his post as a high-ranking military Coalition officer to warn Jasper that plans were underway for an invasion of Earth. Despite several attempts on his life by an interstellar assassin, now presumed dead, and the almost-fatal destruction of the computers implanted in his body caused by the attacks, Far Star has apparently triumphed, Jasper at his side.

"I wouldn't get your hopes too high," the popular senator warned officials after leaving the remote location where she and Far Star are said to have battled the alien fleet. "It was a delay tactic, not a permanent fix. It buys us time to prepare and that's all."

"These Coalition forces are coming back, no doubt about that," advised Jared Jasper, thirty-six, the senator's brother. "And whether we like it or not, all of us

will be on the front lines when they do."
The Sacramento real-estate developer and
national guard fighter pilot assisted in
turning back the alien invasion, although
details on his role in the operation were not
available due to security concerns.

A press conference is scheduled for later
today at Mercy Hospital in Sacramento,
where legendary Jasper patriarch and
former California governor Jake Jasper
was rushed early this morning after suffering a massive stroke.

CHAPTER ONE

Meanwhile, on a planet far, far away...

THE NEWLY INSTALLED minister of Coalition intelligence listened in astonishment as an unexpected visitor vented his spleen.

"Far Star must be terminated!"

The minister couldn't quite get over the coldness in his superior's eyes. *You look as if you could do the job with your own two hands.* He made a fist in his lap behind his desk where no one could spy the symptom of his nervousness—or his grogginess. He'd been summoned straight out of bed and a deep sleep, made necessary after a hastily arranged meeting regarding a shocking encounter with a small, isolated world known only as Earth had kept him up far too late. "Far Star? As in Prime-major Far Star?"

"Yes, that one!"

The minister couldn't remember the officer ever causing any trouble. In fact, quite the opposite. Far Star seemed an affable sort, young and handsome. Intelligent, with a bright future. But his superior had been in the government since before he was born. Who was the minister to question that experience?

You ought to be standing, he realized suddenly, and started to get up. He'd been the minister of Coalition intelligence for all of a week, not long enough to get over being a little starstruck dealing so personally with palace leaders—Supreme Commander Neppal, Supreme-second Fair Cirrus, Prime Minister Rissallen and the eunuch Tibor Frix, captain of the Palace Guard—although he'd not yet met the queen, thank the gods.

At the thought of Queen Keira, the minister winced. Other men might like gorgeous, spoiled, willful, wildly unpredictable women. He did not.

"Be seated," his superior commanded. "Please. I'm here off the record."

Indeed. There was nothing lawful about an in-house assassination.

"The order was put in three Septumdays ago!

Receipt was confirmed by one of your REEFs—
the very best, I was promised. Yet we've heard
nothing, and now Far Star is missing. I had the late
minister insert a code in the kill order giving the
REEF a time limit to track down and kill Far Star.
One week! The time is past. What happened?"

Barbaric, the minister thought. He knew it was
possible to rig an assassin to self-destruct but
had never heard of it being done. Though with a
crime this heinous, one wouldn't want tracks
leading back to the source, would they? Better to
kill the killer and eliminate any messy evidence.
"I'll see if I can contact the REEF." He swiveled
his chair to access his computer. His communication would be delivered directly to a computer
implanted in the individual assassin's brain,
giving a level of security unmatched by other
means. After several tries under intense scrutiny,
there was no answer. As a last-ditch effort, the
minister pinged the REEF's ship. Nothing.

"I am unable to contact him. Since the REEF
hasn't reported back within the prescribed time
limit, I'm afraid he's likely suffered a total
breakdown of his internal computer systems."

"Gods be damned. He's dead?"

"Or a vegetable."

"Hire me another one!" His superior slammed a hand down on the desk, scattering the most recent panicked communiqué from the fleet commander fleeing planet Earth's unexpected wrath. *That is the true threat here, this new and powerful world, not Far Star.* Yes, the minister needed to devote his attention to galactic matters, but at home trouble was brewing, kill orders were flying, and despite being the supposed overseer of intelligence, he knew nothing.

There was something innately humbling about being kept in the dark. But he summoned patience. "I'll find you a new REEF, though you'd better give him a longer rope, because we don't know where Far Star is." Probably lying dead somewhere with the broken REEF nearby. "Meanwhile, as a safeguard, I will leave the viewer on the original REEF's ship set to automatic two-way. The moment he powers up his ship, his image will be displayed on-screen in my office. Then we will have our answer."

"No. Set it to appear on my personal screen, and only my screen."

"As you wish."

The minister's comm device chimed and he unfurled it and laid it on the desk so that his superior could also see who was calling. The individual wore a hooded cloak covering his or her face. "I understand there is a problem, Minister." It was a man—a young man by the sound of it. The voice was regally modulated with an accent that sounded familiar, but not familiar enough that the minister could place it. "Is it true? Far Star lives?"

"Far Star is *missing,*" the minister said. Again, he thought: *I should be concentrating on the humiliating rout on Earth, not this.*

"You sound distressed, Minister."

"Besides the fact that you have chosen not to identify yourself, I cannot understand this sudden interest in Far Star. He is missing. Gone. Vanished without a trace. Isn't that satisfactory?"

"Alive, he remains a major security risk," his superior explained. "It is why we must locate him. He disappeared before the news was formally announced, but Prime-major Far Star has been chosen to be consort to the queen. This marriage must not take place."

"Far Star? Royal consort? Good gods. The poor bastard. Years ago, I heard a rumor that the queen killed a man who tried to take her by force by hacking off his male parts with a plasma sword."

"Almost killed."

"So it is true, then."

"After she sliced off his bullocks, she decided that killing him would be an act of mercy. He lives on at the palace as a eunuch—and as a reminder for those suitors who would attempt to take liberties with the queen."

The minister winced. Perhaps Far Star's termination would not be so terrible, after all. Like euthanizing a sick dog to save it from further misery. "I would think, however, a military man like Far Star would make an ideal consort. With martial arts and weapons training, at least he'd stand a chance at defending himself against her."

"A military man would make an excellent consort indeed. The *right* military man." The man on-screen threw back his hood. "Me."

Good gods. "You're…you're…" If Queen Keira were to marry this…this boy, this *creature*, how would the Coalition survive? *These conspirators don't mean for the Coalition to survive.* "I will not be part of this!"

"You've already done your part, Minister.

Thanks to your help, the queen and I will enjoy a long and productive marriage."

Something hard pressed coldly against the back of the minister's skull. While he'd been focused on the comm, his superior had rounded the desk. Reflected in a crystal souvenir of the minister's last assignment on New Darva was the image of a gun being held to his head.

Of course, you fool. You know too much to be left alive. Briefly, he wondered what had happened to his predecessor. The woman's death had been ruled a tragic accident, but now he wondered. Perhaps, after issuing the original kill order, she, too, had known too much. Or perhaps the previous minister had been more courageous and refused to do as these men asked.

Does it matter what path you chose? The final result will be the same.

The minister stared at his desktop and waited for the burst of light that would end his life. It was a plasma gun: a merciful choice in weapons. The end would be quick and clean. Everything the demise of the Coalition *wouldn't be* if the circumstances of the queen's upcoming nuptials were any hint.

But if the monarch knew of the conspiracy, perhaps the result would be different. It was worth a try. With his heart thundering in his ears, the minister brushed a fingertip over the data-input port on his command center, secretly linking the automatic two-way visual to the queen's private chambers. If the REEF ever checked in, it would be with the queen. With any hope, and it was a tiny one indeed, she'd learn the assassin's purpose—and the treachery behind it.

And if not, despite the confidence of her hopeful groom, Queen Keira would not go down without a fight. The image of the petulant goddess's likely reaction to his marriage proposal was so satisfying in the minister's mind that when the fatal shot was fired in the beautifully appointed office, he died with a smile on his face.

CHAPTER TWO

Back on earth

TALK ABOUT A MORNING AFTER, Jared Jasper thought as he shoved on a pair of mirrored Oakley sunglasses. He felt as if he'd been run over by a truck. An eighteen-wheeler. Fully loaded.

His aching head and dry mouth weren't from a hangover. The single bottle of beer he'd sucked down twelve hours earlier had metabolized out of his system so long ago that he barely remembered drinking it. It was post-saving-the-world syndrome, he decided, reaching for a little elusive humor to carry him through the day. Saving the world wasn't for the weak, especially when it was followed by losing a grandfather whose passing would leave a gaping hole in his life. Not to mention having to make an appearance in front of a cheering crowd of thousands outside the hospital an hour later. After losing a loved one, you craved privacy; it was only human. But his family didn't enjoy the kind of privacy others did. The Jaspers were a political dynasty. Senators, congressmen, governors, both at the national and state level, they were called California's "First Family."

But no fund-raiser or election victory party had ever come close to matching yesterday's spontaneous celebration in front of the hospital, a celebration Jared would love to have shared, but he knew too much. He knew the aliens were coming back. He knew they were so territorially ravenous that they combed the stars scooping up habitable worlds like pieces in a chess game so they could stay one up on their opponent, the Drakken Horde, overseen by an aging Darth Vaderish warlord named Lord-General Rakkuu.

Yeah, he'd have celebrated if he didn't know the Coalition considered what they did *acquisition,* not *invasion,* even though it meant removing the entire native population and shipping them somewhere else. Not anywhere the good real estate was located, Jared was sure.

He made a sound of contempt in his throat as

he pulled on a sweatshirt and prepared to leave the family ranch where everyone else was still sleeping. Give him half a chance and he'd teach the Coalition a thing or two about acquisitions and hostile takeovers. They wouldn't like it. He guaranteed that.

Problem was it wasn't up to him—or guys like him. He considered himself more of a scrappy mediator than an eloquent boardroom negotiator. When it came to politics, too many people in his family did it better. Or at least they enjoyed it, which was more than he could say about his feelings on the subject.

The elder Jaspers hadn't tried to stop him when he'd decided to pursue dual careers in commercial real estate and military flying. His grandfather, while accepting of his choice, had been somewhat disappointed, but soon he'd had Jana to groom, whose success had brought the old man immeasurable pleasure up until the day he died. But in Grandpa's view, *every* Jasper was a public servant, politico or no. "Our duty to others comes before our own interests and ambition," he'd say, and had drilled it into each one of them since birth.

Jared was no stranger to duty—his national

guard career testified to that; he just wasn't cut out for the "sacrifice your life for the greater good" thing. He'd fight in the trenches to the bitter end, but he wasn't going to lead the charge.

The sun was barely up as he grabbed the keys to his Bronco and walked outside. The threat of alien invasion seemed to hang over the world like summer smog in the L.A. basin. He made up his mind to stick with his routine: Starbucks then the gym. After working out, he'd head to the office, although his eerily efficient staff would probably ask why he'd bothered.

How would he answer the question? That he was restless? Sleep-deprived? That somehow his view of life, his future, had shifted, and what used to feel comfortable about his existence now felt like a new pair of shoes that rubbed? He doubted he was the only one on Earth feeling this way, but his deeper involvement magnified the symptoms.

Jared sat in the idling truck, gripping the steering wheel as he watched the sun rise over the ranch-house roof. Everyone who mattered to him was inside that house. His parents, his sisters. And now Cavin. His family all maintained separate residences, but somehow they always gravitated back here, where they'd grown up.

Where all the good memories live.

As firstborn, the ranch would be his someday. He'd raise a family here, and his children would run through the fields and climb the trees, riding the old tire swing to splash landings in the year-round pond. Sure, he was a ways off from settling down, but it was comforting somehow, knowing that life waited for him.

Waited for him? Was he freaking hallucinating? An alien army was off somewhere, regrouping. Unless Earth figured out how to keep them away, extraterrestrials would be taking up residence at the ranch, not him. Not his family.

He jammed the idling Bronco into Drive and skidded around the arc of the gravel driveway. Before he could drive off, the front door opened and his younger sister burst outside. "Jared, wait!"

Dressed in tight brown yoga sweats with a little purse tucked under her arm, Evie trotted down the driveway in her flip-flops. "I'm on my way to Starbucks," he said.

"I was hoping you'd say that."

"Hop in."

A whiff of vanilla followed her into the seat.

Evie always smelled good. She smelled like home. "What a night," she said.

"Yeah. Couldn't sleep. You?"

"I popped an Ambien and slept like a baby. I've got more for later if you want one."

"A ten-mile run followed by a few shots of Johnnie Walker and a hot bath is more my kind of nightcap."

Her laughter made him smile. If Jana was the heart of the family, Evie was the warmth. The body heat, he sometimes told her, but that usually got him a dirty look because she took it as a comment on her weight problem, which in his mind wasn't a problem. Something was wrong with society if a woman sweated being a size fourteen. But lately she'd been hitting the gym for Pilates and yoga. It was the best sign yet that she was getting over divorcing the asshole who'd cheated on her. For a domestic goddess whose home was the heart of her existence, seeing it break up had to be rough. It didn't seem right that the world was now threatening to come unglued just as Evie was thinking about rejoining it.

She slid her window down and inhaled. Her thick, dark-brown hair blew around her shoulders. "Springtime, finally. Thinking it's too early for poppies?"

"Let's check it out." He pulled off the road and four-wheeled it through the meadow. Evie's shrieks of delight echoed in the morning calm as they flew over hills and plunged down gullies. He knew without talking about it that this was what they needed after suffering such a devastating family tragedy and nearly losing their youngest sister. But they'd always been a lot alike, he and Evie. Evie was even more disinterested in politics. While he'd gone to Stanford, Evie had suffered through two years at a junior college before realizing her lifelong dream of becoming a wife and mom. They might be Jaspers, but they wanted no part of the glory themselves.

The Bronco creaked as it bounced along over dirt and rocks. It was hell on his shocks, but in light of everything else, who cared? Evie pointed to a long ditch ahead. "That one," she cried. "Jump it."

She screamed as he goosed the gas. The Bronco soared over the first ridge and with a jolt came to an abrupt stop with the bumper digging into the mud. His hand flew out automatically to keep Evie from hurtling forward, though her seat belt had locked.

"Sorry about that." He hoped he hadn't bent the front end. "You okay?"

But Evie didn't answer. He followed her gaze to the right. Something large and heavy had dug a long scar in the ground. It went on straight as an arrow for about a half mile.

"The assassin's spaceship," she said. "That's where it crashed."

During the chaos of the past few days, no one had spared the time to look for the wreckage of the dead assassin's spaceship. Like Cavin's ship, it was invisible behind its protective cloaking. But here it was in the middle of acres of grassland, scrub and oaks, along with a convenient trail leading right to it.

Convenient enough that you crammed your front end into it, he thought, frowning, and put the Bronco in Reverse. The tires spun in the mud. He killed the engine before he dug in any deeper. "I don't f-ing believe this. We're stuck."

"So much for Starbucks," Evie said mournfully.

He got out and took a look at the rear tires. "I'll need a pull." There was another four-wheel drive parked in the garage back at the house. He flipped open his cell phone, saw the time and closed it. "It's not even seven.

Everyone's sleeping." He doubted Jana and Cavin had done a whole lot of sleeping last night, either. Whatever time they could steal together, they deserved. Cavin was the first man Jana had chosen that Jared trusted to make his sister happy.

"We've got a little time to kill." Jared sent a longing glance down the furrow to where the spacecraft would be if it were visible. "Come on. Let's take a closer look."

"What look? It's invisible. You can't see it."

"Not if we open the hatch and go in. You can see when you're inside."

"Jared, no."

"Aw, come on. Aren't you curious?" It reminded him of the times he and Evie had gotten in trouble as kids. They'd always been going where they weren't supposed to, giving and taking dares, playing with gusto. Jana was the serious one. Except for the night she'd met Cavin, she'd always behaved.

Supposedly the ship was pretty nice. A fighter. Cavin's ship, on the other hand, was a troop transporter and ugly. Jared started walking along the furrow. Evie followed. There was a bounce in her step now. Her hesitance to view the spaceship was crumbling. "But didn't Cavin say something about staying away?"

"That was when the REEF was alive. The risk's gone now. In fact, in the interest of national security, I say it's our citizen's duty to check it out."

"Trespass, you mean. I like the sound of that. I'll tell you what, Jared. The guy broke into my house, went through my things and scared my dog. I'd be happy to return the favor. This is the next best thing. Let's go see his ship."

While hunting for Cavin, the assassin had sneaked into Evie's house looking for evidence. Evie's house was holy ground—you didn't mess with it, you didn't criticize it and you definitely didn't invade it. The killer was probably lucky to be dead. If Evie got her hands on him, it wouldn't be pretty. Especially after learning her psychotic, girlie dog, Sadie, had been completely traumatized by the incident. Even staying at the ranch, surrounded by familiar people, the Chihuahua continued to tremble and growl at nothing. Well, tremble and growl more than usual.

Jared helped Evie climb over a toppled, shattered oak tree. Beyond, the gouge in the dirt ended. The grass was flattened in a vaguely triangular shape. "There she is," he said.

Jared and Evie walked forward, arms stretched out. It was like playing pin the tail on the donkey, except with eyes wide open and without the donkey.

His hands impacted something solid. *Bingo.* His pulse kicked into overdrive with a spurt of adrenaline. "Say hello to the Prince, baby."

"Say hello to the who?"

"The Prince."

His sister gave him a pitying look.

"It's my call sign. The Prince. I know what you're thinking, but every fighter pilot has one. It's part of the tradition. No one in the squadron calls anyone by their first name." He'd hated "the Prince" at first. He'd won the name because of his privileged upbringing, his family's celebrity. But over time, he'd made the name synonymous with shit-hot flying and unwavering professionalism. Now he wore it proudly.

"Okay, Prince. How do we get inside?"

"I have to find the hatch." He ran his hands over the cool, smooth hull. Cavin had shown him how to get inside his dormant ship. He assumed the same technique would work for this one. The fuselage was rippled here, dented there, but not as damaged as he'd expected. He bumped up against what felt like a wing and climbed onto the surface.

"Careful, Jared."

"Don't lose your nerve, girl. This was your idea."

"My idea? All I wanted to see were poppies."

Jared found the seam of the hatch just where he expected it to be, and the release. It opened smoothly. He swung his legs over the edge and dropped down.

The cockpit was snug and dark with room for only one person. But the craft had enough bells and whistles to make his little fighter-pilot heart roll over. As his eyes adjusted to the dark, more of the details became visible. Graceful, unfamiliar symbols labeled the smooth panels. An alien language.

God, you're beautiful. "Say hello to the Prince, baby," he murmured. "Say you're mine." He slid into the seat. It made a whirring noise and molded to his ass.

He jumped. "What the f—?"

"Jared!" Evie cried out from the open hatch.

"It's okay. The seat moved. I didn't expect it." He was damn embarrassed to notice that his pulse had doubled.

Enthralled, Jared took hold of the control stick as the ship continued to come alive. Lights came on, slowly, a clean, white glow. One by one, the panels of instrumentation powered up. In front of him, a large, rectangular screen with rounded edges glowed smoky-gray. In a blink of an eye, it became transparent and he was looking outside at the fields. "This is how they see where they're going," he explained.

"Don't be a spaceship hog, Jared. My turn."

"Not yet. Wait until it finishes powering up." They watched in wonder as the ship's systems unfurled. He'd give his right testicle for a chance at taking it up for a spin, to leave the stratosphere at Mach twenty…to view the curve of the Earth…to experience weightlessness for longer than the top side of a reverse loop… Hell, maybe he'd throw in his eyeteeth, too.

Suddenly, all went still. A silky female voice murmured something in a language he didn't understand.

"What did she say?"

"I don't know. It's the ship's computer, I think. Probably waiting for voice recognition." One light blinked on the left hand rest. It resembled the incoming message light on his laptop. It was too irresistible to ignore. He tapped his finger against the light and the screen turned white.

"Jared, what's happening?"

"I'm not sure." The forward screen was milky bright and rippled like smoke. A part of him wanted to beat feet out of the ship, but curiosity kept him rooted in place. He extended a hand. "The light...it's so beautiful," he joked.

"Not funny. This is freaky. Come out, Jared. Please. Call Cavin."

"Evie, check this out." The milky screen slowly cleared. It revealed a large room sumptuously decorated in warm, cozy colors. Soft, comfortable-looking furniture blended with what was obviously tech beyond anything they had on Earth: a small, round sphere resembling a volleyball floating along near the floor; an entire wall glowing with rippling colors. "A window into another world," he murmured.

Then voices from offscreen erupted, speaking in an alien tongue. His heartbeat kicked up a notch.

"Uh-oh. Jared."

"I know. I hear them."

The closer and louder the voices got, the more Jared hoped to God the screen wasn't two-way. If it was, they were busted.

CHAPTER THREE

IN HER GYMNASIUM DEEP within the largest palace in the galaxy, Keira, Queen of Sakka, swung her plasma sword at an imaginary opponent. Working through a series of choreographed moves designed to hone and strengthen the body and bring focus to the mind, her long, thick hair whipped around her shoulders with every slice of the heavy sword. To her left and right, massive columns soared to the ceiling, the space between them open to various chambers—a meeting room, her bathing hall, an entertainment alcove where she could take visitors and watch troubadours perform. She took little interest in the rest of the palace. This was her sanctuary and she'd had it decorated in every color opposite the reality outside the thick castle walls: a world of ice and towering glaciers; a land of white, ice-blue and steely gray, where it snowed almost all year round except for a fleeting summer.

Sometimes she wished she could wall herself off from the rest of the palace in much the same way.

The captain of the Palace Guard, the hulking eunuch Tibor Frix, stepped through the door. She'd known him almost her entire life. Not once had she ever seen him look anything other than as he did now: immaculate in a flawless uniform and gleaming boots. He snapped his fist over his chest and dipped his head in a bow. "The visitors have arrived, my queen."

"Send them in." Gripping the heavy plasma sword in two hands, Keira whirled on Prime Minister Rissallen and the individuals who had accompanied him: the commander of the Coalition army, several unhappy-looking officers and the highest ranking members of parliament. His usual cronies.

Tibor Frix stepped out of the way, his hooded eyes ever watchful as the prime minister stepped forward and crossed his arms at the wrist over his chest, bowing low.

Keira took a moment to catch her breath. "Rise."

"I'm afraid I have disturbing news, Your Highness."

"Do you really, Kellen?" Rissallen's lips twitched. He hated when she called him by his given name. She held her sword up to the cold winter light filtering through the skylight and admired the sparkle of tourmaline. Then she sliced the weapon through the air. It made a humming noise as it arced in a half circle. The green glow of plasma reflected in the men's nervous eyes. Simultaneously, they took a step back. All except Supreme Commander Neppal, who simply regarded her as if she were a useless figurehead.

Wasn't she? After all, these men came to her only under the most unusual circumstances— and never to ask her advice. They fed her the information as if worried they'd upset her, and had done so ever since she'd taken the throne as a child, thrust into the role after her entire family had died in a tragic accident.

But even though they often kept her ignorant of their silly facts, she frightened them, and she liked that. As long as she inspired fear, she maintained her power over them. If they ever lost their fear of her…

Don't think of that. You're strong, a warrior. Keira stabbed and parried an imaginary opponent, finishing with a vicious lunge at the supreme commander's heart.

Neppal didn't even flinch. She moved forward until the pointed tip of the blade made a hissing sound as it pressed ever so lightly into the officer's gaudy, beribboned uniform. Pinned over his heart were medals and commendations that he'd probably earned but, regardless, his condescending attitude irritated her.

Her mouth tipped in a smirk as she withdrew the blade and noticed the fleck of charred fabric around the tiny tear. *That is for thinking you are better than me, you arrogant bastard.* But she said coquettishly, "Oh! I must be more careful. You'll be visiting your tailor later, won't you?" She dusted a hand over the officer's broad chest. "I'm sure it can be repaired."

Dark brows lowered over angry eyes but Neppal knew better than to stare her down. A second later he turned his eyes to the floor. *Good boy.*

"Taye!" Keira snapped her fingers to summon her favorite attendant. The slender, baby-faced eunuch took the sword and replaced it with a scented towel, which she used to blot perspiration from her face. It had been a brutal workout. Her skin gleamed, her muscles trembled. She'd worked her body to the limit, and gods, it felt good. She wanted nothing less than total control over her body, and so she pushed it, sculpting it, emulating the warrior queens of the distant past. A time when being a queen had meant something more than being a gorgeous creature bred to produce princes and princesses.

An heir factory—that was what she was to them. A breeder. All because she was the last of her line, and they wanted more. If it wasn't a sin, the Coalition would have cloned the holy Sakkaran bloodlines by now to be done with her. Her pedigree was probably the only reason she was still alive. As the last surviving member of her family, the Coalition needed her—needed her because her ancestors were gods to trillions of religious citizens and no one wanted to risk taking that away and destabilizing the Coalition, especially when the murderous Drakken Horde was breathing down their necks.

But that was what generals were for. It was their job to play war games with ships and guns, not hers.

Keira tossed the towel over her shoulder. Taye rushed to retrieve it. The men followed her through an arched doorway to an expansive polished-crystal table. Sheets of gold trapped inside the crystal reminded her of autumn leaves kicked up in the wind. Fall was a short season on this world, like every other season that wasn't winter. In fact, she'd missed autumn completely this year. First there had been summer, then fall had sped by before she'd next had a chance to step outdoors.

Now it was too frigid to venture past the palace doors. The cold of this world had long ago seeped into her heart. Maybe it was why she cared less and less about venturing outside. Or perhaps having to be accompanied everywhere by Tibor Frix and his merry band of eunuch guards had taken the enjoyment out of it. They were present at all times, except when she had to relieve herself, and only then because she'd protested.

She was the last of her line. What did she expect?

Her smart-chair floated away from the table and folded around her comfortably when she sat in it. The officials waited until she was seated before they did so. *Goddesses first.* "Sit, gentlemen, please."

She threw a longing glance at the door to her private chambers. Steam floated out of the room as the attendants prepared her post-workout bath. She should be soaking in cloud-bell scented water, not putting up with these insufferable men who wanted to talk about the most boring subjects imaginable.

"Your Highness, the news we bring you today is troubling," Neppal said, dragging her glare away from the irksome prime minister. The supreme commander was the leader of the entire army with an ego to match. Good thing it was never proposed that she take Neppal as her mate. What a disaster that would have been. "There is a new and serious threat to the Coalition. I have confirmed reports of an encounter between a planetary acquisition force and a rogue planet at the edge of civilized space. The intelligence minister, in fact, was working on this when he met his tragic fate. The world is known as Earth, and they appear to maintain a substantial battle fleet. We cannot as yet determine the types of vessels, nor their technological level, but we have teams working on it."

Tibor Frix interrupted. "Is the palace at risk?" The sharpness in his tone caught Keira's attention. He rarely spoke up, but his eyes were focused like lasers on the commander.

"Absolutely not. Their fleet formed a defensive barrier, preventing the acquisition force from landing, but made no move to attack. We are still the larger power by far, but they are respectable in their own right. That we didn't know about them before is the issue that disturbs me. Where do their loyalties lie? This we must determine."

"But they're nothing but a frontier world," Keira exclaimed. "Country bumpkins. Yet you act as if they have the ability to swing the balance of power in the galaxy."

"They could." The warning in the commander's dark eyes made her shiver. "*If* they were to align themselves with the Drakken."

Keira went very still. She refused to admit to fear—she'd rather die than do so—but the mere thought of Lord-General Rakkuu bringing his army to the palace gates stabbed fear deep into her heart. Not only would he want to conquer her Coalition worlds, he would want to conquer *her*. He was growing old, but he had a son nearing adulthood, she'd heard. It was said the boy would likely grow up to be worse than his sire.

"No more talk of the Horde," she commanded. "Earth will join us. You will find a way to make it so."

"I've called an emergency session of parliament," said Rissallen. "In light of this threat to our national security, it would reflect well if you attended."

"Attend…" He wanted her to go into that chamber? Keira fought a wave of dizziness. The thought of the cavernous room, the noise of many voices… *Her head spinning in confusion, the grief choking her, the fear.* She could not. It would be all too reminiscent of when she'd been summoned before a full session of parliament the day she'd learned of her family's fate. She'd felt so small, so frightened. Helpless. She'd never again set foot in those chambers.

She tossed her hair and sniffed in disdain. "I have no patience for politics. Send me a summary." Which she'd have Tibor summarize even further, while her attendants gave her a post-bath massage or painted her toenails. Every government communiqué was condensed by Tibor. He was invaluable. Without him she might actually have to pay attention to what was going on. "You are dismissed."

The visitors bowed low, mumbling the usual respects, and left.

Only Tibor remained behind, silent, ever watchful. "What?" she demanded when he continued to ponder her. She couldn't tell if there was censure in his scrutiny or pity. If he didn't agree with her aversion to politics, so be it. She wasn't going to change for anybody. She had her reasons for doing things, and they were private. She had no desire to share her inner thoughts with anyone, especially a man.

She shoved away from the table and stood, sending the chair spinning. It collided with a display shelf and sent a priceless vase crashing to the ground. What did it matter? Everything was priceless around here. They'd find another trinket in the museums. Unlike people, objects could always be replaced. "Taye," she yelled.

The boyish eunuch scurried forward. "How may I serve, my queen?"

"Bring me my daggers."

The eunuch returned with a set of ancient throwing knives. She snatched the box and stormed into her private chambers. The only way she could ease her apprehension about the rogue planet was to work with weaponry.

A breath exited her tightened mouth as she hurled a dagger at a padded wall. She selected another. The knife went hissing through the air. It landed in the same spot as the first, shattering the ivory hilt. Another replaceable object, she thought, hefting the next dagger.

Keira kept burying daggers in the wall until she'd exhausted her supply—and herself. Muscles trembling, she raised her arm to throw the last knife when the communication screen taking up half of an adjacent wall grabbed her attention.

The screen was illuminated, signaling an incoming visual.

Damn politicians. What more could they possibly want to bore her with? Furious at the annoyance, the invasion of privacy, she whirled on the screen. "Display message!" The visual came to life.

She stormed forward. "I thought I made it clear that I'm not interested in—"

The sight of the gorgeous man slouched in the cockpit of a fighter craft brought her up short. Their shocked eye contact was instant and intense, and for one dizzying moment, the room around her faded away, the sounds becoming muffled. In those few beats of her heart, she didn't know what to say or think.

Swiftly, the trespasser's shock slipped into curiosity and a dark, amused flicker of male appreciation, which made her acutely aware of how formfitting her workout wear was when damp. In his gaze, she felt naked, a sensation that was unexpectedly, breathlessly and infuriatingly arousing. "How dare you?"

How dare he *what?* She didn't have any idea, but she felt utterly…invaded. *By the gods.* "Identify yourself immediately!"

Keira gripped the dagger and strode forward to confront the trespasser, intending to make her displeasure perfectly clear.

CHAPTER FOUR

WHOA, BABY. Jared sat up straighter in the pilot's seat as he stared at the striking alien woman on-screen. Heavy, dark and long, her hair whipped like Medusa's snakes around her shoulders and breasts as she turned to face him.

Shouting something, the woman shoved a hand through her wild mane of hair. A thick, intricately jeweled band glittered on her upper arm. This was no shopping-mall purchase. The workmanship was exquisite and matched the earring dangling from her left ear. The chick was buff, sculpted muscles flexing. She wore a black jumpsuit so formfitting it looked painted on. Jutting nipples pushed up against the fabric by one unforgettable pair of breasts as her chest literally heaved.

So much for any doubts as to the two-way feature of the ship's TV. She could see him, no doubt about that. Her eyes had opened wide at the sight of him, her mouth forming a luscious circle of surprise.

The moment hung in freeze-frame. He didn't move. He had the wildest impression of having startled a rare and beautiful mythical being like a mermaid or fairy: a few seconds of intense eye contact before she escaped forever.

"Jared," Evie whispered. "Put your eyeballs back in your head."

He lifted a finger to his lips. He didn't want to scare the woman away.

The alien woman must have taken his gesture as if he were telling *her* to be quiet. Wielding a knife, she stormed the screen. So much for thoughts of a fairy or mermaid; she looked more like an avenging warrior princess off the pages of a manga comic book.

"Uh-oh," Evie said. "Now she's pissed."

"Actually, a little more than pissed. Given half a chance, she'd probably cut out my heart and eat it for dinner."

This is the face of your enemy.

And mine is the face of hers, he thought. Against his better judgment—and Evie's—he stayed put.

The woman stopped inches from the screen to finish telling him off, but he couldn't understand a word she said. "What we need is a little closed-captioning." Lights blinked on the armrests. "Maybe one of these is a translator."

"What if it starts the engines? What if it makes it fly?"

"Don't panic. The tech may be a lot more advanced than what we have, but some things stay the same. Controls on a seat are usually for convenience or comfort items."

He tapped them one by one, figuring he'd keep trying until he found one that translated. It was worth a shot. Cavin had a translator implanted in his brain for two-way language understanding, so likely there was something similar in the cockpit. Down the bank of lights he went. "Talk to me, baby. Talk to me…"

The alien warrior-chick reared back, startled. A spark of fear in her eyes disappeared almost as quickly as it showed up. "Earthling," she spat.

"You got that right."

"Trespasser. Barbarian!"

Jared coughed out a laugh. "There's only one barbarian around here, and it's not me. Look at you. We stopped dressing like that a thousand years ago. Daggers are pretty much passé, too. So, is this a retro fashion trend, or are all of you Coalition types this primitive?"

"Jared, you're going to start a war," Evie hissed.

"We're already in a war," he whispered back. "I'm just adding a little fear and awe."

"I will see you brought to me in chains, Earthling!" the alien chick yelled to him.

"I haven't had an offer that exciting in a while. Do I get to see you in chains, too?"

The woman's mouth dipped in a sneer as she looked him over from head to boots. Stripped naked, he doubted he would have felt more exposed to her scrutiny. "I'd rather cough up blood."

"Nice."

"Jared," Evie warned. "Don't make me come down there and get you."

"I've got to go," he told the alien woman. "But I'd like to chat more sometime. I have to admit, the chains thing really got my imagination going."

The woman's mouth tightened. She had very expressive eyes, Jared noted. In them, it was very easy to see every detail of his excruciating death should she get her hands on him. But that

would never happen because he'd fight to the
death to keep her people from taking over his
world. Even if every Coalition woman was as
hot as she was.

"Jared?" Evie interrupted. "You're doing it
again."

"Doing what?" he whispered back.

"Staring at each other." Evie's face was
centered in the open hatch above, framed by
blue sky. Her hair swung just above his head.

"I'm not staring at her. I'm contemplating
her contemplating my death."

"Who are you talking to?" Warrior-chick
demanded.

"My staff. And some members of my harem."

Evie made a sound that was strangely close
to the one Warrior-chick made.

"Who are you?" the woman asked.

"You don't know?"

"Careful, Jared."

I know what I'm doing, he told Evie with a
frown.

He leaned forward. "You can call me the
Prince."

"Oh, jeez," Evie muttered. "I can't listen to
this anymore."

"You are *a prince?*" Warrior-chick's chin came up as she asked the question, her nostrils pinching.

"I'm *the* Prince. And my message to you is this—if your people come back for another try at landing on Earth, we'll be waiting. A billion more guys like me, waiting." Trash talk. But sometimes the most effective weapons were psychological. "Mess with Earth and your defeat will become your reality. Got that? Now, have a nice day, baby," he said and powered down the ship.

Jared pushed free of the pilot seat's glove-tight hold. He pulled himself out the hatch and slammed it closed behind him. "What the hell just happened?" He rubbed a tired hand over his face. "I need a shave."

"What just happened? I don't know, Jared, you tell me." Evie dropped down next to him on the fighter craft's invisible wing. Side by side, they sat, legs dangling. "Who are you? Because whoever you were in that cockpit, I didn't recognize him."

"It's not someone you'd know unless you flew on my wing in an F-16. It's how I deal with the stress of combat. It's how most of the guys do, I think. Maybe it's why we have the call signs, to differentiate who we are inside the cockpit from who we are outside of it. An alter ego. But when I leave the unit, he stays behind. Ol' Prince is not exactly family friendly."

"He's a jerk."

"But he's perfect for dealing with uppity Coalition bitches." Jared shifted his focus to the closed hatch. He couldn't believe the argument had actually turned him on. "What a woman, huh? Totally not my type, but…wow." He thought of her hair whipping around her shoulders, pictured her naked, that long hair stuck to her damp skin, letting tantalizing peeks of her breasts and stomach show through. Her skin would be damp from having sex with him, not from pumping iron. Or maybe they'd do it after they worked out…and before…and…

"Jared."

Evie's voice jolted him out of a fantasy of the alien woman bent over a table, her lush breasts in his hands as he thrust into her. By now he had such a hard-on that he hunched over, grateful he was wearing thick sweats. What the hell was wrong with him? He wasn't in high school anymore. "Say again?" he said with a trace of hoarseness in his voice.

Evie's dark eyes sparkled. "Chemistry. I said it was amazing that you can feel it across light years of space."

"Chemistry?" He choked out a laugh. "I have a few ideas on what to call it, but it's not that."

"Denial."

"Sanity."

"Jared, you're so unromantic."

"She's the enemy."

"So? Woo her over to the dark side. Use the force."

He pulled out his cell phone to call Cavin and brief him on what they'd discovered. "Force or no force, Miss Sunshine lives in a galaxy far, far away. And after our little conversation today, I'm doubly determined to keep it that way."

KEIRA WAS STILL SHAKING as she addressed the leaders she'd summoned from their ridiculous emergency meeting. *This was* the emergency! "The prince of Earth insulted me. Challenged me. Me—the queen!"

She'd bathed and changed into an exquisite bright-yellow ceremonial gown. It constricted her ribs to the point where she couldn't inhale fully, which contributed to her swimming head. But it helped constrain her temper, as well. "He's a frontiersman, a barbarian, and yet he broke every level of security we have, forcing his image onto my personal view screen." Searing it into her mind.

Gods, he'd affected her, and in more ways than she cared to admit. She'd thought herself immune to sexy, good-looking, arrogant, supremely confident men and their charms. Particularly those well beneath her social standing.

"How could you let this happen? He taunted me. Your monarch. Your *goddess.* I'm humiliated and disgusted. I'm…I'm furious!"

Light-headed, she gripped her rustling skirts in shaking hands. The fabric blotted her sweaty palms, effectively hiding the roiling fear she tried so hard to suppress and hide. *You are strong. A warrior.* "I want an explanation, and I want it now, or I'll have every last one of you fools executed."

"We have put the entire planet on full alert," the new minister of intelligence, Ismae Vemekk, offered. "No craft can get in or out."

Keira glared at the unfamiliar woman with

contempt. What were they doing, alternating boy-girl-boy-girl as they replaced intelligence ministers? Spicing it up for variety? Usually the cronies stayed on in their posts for life. "Who cares about spacecraft when an Earthling can invade my privacy and taunt me at his convenience? Isn't a physical invasion the next step?"

"Earth does not have the power to invade the heart of the Coalition," Neppal said.

"How do we know this? You yourself said that if they align with the Drakken…" She couldn't finish the thought. "How are we to make an impression on Earth when they so easily make fools of us? Damn you, Neppal. Where were your troops when that signal came in? I was alone. Alone!"

Alone…

A memory ripped through her mind in dark, violent snatches. The smell of her mother's skin. The sound of her fear-filled voice. They were on a ship and something had happened to it. Her mother stuffed Keira in a dark pipe barely large enough to fit her. *Stay here, Keira. Do not move. Do you understand me? No matter what you hear, do not come out.* And, oh, what Keira had heard. Awful things. Unforgettable things.

Keira realized she'd brought her flattened hand to her chest to quell her thumping heart. Ashamed, she made a fist. "If I cannot be safe in my own home, then where can I be safe?" She detected a slight thickening in her voice and cleared her throat. They mustn't see her fear, they mustn't. She picked up a wineglass Taye had filled with snowberry liqueur, knowing that it calmed her. In one gulp, she emptied it and was about to slam the glass on the table when something more satisfying came to mind. Sneering, she hurled the glass at the supreme commander. Years of training with weapons had given her dead-on accuracy.

The officer blocked the glass with his arms, fists pressed together. The heavy goblet crashed to the floor and shattered. "The next one will hit the target, I swear it," she hissed, glowering at Neppal.

Carefully, the prime minister broke in once more. "Perhaps we can see the offending visual ourselves?"

She actually felt a quickening of her heartbeat at the prospect of watching the recording again. Was the prince as proactive and forceful in the other, more personal areas of his life? He'd mentioned a harem. An image of him making love to several women threatened to take her breath away—one: because she didn't like the thought of other women touching him, and two: no man should look that good naked. Trying to act as coolly as possible, she sashayed to her throne and sat on it with a whoosh of yellow skirts. "Show visual," she commanded from the enormous, bejeweled chair to the leaders gathered in a half circle around the huge screen.

The recorded image was stopped and brought back to the beginning. Every one of the palace leaders present focused on the display—and the Earthling prince. It grew very quiet in the chamber. All were sizing up the man, seeing if concern was justified, and if so, to what level.

Keira sat rigidly, her hands clasped demurely on her lap, until she noticed her fingers digging into her flesh and slipped her hands under her thighs.

The Earthling's voice filtered through the translator. His surprise slid into interest, male interest, when he first laid eyes upon her. *He finds you attractive.*

It took everything she had not to let his appraisal of her matter.

"How dare you?" Keira stiffened at the indignation and shock in her recorded voice. And the anger—anger at herself. That was new. Usually she was angry at other people. Another reason to despise the Earthling prince.

"Trespasser. Barbarian!"

He laughed at her then, called *her* the barbarian. How dare he treat her with such disrespect?

On-screen, the Earthling prince leaned forward, his mouth formed in that half smile that so unsettled her. She couldn't be further from naked, dressed to her chin in the layered and laced traditional gown, but every time the man's eyes swept over her, she felt exposed. She shivered as she always did when hit with a sense of vulnerability, but this time the trembling was different. Quite…different.

She imagined his muscled body sweaty and naked as he struggled to free himself from the cuffs with which she'd bind him. He'd be hers, all hers, and at her mercy. She imagined tasting his skin, touching him wherever she pleased. "By the gods and goddesses," she whispered.

Keira closed her eyes and prayed to get through this session with her dignity intact. Sometimes, it felt as if her dignity was all she had. In the frightening, lonely days after losing her family, dignity had served well as a protective wall, one as high and as wide as those surrounding this palace.

She fought to keep that wall around her now, listening to the prince rage, "My message to you is this—if your people come back for another try at landing on Earth, we'll be waiting. A billion more guys like me, waiting."

The visual ended soon after. Everyone was briefly silent. No one questioned her rage now. They appeared to be as shocked as she was.

The new minister of intelligence was the first of the leaders to find her voice. "I am deeply sorry at the distress this invasion caused you, Your Highness. I do not know why the transmission appeared on your screen, bypassing all our security. You have my word we will work ceaselessly on this until we have an answer."

Keira nodded her thanks yet regarded the tall woman with pity. If the fates of her predecessors were any indication, Ismae Vemekk's life span would not be noted for its longevity.

Supreme-second Fair Cirrus frowned, rubbing his knuckles across his chin. "Indeed, this proves Earth's cleverness. That cleverness could very well lead them to be reluctant choosing sides in a war they know little about."

The age-old war with the Drakken.

"There is one way to avoid uncertainty as to their loyalties," Rissallen said. "A fail-safe way."

"Nothing is fail-safe," Neppal barked.

"This is nearly so. A treaty to take precedence over all treaties." The prime minister's mouth slid into a winning smile, revealing perfect, if a little large, teeth. Rissallen could be so oily. What did he have up his sleeve this time? That they simply cut off the power to her visual communications screen? That they eavesdrop on all her private conversations from now on?

Keira slammed her hands onto the armrests of her throne. The jewels on her fingers clattered against the jeweled precious metal on the armrests. "I'll have you know, Kellen, that I will not be coddled, or talked down from my concerns."

But the leaders seemed not to hear her. "I wonder," Fair Cirrus said to Rissallen, "is the prince unmarried?"

Rissallen waved at the blank screen. "He did not have a wrist tattoo indicating he was married."

"Earth tradition may differ."

"Nor did I see any such jewelry that could possibly signify his marital status."

"He mentioned a harem," Fair Cirrus noted.

Keira bounced her gaze from man to man. She expected them to be counting Earth's warships, not counting the prince's wives.

"That's not unusual for a man of power, no matter what his marriage status," Neppal said. "If single, he'd maintain a harem for sport and for variety. If married, he'd certainly be entitled to additional females to ease the boredom."

Keira snorted. "The only one bored in your bed, Commander, is the woman you take to it."

Finally, Neppal met her gaze. A hint of malice glinted in his eyes. "I do not like the idea of bringing in an outsider to be the queen's consort, but the more I ponder it, the better it sounds," he told the group.

"Consort?" she croaked.

Rissallen dipped in a small bow. "A treaty of marriage would put all our fears to rest. It would link Earth to the Coalition. Permanently."

"At least until death do they part," Neppal said smugly.

"Gods," Vemekk said. "Tell me you're not considering mating them."

Mating? Her and the Earthling prince? Keira gave a little squeak. By now, her pulse was making a strange whooshing noise in her ears. "I thought plans were being made for my betrothal to a high-ranking military officer." Not Neppal, but someone as easily dismissed. "Where is he? Why have I not met him yet?"

The group shuffled their feet and cleared their throats. "Prime-major Far Star is missing," several admitted at once.

"What happened? Did he run away? Was he too terrified to marry me? Did he hear rumors of my skill with a sword?" Of course, they weren't rumors, but they served her well as a man deterrent.

Rissallen smiled. "We simply don't know, my queen. But he is old news now. Now we have a new and better man for you to consider."

The Earthling prince, she thought, struggling to breathe in the constricting dress. Although she wouldn't truly be allowed to consider him, would she? They'd pretend to include her in the process but ultimately, they'd make the decisions as they always did, as they had ever since she'd taken the throne as a child-queen, a frightened little girl lost in a sea of what she didn't understand.

You're still that girl. Wasn't she supposed to hold absolute and holy power? Some goddess she was. She had no free will, no control over her destiny, no *choices*. Not since childhood had she ventured off this world or mingled with the people who worshipped her daily in their temples. She was a prisoner in this castle, born and bred to breed, and nothing more. She'd never really matter, not the way she longed to matter.

Keira strode to the huge window that looked out onto a glacial landscape, which held about as much warmth as her blood did in that moment. Her breath formed mist on the glass, obscuring the dramatic views. "I wish it were summer," she whispered, dragging a finger through the circle of vapor. For those few fleeting weeks out of the year she felt alive. She spent the glorious weeks outside and especially the nights that never grew dark. Sometimes, she even evaded the guards, if only for a few moments.

Her mood darkened. She'd evade her future husband, too. And as often as possible. Once he'd planted a baby in her belly, there was no further need to be with him.

What if he didn't agree to the treaty of marriage?

Of course, he would. For him, it would be a huge step up. She was a goddess. The blood of Sakkara flowed in her veins. She could trace her ancestors back to the beginning of recorded time. Her family was revered as gods by trillions of Coalition citizens and billions more undocumented believers who lived across the border in Drakken space. *She* was the goddess they worshipped.

A goddess who felt very human most of the time.

She heard a throat being cleared, and the shuffling of feet as the leaders waited for her to turn around. They would make the decision for her if she didn't, citing reasons of national security. She might as well hold on to as much control as she could. She took a breath, her hands fisted at her sides. Then, with dignity holding her smoldering rage in check, she turned around and squared her shoulders. Her ornate dress rustled. "It must be done. For the sake of my people, I will take the Earthling as my royal consort." She wasn't very convincing at altruism but nonetheless, she tried. Luckily, no one snickered.

Unlike the others, who seemed relieved,

Vemekk and Neppal continued to act unhappy: the minister quite shocked and dismayed, and the supreme commander simply angry. Keira could explain the commander's reaction away as sullenness over not having had the chance to go to battle against Earth with his army, but the minister's reaction was more puzzling.

"Find out the prince's status," Keira said. "And if he is free—" her hands opened and closed, itching to throw daggers "—strike a deal with Earth. Tell them they may offer their prince as the price for peace and the opportunity to keep their planet."

Rissallen slapped his hands together in delight. "Together the Coalition and Earth will present a united front to the Drakken Horde."

As for *her* united front with the Earthling, it need not exist. He'd be given a life of comfort and riches in the galaxy's most luxurious palace. All he ever needed to sate his appetites would be available to him, so he need not look to her for all his satisfaction. And if he were to persist, well, her skill with a plasma sword was legendary.

JARED AND EVIE WERE MET by Cavin and Jana as they pulled up to the crash site. Cavin hopped out of the car and walked around the front to meet them. His step was as brisk as ever, as if the past few days hadn't happened, as if he hadn't been treated for extensive injuries only the day before, cleaned and stitched up before accepting a few Advil to swallow. He'd refused anything stronger, said it might interfere with what few nanomeds he had left—microscopic computers that remained in his bloodstream to assist in healing. The guy, for lack of a better word, was a stud.

"I'll cut to the chase," Jared told them. "We went inside the spacecraft."

Cavin didn't seem fazed. "You are one step ahead of me. I intended to do the same today— and take you with me. I wondered about the condition, whether or not we can power it up."

"Trust me. It powers up just fine."

Cavin lifted a brow. "To be honest, I'm impressed that you figured out how," he admitted with no trace of condescension. "After all, your only experience was manning my transport—an inferior vessel."

"As much as I'd like to take the credit, I can't. I sat in the pilot's seat and the ship powered up on its own. Then the visual came on, also on its own. At first it was an image of the field, then it changed to a room."

"Not an Earth room," Evie said. "It was beautiful, too." High praise from the Domestic Goddess.

Cavin walked around to the back of the Jeep. He opened the trunk and lifted out a toolbox. "The screen must come out and be stored in a more secure location. We might need the technology at a later date."

Yeah, like for when the aliens return. "But, it's our window across the galaxy," Jared said. It didn't seem right, ripping it out by the roots and hiding it in a closet.

Jana threw him a funny look. "A window across the galaxy? Since when did you turn into a poet?"

"Ever since he met her," Evie said.

"Met who?" Cavin asked, a screwdriver dangling from his hand.

Everyone was staring at him. Jared lifted his hands. "A woman walked in front of the screen and saw me."

"She saw you? Are you sure?"

"Oh, very sure."

"He's sure," Evie chimed in. "I'm sure."

Cavin shoved a hand through his hair. "My worry had been using the ship with the REEF alive. It seems we didn't take into account his being directly linked to home."

"Look, buddy, I'm sorry. I screwed up." Jared felt like crap. "I was curious, and since the REEF was dead, I didn't see the harm in it."

"It isn't your fault. You didn't know the screen was set to automatic two-way communication. None of us did. I thank the gods it was you they saw, and not me." Cavin sounded brusque. Just because the REEF was dead didn't mean the hunt for him was over. It had to be disturbing not knowing who'd wanted him dead—or why. "Give me a description of the woman."

Jared did his best to comply without using the terms *hot, bodacious* or *babe.* "She had brown eyes. And long, brown hair." He tried not to remember how wild it had looked falling over her shoulders. Tried not to picture her naked. "She was in great shape, borderline weight lifter but not bulked up, just tight." He cleared his throat and tried to stay on track. "She had a black bodysuit on. It was skintight, almost paramilitary-looking. And she seemed pretty well experienced with weapons—at least the daggers she threw around while she screamed at me. If we hadn't had God-knows-how-many light years between us, I have a feeling I'd be wearing one right here." He pounded a fist over his heart.

"Hmm," Cavin said. "My guess is that she's a REEF."

"A robot? You're f-ing kidding me." A machine had turned him on. What did that say about him?

"REEFs are human, but with bio-implants to enhance physical performance."

He'd thought the alien woman had resembled a manga warrior princess. It seemed he wasn't too far off.

"Was anything specific discussed?"

"Ah…" A little sheepish, Jared rubbed his chin. Like slamming down a few beers with his fighter buddies and getting a little too rowdy, trash talk always seemed appropriate at the moment but a little embarrassing the next day. "I told her to tell her people to keep their greedy little paws off Earth. More or less."

"It was more," Evie said. Jared threw her a dirty look.

"Do you think she was working with the REEF who followed you here?" Jana asked Cavin.

"Likely, yes. Unfortunately, the one person who could give us this answer is dead." Cavin opened the hatch to the fighter and dropped down inside. He studiously avoided sitting in the pilot's seat. Jared joined him, hanging over the lip of the hatch and passing tools back and forth. The ship remained dark as he went to work unfastening the screen from the rest of the instrument panel. He couldn't risk the two-way screen revealing that he was alive, and on Earth. Finally it was free. Carefully, they lifted it out of the cockpit. It was surprisingly light. They carried it to the car's trunk and loaded it inside. "The viewer is still operational, so you won't lose your window into another world," he added with a wink.

"How? Where's the On switch?"

Cavin passed his fingertips over a small rectangle that looked like a checkerboard. "All it requires is a touch. Another reason to keep it in a secured location until we're ready to use it."

"The president's going to want to know about this," Jana said. "And just about every other government agency. Up until now, we haven't had an effective way to communicate with the Coalition. Now we have something that's reliable and portable. Jared, your accidental discovery may just end up being our ace in the hole."

Jana's cell phone rang. She read the number and her face paled. "Oh, God."

Jared's immediate fear was that someone in the family was hurt or sick, but every one of them was here at the ranch.

"It's Connick," Jana said and took the call.

Thomas Connick had been the liaison between the mysterious Gatekeeper and Jana and Cavin. When Cavin had come to Earth, it had been with a plan as simple as it was brilliant: using the legendary Roswell flying saucer to project false images of spacecraft out into space. In the biggest ruse since the Trojan horse, Earth would come off looking like an interstellar superpower, and the Coalition Army would be tripping over themselves in their rush to make a galactic U-turn. Problem was, at first no one had wanted to own up to the little ship's existence.

Only with the end of world as they knew it staring them in the face had they allowed the secret guardian of the craft, a woman known only as "the Gatekeeper," to let Cavin hack into the ship. It was anyone's guess who Colonel Connick worked for, or even if he was a colonel, but he'd met Cavin and Jana in the desert, leading them to an even more remote location from where they'd hiked it on foot to the farmhouse housing the Roswell saucer. Jared had figured they wouldn't hear from Connick again, or at least not until the aliens returned for Invasion, Round Two. If he was calling, it was important. Had the Coalition figured out they'd been duped?

Jana put the phone on speaker. "Go ahead, Colonel."

"The REEF," he began. "We found him. And he's alive."

CHAPTER FIVE

REEF ASSASSINS NEVER gave up. Battlefield
legend claimed that not even death ended a
REEF's desire to kill. Cavin had heard the
stories many times during his career as a Coalition officer. Once, there was a REEF whose
bloodied and broken human body continued to
slither after its target *after death,* its inner com-
ponents still whirring as they dragged the muti-
lated body toward the intended kill.

This REEF demonstrated the same single-
minded determination. Unfortunately, his aim
was to terminate himself. So far, an induced coma
was the only way to keep him from doing it.

Lucky for him, the Gatekeeper and the
Handyman were assigned suicide watch. For
more than half a century, the older couple had
been the guardians of the "Roswell saucer," the
little scout ship Cavin had used to turn away the

Coalition fleet. Now they'd become the guardians of the only other living extraterrestrial. Surely they'd do just as good of a job keeping the REEF safe and sound.

"He's in here, Major Far Star. Hush now." The Gatekeeper led Cavin into the bedroom where the REEF slept. A mass of curly red hair overwhelmed her small body. She wore an apron tied around a floral dress. Flawless skin disguised the fact she was in her sixties in Earth years. But her delicate appearance was deceiving. She was a covert government agent with license to kill anyone who threatened her ability to protect her secret hidden in the basement below the house—and now the one slumbering in a guest bedroom with a gaily patterned quilt pulled up to his chin.

Not how I ever imagined seeing the REEF, Cavin thought.

Sunshine brightened the room. From the kitchen down the hall in the simple farmhouse, the smell of baking perfumed the air. The atmosphere lent a cheery mood that the REEF had no intention of sharing—if the man's expression was any indication.

Cavin raised a brow and the older woman

stirred. "Has he been frowning like that the entire time?"

Nodding, she sighed. "When he hasn't been gritting his teeth in pain, the poor thing."

Cavin took a seat next to the bed. "I need for you to rouse him."

Tubing ran from a bottle suspended on a stick to the assassin's arm, transporting a clear liquid into his bloodstream: nutrients and perhaps medication. For Earthlings it was advanced technology. To anyone else, the items were relics of a far more primitive time.

The Gatekeeper adjusted one of the drips. Cavin got comfortable and waited for his former archenemy to come to.

The REEF groaned and swiped his knuckles across his chin. Cavin guessed pain in the assassin's raised hand drew his focus to his forearm, where he tracked a long scar running from the heel of his palm to his inner elbow. Shock flashed in eyes that Jana once described as blue ice. "My computer," he rasped. "The command center for my entire system... The blasted Earthlings have disabled it!"

"It feels strange, I know. I'm not quite used to it myself."

The REEF swerved his gaze to Cavin. He seemed to have trouble focusing, and at one point, Cavin thought he might pass out again. But he held on, growling, "Far Star..."

"We couldn't stop the seizures. If we hadn't disconnected the computer, you'd have died. At least you still have your hardware. Mine's gone." Cavin pulled up his sleeve, revealing his scarred forearm. While the REEF's scar was thin and neat, his was jagged and lumpy. "Taken out with a pocket knife in the desert with no anesthetic."

The REEF gave a disdainful sniff. "Anesthetic."

Cavin guessed the man's thoughts: REEFs were tough, unlike Coalition officers. "Jana did the surgery." He worked at hiding a smile. "Consider yourself lucky I didn't send her in to do yours."

A bulge in the assassin's cheek told Cavin he was using his tongue to feel for the self-destruct device once buried in his molar.

"It's gone," Cavin said.

"Terminate me, then. You do it. I'm finished."

"Quite the opposite. You're just starting. You have a chance at a new life. Whether you ultimately decide you want this life is up to you, but it will be offered nonetheless."

For a long moment the assassin gazed at him, as if searching for trickery. For spite. "Why are you being kind to me? You have every reason not to be."

"It's selfish, really. I need you healthy and alive to answer my questions."

"Ask fast, because I plan to shut down my systems—permanently."

"I'm afraid you're too human for that now."

The REEF wasn't too weak to shoot him another glare. "If I could kill you, Far Star, I would."

The REEF tried to sit up but he grunted in pain. His eyes rolled back in his head, his body going rigid.

"Seizure!" Cavin shouted, but the Gatekeeper and the Handyman were already there. A mouth guard was thrust between the REEF's teeth to keep him from injuring his tongue. The Handyman used his strength to hold the assassin's still-powerful body in place until the convulsions finally passed.

Once more, he was unconscious. "He needs to sleep," the Gatekeeper warned sharply.

"I must learn what he knows first." Cavin had to find out who the woman was who'd argued with Jared. "The fate of your entire planet depends on it."

The Gatekeeper's small, pink mouth stretched into an unhappy line, but she did as Cavin asked. This time it took more meds to awaken the REEF. When he finally regained consciousness, he opened his eyes for only a moment before squeezing them shut. "Still here...damn it."

"Yes, I'm still here. I need to ask—"

"I meant me, Far Star. With each seizure, I expect to die. Luck isn't on my side, it seems."

Cavin begged to differ, but he knew that if he didn't ask his questions soon, he might forever lose the chance. Complicated as it was to explain, he told the REEF his reason for coming to Earth. "Either they didn't want me marrying Queen Keira or they didn't want the queen marrying at all. It doesn't matter which. Both point to turmoil in the Coalition. I aim to exploit that turmoil to save Earth."

"I can't help you. I don't know the identity of the conspirators. The order came via the Ministry of Intelligence, inserted anonymously into my internal command center."

"Yesterday Jared Jasper and I powered up your ship."

The REEF's eyes opened wide. He focused on Cavin with some obvious difficulty. "But that viewer was programmed for automatic two-way!"

"We found that out," Cavin said dryly.

Now they'll know I failed. Cavin saw the thought as clear as day in the REEF's eyes before he shut them in defeat. The assassin knew he'd forever lost his chance to return home. A REEF who bungled such an important mission would be terminated, even if sabotage was the cause of it.

"A woman appeared on the screen," Cavin continued. "Not the minister of intelligence—the description I was given doesn't fit her, or any other females in high positions in the government—but she was strong, very fit, with long, brown hair and possibly brown eyes. She wielded one or more daggers and acted extremely agitated. She lost her temper not once but several times. Does that resemble any REEFs you know?"

"No. None would be that undisciplined."

"It remains a puzzle, then." Cavin let out a disappointed sigh. "I want to know who she is."

"As do I, Far Star. She very well could be the one who ordered my demise."

The Gatekeeper's hand came to rest on

Cavin's shoulder. "You must let him rest," she said. "I don't know how many more seizures he can suffer before…"

"As many as it takes," the assassin whispered hoarsely in English.

The Gatekeeper pursed her lips, her eyes shining. "No more of that. When you leave here, it's going to be out that front door on your way to a new life."

But not before Cavin and Jana took steps to protect the REEF from certain secretive elements in Earth's government. A chance to open up REEF's body and study his bio-engineering would be a temptation they couldn't resist. Luckily, Cavin had already come up with the perfect hiding place: with Jana's sister, Evie, and her children in a place called suburbia.

THREE DAYS LATER, in the middle of a private gathering of close friends and family back at the Jasper ranch, Jana's beeper went off. She silenced it without looking at it. Dabbing her eyes with a tissue, she leaned into Cavin's embrace, listening as person after person used the microphone to share remembrances in celebration of Jake Jasper's life.

The actual funeral had been a state event. Once again, the Jaspers were on display when they would have rather paid their respects in private. But Jake Jasper had been so well loved, to keep him from his adoring public, even in death, would have been unthinkably selfish.

Jared sipped a scotch and soda as he offered up his shoulder as a mop for Evie's tears. He didn't mind. Comforting her kept him from getting choked up from the sound of the women in his family weeping. He was okay on his own or in the company of men, but put him around the crying women and he was done for.

A moment after Jana's beeper sounded, Cavin's went off. He briefly met Jared's questioning gaze before discreetly slipping the pager from his suit pocket to take a look at the caller. Jana and Cavin's beepers were high-tech twins designed to keep the two most important people to Earth's future tethered to world leaders. But they'd barely gotten here and already someone was checking in?

That was no way to live. Jana and Cavin had been airlifted in by an unmarked chopper only an hour before the gathering had begun, and tomorrow they'd return to the top-secret location in Nevada where they were nursing the badly injured ex-assassin back to health. Supposedly, the guy was on suicide watch. Everyone in the family had mixed feelings about that. Evie, quite frankly, wanted the dude dead, and even more vehemently than ever. Jared, on the other hand, hoped the guy lived long enough to give a hint as to the identity of the woman who'd appeared on-screen in his ship. Unfortunately, what little they were able to get out of the REEF left them no closer to finding out than they had been before. You'd think people would remember a gorgeous, half-naked, crazy woman wielding deadly weapons, but no.

The infamous two-way screen had been shipped to Nevada, where the ex-assassin was recovering, and also the location of the Roswell saucer. A bummer, because Jared would have liked to see her one last time. Maybe then he'd be able to stop thinking about her.

Okay, the alien babe was smokin' hot, but why was she still stuck in his head? He disagreed with Evie that it was chemistry, but it was definitely something.

Whatever Cavin saw on the caller ID was enough to take Jana by the hand and lead her from the room.

"Be right back," Jared told Evie and followed.

He found them in the hallway. Their voices sounded urgent as they did some kind of three-way calling thing on their cells.

Jana hung up first. She stared at the phone in her hand, then into Jared's questioning eyes. Her voice was barely audible. "I'm telling you what's going on because you've been involved from the beginning, but don't tell anyone else."

"No one," Cavin warned.

Jared answered with a curt nod. "It's them, isn't it? They're back."

"Yes." Jana sounded positively ill. "I thought we'd have more notice. I thought we'd have more time."

"Squee…" Cavin squeezed her shoulder as he murmured the nickname he used with such affection. Jana gazed at him with an expression that seemed almost too poignant and too private for Jared to view. "They aren't here yet. They merely contacted the International Space Station."

"Holy…" Jared imagined what chaos had erupted on the space station. The astronauts must have pissed in their pants.

"Why the space station?"

"Our massive battle fleet was off-line," Cavin

said with a pained expression. He rubbed his forehead and continued. "Apparently they have a message to relay to us, and that was the only place they could reach."

"We don't know what was said," Jana added. "We're flying back so Cavin can translate what came in. Tell Mom and Dad we had to go. Don't say why."

"Don't worry. I won't." The last thing they needed was panic among the guests. It'd spread like wildfire through the city and then around the world. There would be plenty of time for panic later.

Jana startled her big brother by throwing herself into his arms. He held her close, his face buried in her blond waves. *Take care of her,* he told Cavin with his eyes.

Cavin nodded solemnly. All too soon he'd taken Jana and hurried out the front door. A helicopter floated down to the ground in a cloud of spring blossoms and dust as the couple sprinted to the chopper. Numb, Jared watched them lift off, watched until they'd disappeared into the clear blue sky.

A message… The aliens had come with a message. What kind of message?

Did it matter? It had to be better than showing up with a bunch of ships with big guns. Surely this was a good sign. Holding that thought close, he returned to the house to explain away Jana and Cavin's sudden departure.

KEIRA STRODE ACROSS her private chambers with a portable viewer held in front of her face. A miniature image of the prime minister informed her, "The messenger has arrived at Earth, my queen. But we could not find their fleet to deliver our message."

"It was not delivered?" A confusing mix of relief and sharp disappointment swept through her.

"On the contrary. But in the absence of the fleet, we had no choice but to leave the message with a small, manned satellite-type object. An archaic vehicle. Clearly, they are in possession of a type of stealth technology we do not have, to hide their entire space force like that. It makes them an even more valuable ally."

"Ugh! Do not bore me with the details. I do not expect to hear from you again until the deal is ready to be sealed."

"As you wish, Your Highness."

Then she would speak to the Earth prince once more, where they would agree to the treaty joining their worlds. She rolled up the thin screen and slipped it back in the pocket of her robes. "Taye, gather the precious oils and ready the massage table." Her workout had not quite eliminated the trembling deep in her belly. Perhaps a long, relaxing massage would.

Keira threw off her silken robes as she glided across the room. Tibor stood at attention, his sword at the ready. A flutter of silk landed on his polished boots as she breezed by. The cool air washed over her naked body. Her breasts bounced freely as she glanced over her shoulder. Tibor's expression hadn't changed. She knew she looked alluring, but he was not even remotely interested. Walking in front of him naked was like being naked in front of a woman. No sexual attraction. She was amazed that such a large, well-muscled man was a eunuch, but perhaps his male parts hadn't been removed until he was well past puberty. When they were removed in boyhood, the result was a very feminine man, like Taye and the others who served her. No intact males were allowed in her presence, save the leaders, and they were always under close watch by her guards, namely Tibor. Pregnancy wasn't the problem—there were technically flawless methods to take care of that. *They don't want you falling in love.* That was it, she knew. No falling in love with an unsuitable man.

Is not the Earthling prince unsuitable?

Somewhat, yes. He was from the frontier. A backwoodsman. An arrogant, ignorant ass. Warmth spread into her lower belly at the thought of his eyes, the way he'd swept that hot gaze over her body.... Even now, with the event held in her imagination, she felt her breasts tingle, felt her body growing aroused. Only in her imagination had she ever felt such desire. In real life, it was always so boring! She'd been with men a few times, suitors all; she'd let them touch her, explore her, just out of curiosity. The one man who'd dared to force himself on her before she'd been willing or ready was now a eunuch. And not by choice. Fortunately for him, the cauterizing effects of a plasma sword had kept him from bleeding to death. She knew rumors had spread far and wide after the incident, but he had deserved it. One did not rape the queen. Not a suitor. And not, she vowed, a husband.

She sashayed to the long table where Taye waited patiently. His small, delicate hands produced the most delicious massages. She stretched out on the table on her belly, sighing in anticipation as she did so. The scent of the oils filled her nose as he kneaded away the tightness from her body.

She entertained herself with sensual fantasies of the Earthling prince chained in her bedchamber, until she found herself pushing her hips against the table. Until she'd grown so wet inside she gritted her teeth.

If she rolled onto her back, Taye would continue his massage to more intimate areas if she asked. She knew royals had used their servants in such ways in the past—the Sakkaran line was noted for its sensuality and powerful sexual drive. The blood of the gods and goddesses ran hot. Taye had been trained in ways to please her, and no doubt the leaders assumed she used her staff in such ways. But the thought of losing control at their asexual hands was so repugnant, she'd never done so, and never would.

"Go now," she ordered the eunuch in a hoarse voice.

"As you wish."

As you wish, as you wish. She was sick of hearing as you wish! No one actually cared what she really wished!

She pushed off the table and grabbed her robes, throwing them around her.

"My queen."

"What, Tibor?"

"The minister of intelligence, Ismae Vemekk, begs a moment of your time."

"Now? For what?"

"It is a private matter, she says."

"Private matter." Keira snorted. "Well, she is the holder of state secrets. Let her in."

Briskly, the woman entered the room. "Thank you for agreeing to see me. It is a matter most urgent." She lowered her voice. "And of utmost discretion."

"Have they not told you of my distaste for politics and policy, Minister? If after the first few words that exit your mouth, I am bored, you—"

She moved closer and whispered in her ear. "You do not have to marry him. The Earthling prince. I can help you avoid having to do so."

Keira jerked back. "What?" Shocked, she sought out Tibor's eyes, hoping to find some guidance there. Some clarification. But, oddly, his gaze was downcast.

"I know you find him distasteful. He is a barbarian. Beneath you. Unschooled in our ways."

"I don't want to marry him, trust me."

"I can help you. My position allows me access to methods known not even by Supreme Commander Neppal."

Keira's brow pulled down in a frown. Or perhaps it was just because the woman had mentioned Neppal by name.

This official was offering her a choice. When had she ever had a choice in the major events of her life? Her mind began to race with possibilities. *You wouldn't have to do this. You do not have to make a choice driven by your fear of the Drakken.*

Tentatively, Keira said, "It has been agreed that this treaty will go forward. Their prince as the price. Our peace as the reward."

"I see you have made up your mind. I will say no more on the matter. Just know you can trust me. You can call me anytime. Ah, you are a brave woman, Your Majesty. I can see the Sakkaran blood flows powerfully in you."

Keira thought of herself as a lot of things.

Brave was not one of them. Not that she'd ever admit to it. She acknowledged the woman's remark with a nod.

"However…" Vemekk dropped her voice to a whisper. "If during the course of the marriage you change your mind, I will help you escape him. Even if you feel you need to get away for a short time. This I offer to you, woman to woman."

Keira was at a loss as to how to react to the woman's compassion. She'd offered more than policy, more than advice. She'd offered friendship. It was something Keira sorely lacked. The queen did not have friends. The queen was above friendship. Tibor was the closest she had to a friend, but his relationship to her was more fatherly protector rather than confidant. Not certain how to react, Keira answered with a stiff nod. "I will remember your offer." Deep down, a small, warm spot of relief blossomed. If she needed an escape, she had one.

The woman bowed deeply and stepped back. Then she hurried from the room. Tibor followed to escort her to the door.

Keira stared after them. The woman's concern only heightened hers. If the Earthling prince thought he could be forceful with her, treating her as barbarians treated their mates, he had a surprise in store. She'd spent a lifetime doing things she didn't want to do. It would not be that way in her marriage.

CHAPTER SIX

NO NEWS HAD TO BE GOOD NEWS, Jared thought in the back of his mind as his basketball game wrapped up. He'd made a vow to keep to normalcy, even though it was killing him to know what the message from the aliens had said.

He exchanged high fives and ribbed a few friends on the opposing team as he grabbed a towel off the bench. They'd won by twelve points. Not too shabby. Ready for a shower, he walked off the court, limping a bit. His right knee was swelling, the result of a snowboard wipeout the year before. He'd ice it in the locker room before heading out. It was just one more mundane detail anchoring him to his normal life.

The rest of the world was carrying on, as well—aside from the usual wackos screaming that the end was upon them all. Jared hadn't done enough of anything lately that would require him to repent. But it was Friday, the night was young and he was single. Maybe a little sin was in the forecast. Hell, he deserved it. After ending things with Gina, no one had caught his eye. Except for Warrior Woman. Jeez. No matter where he and the guys went out for drinks tonight, he wasn't going to find any smokin' hot alien babes.

A hand landed on his back as he pulled open his locker and grabbed his shower bag. "Beers, sushi," Troy told him. "Mikuni's."

"Rog." When they flew together in the guard unit, Troy was Paco and Bob was Gilligan. With the unfortunate name of Bob Denver, there'd never been any doubt as to what he'd be called. It didn't help that he actually looked like the character from *Gilligan's Island.* The pilots were the only ones in the squadron who lived close enough to be part of Jared's local social life. Troy was divorced and always up for action on a weekend—snowboarding in winter and waterskiing in summer. Bob was married with kids, but he usually joined them for a few after-game drinks before heading home.

It was a good life, Jared thought out of the blue as he stood in the shower under the gushing water. Funny how it wasn't until you came within a hair's breadth of losing something good that you stopped to appreciate what you had: good friends, family, a comfortable place to live. He wouldn't change a thing about his life. He liked everything the way it was.

As he dressed, his mind wandered back to the mysterious message the aliens had sent to the space station. He couldn't help but worry. Was it a deadline? A threat? Or, he hoped, a treaty. But negotiation was Jana and Cavin's talent. He rested easier knowing it was in their hands.

Out in the parking lot, he tossed his gear in the back of the Bronco. "I'll drive," he told Paco and Gilligan.

"In your hot car," Paco joked, looking at the dinged up Bronco.

"Hey, so it's not your pretty Porsche." Like Paco's precious machine. "I'm damn glad, too. I like my cars like my women—friendly, un-complicated and easy to repair." In other words, not high maintenance. "I got new tires, though."

"Is that what those are under the dirt?"

"Dude, I drove all over Sutter Buttes today, checking property that's back on the market. There was a road only part of the time." He patted the Bronco before climbing in. "It's a working man's car."

His buddy snorted as he buckled up shotgun. Gilligan hopped in the back. Mikuni's was a typical Friday-night stop and it was only a few blocks away.

Jared pulled out of the parking lot. "You want a Porsche, Paco, we'll make it a Porsche." He cranked up the stereo and rolled down all the windows. The night was mild and the wind smelled fresh. He slipped in a Kanye West CD. In the next minute, the pounding bass poured out the windows.

Jared's laughter died in his throat when he saw a police car trailing him, lights flashing. He lowered the volume. "What's he want?"

Paco turned around as Jared pulled over. "What's the crime? Blowing off steam? Two white guys and a Mexican listening to hip-hop?"

Jared shook his head and he pulled his license and registration from his wallet. "The boys had better be quick, because there's an asahi and a sumo roll with my name on them."

The men who approached the car wore plain clothes. Watching them in the rearview mirror, Jared narrowed his eyes. They hadn't come out of the police car, but out of a dark, unmarked car that had slid in behind them while he'd been digging out his license. "Look at this," he said quietly. "Feds."

"What do you think they want?" Gilligan asked.

"I have no f-ing idea." Jared forced his annoyed frown into a smile as the first man stopped outside the open window. "What can I do for you, sir?"

The man wore a poker face and a black suit. His tie was the perennially unstylish kind favored by men who'd been in Washington too long. "Brad Sarto, DHS. How are you tonight, Mr. Jasper?" he asked, reading the license. Turning, he sent a brief nod to the other men, one of whom got back in the dark sedan.

DHS... That was the Department of Homeland Security. "How am I? I'm a little curious as to why you pulled me over."

"Can you step out of the car, Mr. Jasper?"

For the first time, his pulse picked up a notch. "Show me some ID first."

With the faintest hint of irritation, the iron-faced man handed over his identification. It looked legitimate enough. Sighing, Jared killed the engine and handed Paco his keys. "Hold on to these, will ya?"

"Yeah, no problem." His friend's face showed a mix of confusion, outrage and frustration. "You want me to call someone?" A cell phone was gripped in his hand.

"Let's see what they want first."

"Sir, please," Sarto persisted. "I need you out of the car."

With a major effort to keep his temper in check, Jared did as he asked. "What seems to be the problem—?"

Sarto linked his arm with his. "Come quietly. Don't make a scene. We're in a public place and we don't want to draw attention."

"Like hell we don't. You have no reason to arrest me."

"You are not being arrested."

"Could have fooled me."

"Sir, please."

Jared swallowed the rest of what he wanted to say. The relentless training he'd gotten from his parents during his upbringing to be polite to public officials and those in positions of authority was wearing thin, way thin. "Aren't you supposed to tell me what I'm under suspicion of doing? Isn't that how it works?"

Sarto hustled Jared to the idling, waiting car.

The man behind the wheel was a shadowy figure.

"Hey!" Jared dug in his heels. "This is America. You just don't abduct people off the—"

Something jammed into his kidney. It felt like a gun. The next thing he knew he was sliding along a smooth vinyl seat, face-first. He heard the sounds of a scuffle, shouts that told him Paco and Gilligan were fighting back. But the car skidded back onto the street and away from his friends' agitated shouts.

Someone grabbed Jared's collar and pulled him farther into the speeding car and he struggled to get up. The door behind him slammed shut now that his feet were no longer hanging out.

The car weaved, throwing him off balance every time he tried to get up. He did a pushup, and a hand pushed him back down. "Don't get up!" Sarto ordered.

Something cold pressed lengthwise across the back of his neck. A pipe? Gasping for air, he tried to figure out what Sarto was using to keep his head down. *It's a gun.*

Jared tried to get his wits about him. Carefully, he turned his head slightly to get more air. The sedan was speeding, and the wails of a police car told him whatever they were doing and wherever they were taking him had been sanctioned by the law.

The only thing he could think of to explain what was happening was that Jana and Cavin wanted him to babysit another spaceship. No one else was trained to do it. But what kind crazy deal was this? Abducting him off the streets at gunpoint? No, it didn't smack of anything his sister would approve of. And then why take Sarto's word he was DHS? He sure wasn't playing by the rules—any agency's rules. Likely, the guy was a covert operative. *You're in deep shit, Jasper.*

He could tell by the change in vibration that the sedan had pulled onto the freeway. The agent lifted the gun off the back of his neck. Jared sat up, rubbing his neck.

"Sir, you need to stay in the car."

"We're going eighty freaking miles an hour. Where do you think I'm going to go?"

The man's lips compressed. It was the first expression the man had made the entire night so far, and it wasn't much.

They were heading east on Highway 80, toward Reno, Nevada. "Okay, you're aliens and you're abducting me. But instead of using saucers, you use late-model sedans with tinted windows."

No answer.

"Okay, you're really from the IRS, not DHS, and you're suspicious about all those real-estate deductions I took last year. Got news for you— they were legit, every one."

No reply.

Jared dragged the back of his hand across his face. "So, where are we going? Or do I get to find out before we get there? Actually, if you're looking for a good place to dump my body, we just passed Folsom Lake. You'll need concrete, though. Otherwise I'll float."

"Please, Mr. Jasper. Remain calm."

"I am fucking calm!"

In the ensuing silence, Jared felt like an idiot. *Easy, bro. Stay cool.* He exhaled and sagged against the backseat. He had no choice but to hang on for the ride. No sooner had he formed the thought than the sedan pulled off the highway and onto a dirt road that wound through a mandarin-orange orchard.

He decided then he wasn't going down without a major fight. They were armed; he wasn't, but that didn't faze him. It wasn't ending this way, that he was sure of. He had a good life and he wasn't ready to give it up. He liked it too much here on Earth. The Pearly Gates could wait.

The sedan bumped along a dirt road. Jared watched, waiting, fully alert. There were small lights ahead. They seemed out of place in the dark orchard. As the car came closer, Jared made out the outline of the form. It was a private jet, an expensive, late-model Citation. It sat at the edge of a narrow, unlit runway. The engines were running.

This was too much. They stopped the car. Sarto hopped out. His gun was back in his holster. "After you, sir."

Jared got out of the car and patted his pockets. He didn't have his cell phone or his wallet; he'd forgotten them in the Bronco , never thinking he wasn't going to return anytime soon. He'd worked all day with clients on a development project. He was tired. His knee was aching, and his chin had vinyl-seat burn. He was hungry and he wanted that asahi, damn it. He wasn't the type of guy to complain, but, hell, after tonight, who wouldn't do a little whining?

At the jet, a pilot stood at the bottom of a

small, fold-down staircase. He was as poker-faced as Sarto—where did they find these people?—and he wore an air-force flight suit. So, his kidnapping was military-sanctioned, huh? Then Jared saw the guy had no name patch and no visible rank. Maybe not.

"Good evening, sir. If you would, please take seat 2B next to the vice president."

The who? Jared climbed up the couple of steps into the small, elegant cabin. The man in 2A smiled at him, extending his hand. "Jared Jasper. I'm Ed Greer. We're damn glad we found you right away."

Jared swallowed hard and shook his hand. "An honor, sir." The man needed no introduction. He was the vice president, all right. Vice President Greer of the United freaking States. "What the hell is going on, sir? Did something happen to my sister—Jana Jasper? *Senator* Jasper. Is Major Far Star okay? Or my father?"

"Everyone is fine, son," answered a new voice. Jared was so rattled and the cabin so dimly lit that he just then noticed a bald, buff guy sitting across the aisle. "And I must say, Mr. Jasper, it's an honor to meet *you*."

The man wore an army uniform with rows of

medals that seemed to stretch from his square chin all the way down to his shiny black dress shoes. Four gold stars shone on each shoulder. No. It couldn't be...

"Nathanial Brown, chairman of the Joint Chiefs of Staff." He popped a can of beer and handed it to Jared. "But you can call me Nate."

Numbly, Jared shook his hand. He was a lowly major in the air national guard. A weekend warrior. And the top military officer in the nation wanted to be on a first-name basis. Sure, benefits came from his family's celebrity, but this was too much.

He took the offered beer and plunged into a comfortable leather seat. He stared straight ahead, barely aware of the flight attendant—who, curiously, but somehow not surprisingly, resembled a martial-arts expert—and buckled his seat belt across his lap.

He didn't ask any more questions. He knew somehow they'd be ignored. The most important one—the welfare of his family and Cavin—had already been answered.

The sleek jet took off into the night sky. In disbelief, Jared closed his tired eyes. One thing was for certain: wherever his final destination was tonight, they hadn't skimped on the escorts.

"WHO THE HELL GAVE YOU authority to apprehend my brother? *Who?*"

Jana's voice carried from the other side of the closed door in a reasonably comfortable waiting room in a small, empty passenger terminal at a tiny, unmarked airport in the middle of nowhere. After escorting Jared here after landing, Sarto had disappeared. The flight attendant had come in sometime later with coffee and a vending machine doughnut. Real gourmet chow, Jared had thought sullenly and wolfed it down. When Jared had tried the door, it was locked. They didn't tell him where he was, but judging by the amount of hours they'd spent in the air, it was somewhere on the east coast, but not near a city he recognized—or near any city at all. Awaking from a bleary sleep at dawn, he'd seen nothing but emerald-green hills rolling by below.

"This is bullshit!" Jana yelled. "Total bullshit."

Jared didn't think he'd ever heard his sister that furious. The woman was a Girl Scout when it came to using bad language. *Dang* could make her blush. For her to cuss, well, it had to be ugly. He was glad he wasn't on the receiving end.

"If anything else is done without my or Major

Far Star's direct authorization, we're pulling up the stakes and leaving Earth to fend for itself, General. Go near my brother again without my knowing and you can save your own ass from the invasion!"

Ooh-ee. Jana, it seemed, could trash talk as well as he could. She'd never abandon the world, but the threat sure did sound convincing.

"Sure. Tell the president what I said. I don't care."

To the sound of mumbling voices and sincere apologies, the door burst open and Jana stormed inside the room. Her hair was spilling out of what had probably been at one time an upswept hairdo. Her mascara was smeared, and her suit was wrinkled. She looked as if she'd slept in her clothes. Scratch that. She looked as if she hadn't slept at all.

Cavin strode in on her heels. While he hadn't said a thing, he didn't need to; his angry eyes and tight jaw gave it all away.

"Hey, you two," Jared drawled. "Maybe you can help me out here. A couple of goons grabbed me off the street, threw me in a car, stuffed me in an airplane, and, voilà, here I am. What's going on? If you needed help babysitting a saucer sending out a few false signals, you shoulda said so—"

"Jared, I am so sorry," Jana said before he'd finished his sentence. "I was supposed to escort you, then we got sidetracked with some last-minute arranging—where to hold the meeting, the protocol involved—and the next thing I know, they went to find you. I guess they were terrified you'd go missing."

A few seconds ticked by. "And I'm suddenly Mr. Popular because…?"

"Because you're crucial to our survival. Our future. Jared, this is big. Really big. No one expected this, least of all Cavin or me." Jana crouched by his legs. "It's going to be a bit of a shock, I know. It was to us, trust me."

"Are you sure you have the right person? When I climbed out of Cavin's ship, my involvement with this mission ended."

"Not quite." She rubbed his hand as if not sure what to say next.

The woman was many things, but never speechless. The first real flickers of unease filtered through him. "What happened to that gift of gab?" he joked nervously.

When she lifted her eyes to his, they were

tear-filled. Jared tightened his abs. Whatever she was going to say couldn't be good. "This has something to do with that message the aliens delivered to the space station, doesn't it?" he asked.

"Yes. They offered us a treaty—a *peace* treaty."

Jared grinned. "This is great! Fantastic…" His excitement faded the minute he saw Jana's expression. If he wasn't mistaken, she looked guilty. "Aren't we supposed to be at least a little happy?"

Cavin stepped in. "The terms of the treaty are specific—in exchange for peace, they want you."

He glanced from Cavin to Jana and back again. "That doesn't make sense."

"Recall when you encountered the woman in the REEF's fighter on the comm screen?"

"She's been a little hard to forget," he admitted.

Cavin slipped a PDA from his pocket. He turned it around and showed Jared the screen. It was an official portrait, a royal portrait. A young woman dressed in ornate, multicolored robes sat on a throne. Her dark hair was coiled in braids wrapped with jewels and fabric, and piled on the top of her head. The picture was taken at some distance. Her oval face was pale. She looked very stiff, almost like a mannequin. If he had to guess, those clothes were pretty uncomfortable.

"She looks, ah, queenly. Very nice. And I'm still confused."

"You don't recognize her?"

Jared honed in on her eyes. Haunted, they made her look as if she felt she were trapped and scared and had no other way to get the message out. But there was a spark of defiance, too, an attitude reflected in her stern little mouth. "Aw, hell," he said. It was the smokin' hot alien babe. The one he'd called a barbarian.

Cavin regarded him solemnly, and Jared knew the other shoe was about to drop. "The treaty is one of marriage to unite the royal families of Earth and the Coalition."

"The queen of the galaxy wants to marry me?"

"Badly," Cavin said. "And soon."

CHAPTER SEVEN

IN SHOCK, JARED WALKED with Cavin, Jana, his father—freshly rushed in from Washington—and a bevy of secret-service agents across an expanse of emerald-green lawn. The Kentucky mansion belonged to software mogul Bill Bates. Apparently, on short notice and needing discretion, a quick decision was made to use the billionaire's palatial Kentucky home as a backdrop for Jared's meeting with Coalition leaders. It was the closest to a palace they could come up with in a pinch. For future broadcasts, they had the Chinese premier's residence and Buckingham Palace lined up. Earth's prince had to look the part.

Jared squeezed his eyes shut for a few seconds. Whoever would have dreamed a little trash talking would land him in this dilemma? The woman believed him—actually believed he was prince of Earth! And who would have guessed she was the queen?

Jared figured the little stunt with the shadow space force had startled the Coalition, only he didn't understand how much so until now. They'd offered up the only remaining member of their royal family in true Dark Ages fashion to unite the two sides as a way of canceling out Earth's perceived threat. Only "offering" their queen wasn't exactly how it was going down. It was more like the queen demanding *him*. Cleaned and pressed and tied up neatly with a pretty bow, he was the perfect gift, according to every world leader.

Jared frowned. They picked the wrong guy for this plan.

Go with the flow. Yeah, it was all he could do. He wanted to get out of the center of this hurricane and go home to his happy, *normal* life.

They entered the grand foyer. Twin sweeping spiral staircases soared in both directions. The floor was white marble shot through with black. A French king had never lived here, but it sure looked like it. Everything was either royal-blue velvet or had gilt touches, or both. It was a gaudy display of mind-boggling wealth. "This is the first impression we want to give these people?" Jared asked out the corner of his mouth.

"This is what our world leaders agreed on," his father said.

Jana nodded as she took messages on her PDA. "We were too amazed that they came to a consensus and did it so quickly that we didn't argue."

A man hurried up to Jared and placed a hand on his velvet-clad shoulder. He wore an outfit flown in for the occasion by the king of Denmark and the stiff collar itched like hell.

The older gentleman grinning at him was about five foot six, and looked vaguely familiar. He wore a pin with the Chinese flag and spoke to Jared in Mandarin. His eyes watered. Tears? Something told Jared he wasn't the type of man who cried. A young female translator filled in the blanks. "The premier thanks you with all his heart. Everything he has is yours. He would offer his daughter but you are already taken."

The pair beamed at their joke. The shorter man gripped the sleeve of Jared's royal outfit. "You save world," he said in a thick accent. "You save us." He gave one last emotional squeeze before letting Jared pass by.

Jared watched them walk away. "Who was that?"

"The premier of China," his father answered.

"The head dude? The leader?" He'd already been greeted by President Ramos and the British prime minister. "But this is Kentucky."

"It's now ground zero in the fight to save Earth."

A group of plain-clothed feds with dark glasses and no expressions met them at the entrance to the room where the screen from the REEF's fighter was set up to receive an incoming message from the Coalition's Royal Palace. They gave Jared a box.

"The betrothal gift," Cavin explained.

"An engagement ring?"

"The stone is too large for a ring. But it can be cut down if she so desires. Coalition brides wear wristlets to signify marriage status, and the men tattoos."

Jared lifted the lid and peered inside the box. "Holy… You weren't kidding when you said too large."

"It's a pink diamond," Jana explained. "Almost two hundred and seventy-four carats. At first, everyone thought the Hope Diamond would do because it's in the Smithsonian and easy to get hold of, but then some experts reminded us the stone was bad luck. Someone talked to someone else and we ended up with this one. It's called the Pink Sunrise—rare, flawless pink and—"

"Huge." Jared shut the lid. "The little diva better say thank you."

As they hustled him into the room, the enormity of what he was about to do struck him. "I don't feel ready for this," he said under his breath. How the hell had saving the world fallen on his shoulders? *Your big mouth, that's how. A throwaway remark got you into this.*

"Follow the script," Cavin reminded him. "It's all right here. Coalition protocol."

"Why their protocol? Why not our way?"

"We don't have a way," Jana pointed out.

"We don't have a prince of the planet, either."

Cavin urged him forward. "Prime Minister Rissallen will most likely begin the proceedings. When the queen appears, he will be the one to introduce her. Don't say anything until they're done. And when it is time, you will tell them this…." Cavin's finger traced along the lines Jana had scrawled for him—he hadn't yet mastered the written form of the language.

"You'll say you're humbled and honored by her generous offer of marriage—"

"Humbled?" *Not.*

"—and pleased to accept their offer of peace."

Jared held up his hands. "Hold on, cowboy. I didn't agree to anything yet."

Jana reassured him. "Remember the shadow fleet—the battle force of false signals? This is the same thing. A shadow engagement. You're not agreeing to anything at this point, not really."

"Right. We're lying."

"We're setting the bait."

Jared took the script and sat in an expensive leather recliner in the middle of a marble-floored room that had been cleared of all other furniture. People fussed all around him, testing the light, the sound, the position of his medals—rather, the king of Denmark's medals. A woman dusted his face with a huge, powdery brush. "No." He pushed away her hand as tactfully as he could. "No makeup."

She seemed to sense his coiled tension and backed away quickly.

At the appointed time, the screen went from opaque to clear and the room fell silent. There was nothing to see yet on-screen, just an empty throne.

"Maybe she got cold feet," Jana whispered.

"Maybe she's getting her daggers out." He glanced over at Cavin. "It feels a little strange meeting your former fiancée and pretending I'm going to marry her. You okay with that?"

Cavin snorted. He lifted fingers to the back of Jana's neck, massaging her with unconscious possessiveness. "Our betrothal was never official, nor did I ever meet her. Although not many years after I visited Earth for the first time, when Jana and I first met, I remember seeing images of her coronation. Queen Keira was very young. A child of six or so of your Earth years."

That put Keira in her midtwenties now. "Where were her parents?"

"She lost her family at a young age. A tragic accident."

Gone, in one fell swoop. Life could be like that. One minute everything was okay, and in the next the rug got pulled from under you. What a rotten break, losing your entire family like that and then having to take over the reins of a kingdom. What if you didn't want to be a queen? Jared imagined what it would have been like if his father and grandfather had forced him into politics. Not pretty.

Unlike the queen, who was gorgeous. "Why isn't she married?"

Cavin made the kind of face that would worry a guy. "It's not been for lack of trying. Since she was a teenager there have been a parade of potential consorts. She's refused all of them or they disappeared in lieu of refusal and the consequences of that. It's widely known that she sliced off the male parts of a man who tried to rape her."

Jared winced. "That hurt."

"Since she felt that killing him would be an act of mercy, he lives on as a palace eunuch as a reminder for those suitors who would attempt to force themselves on the queen."

Jared resisted the urge to grab his package and shift position. He wondered if they made plasma-retardant jock straps. The lucky guy who did end up marrying her was going to need a pair or two.

"Good luck, Jared." Cavin gripped his hand in a heartfelt squeeze.

"Thanks, bro. I won't let you down. I won't let Earth down."

"I know." Cavin's eyes filled with respect. Then he walked out of sight of the screen. He'd keep in touch with Jared throughout the ceremony through a tiny earpiece transmitter. With Cavin's name still on the books as a termination target, it was best no one in the Coalition saw him.

Jana would play the part of Jared's adviser. Dressed in a uniform juiced up with gemstones, her blond hair gelled and scraped back into a cascade of stiff curls, his baby sister resembled a decadent, third-world despot. What kind of message were they sending the Coalition?

The screen cleared and a tall, thin man appeared. Jared tried not to draw comparisons with this serious situation and popular culture, but damn if the guy wasn't dressed in the robes of a Jedi master. He half expected Yoda to appear next. "Prime Minister Kellen Rissallen," announced the computerized translator. The name echoed in the empty room.

Everyone remained silent, here on Earth and across the light years, poised at the brink of forming an alliance between their two civilizations. An alliance based on a lie, Jared thought. The whole thing made him uncomfortable. Keira believed he'd eventually marry her and he had no intention of ever doing so. The further they went with this ruse, the worse he felt. It was like a lie that started off small but dug you deeper and deeper. Every leader on the planet was in on it, even the rogues and crazies. Was Jared the only one bothered by the deception part of it? Apparently so. With stakes like a world invasion hanging over their heads, everyone was happy to lie their asses off.

A tingling in the back of his neck and a squeeze in his gut unsettled him, but he sat tall in his leather throne, reminding himself that this was war, and in war you did what you had to do. The queen didn't need to know this was a shadow engagement. And that it was going to be a very, very long engagement. An infinitely long engagement.

The prime minister crossed both arms over his chest and dipped his head. "We bring good tidings and greetings of peace to Earth."

Next, Jana took a deep breath and called out, "Jared Jasper, Prince of all Earth."

So far, the exchange followed the script exactly.

Jared readied himself for what was to come. This had to go well or Earth lost its future. The pressure was on.

KEIRA CAUGHT SIGHT of herself in a mirror, and her breath hitched. She looked...like a bride.

Gods. She gulped. This was all rushing at her so swiftly, she hadn't had a moment to feel scared. But now the fear simmered beneath the surface. She tried to keep it in check. This had to go well. The future of the Coalition depended on it.

But she was a skilled actress, and she'd use the ability today. She'd acted all her life, rarely showing anyone who she really was. She'd have no problem hiding behind a veil—literally and figuratively—today, the day of her marriage.

Attendants fluttered around her. She shooed them off to finish primping in front of the mirror. Her hair was a pile of ornate braids woven by a team of hairdressers. Her gown was traditional: midnight-black shot through with opalescent threads of every color in the rainbow. Tinted nano-computers created a three-dimensional prism effect, shimmering as she moved. The bodice was snug with a high neck. Sleeves hugged her arms to the wrist. Where they ended in a point, rare black pearl-orbs dangled, reaching almost to the hem of the lushly flowing skirt sweeping the floor. She was the perfect Sakkaran bride.

"It is time," Tibor said. His eyes were deep and dark as he nodded at her. Uncharacteristic emotion tugged at his features. Her father was long dead. If he had been here, he'd have looked a lot like Tibor. To her guard's right stood Fair Cirrus, Neppal and Ismae Vemekk. *Remember,* the woman's eyes said, *I can help you escape him.*

Keira knew something the minister didn't: after the first-mating night and the games she had in store for the Earthling prince, perhaps it would be he who would want to escape *her.*

Somberly, Keira lowered a drape of black, semitransparent fabric over her face. With eunuchs and assorted palace staff trailing her, she glided into the chamber where she would bind herself to the Earthling prince for a lifetime.

There, Rissallen addressed a man and woman displayed on a huge screen. The prince! Keira halted, her breath catching. Dressed in royal ceremonial regalia, the Earthling prince looked as handsome as he did confident: a completely self-assured male in the prime of life. In control. *This man will share your bed. He will share your body.* Her simmering fear began to bubble.

You are strong. A warrior.

Rissallen saw her standing in the doorway and beckoned her forward. She hesitated.

Maybe Vemekk's fears were justified. Perhaps this was a Drakken trick, and the Earthling prince belonged to the Horde. After he came to live in the palace, he'd lock her away, raping her to impregnate her with half-barbarian heirs to spread Drakken influence throughout the galaxy.

Keira scowled. No! The only half-barbarian babies she'd be birthing would be the Earthling's.

Grasping the fabric of her skirt, she fought to keep her hands from trembling as she walked forward, step by reluctant, regretful step. Rissallen extended his hand to help her up to the dais. As required by tradition, the origin of which was lost in the mists of time, seven white-robed priests and priestesses formed a half circle around the platform. Incense floated into the air as the soft chanting began. "We come from the light, we will return to the light," the holy ones whispered, over and over.

Keira's rapid breathing made the diaphanous black fabric in front of her face flutter. Why was she so nervous? This ceremony wasn't supposed to matter. She wasn't supposed to feel the gravity of this day, its importance in her life. It was just a treaty. Just a marriage. A formality, really. Yet her heart slammed and her palms sweat. Why did the prince affect her so? Was it because he was an unknown quantity, a man from so very far away? Was it because he wasn't afraid of her the way everyone else was? *Or is it because when he looks at you, he seems to actually see you?*

Gods help her. Eyes downcast and scared to the bottom of her soul, she waited for the ceremony to begin that would bind her to a man located light-years away.

CHAPTER EIGHT

JARED ATTEMPTED TO reconcile the stiff, silent, black-draped woman with the fiery beauty he'd met online only days earlier. "Couldn't she have chosen a better color?" he muttered to Jana. "It looks like she's on the way to a funeral."

"Protocol," Cavin whispered from offscreen. His voice came over a tiny microphone jammed in Jared's right ear. "It's the color worn to a betrothal ceremony."

"Great." Black. What a cheerful tradition.

"Keira, Queen of Sakka," the prime minister intoned from on-screen.

After the appropriate amount of time passed, Jana announced, "Jared Jasper, Prince of Earth."

As the formal exchanges back and forth droned on, Jared reviewed his part of the routine. A dull headache didn't help his concentration. Some prince he was. Where was his staff? His servants? All he'd had to eat since yesterday was a doughnut and coffee. Jana owed him big-time for this. In fact, Earth did. The Japanese emperor was probably here. Surely he could arrange for some sushi and ice-cold Japanese beer to be flown in to ease the craving from last night that had never gotten satisfied. His stomach growled, and he cut off that train of thought. No use letting food distract him from saving the world.

As the pleasantries dragged on, Cavin paced out of the line of sight of the screen. And if that wasn't enough pressure on Jared, the president of the United States, the prime minister of the U.K., the Russian president and the Chinese premier sat rigidly in a row, listening intently.

Finally, it was time for Jared to address the queen. *I bestow upon you blessings from the planet Earth,* was what he was supposed to say. Was *expected* to say. As he hesitated, he sensed tension building, both among the dignitaries sharing the room and the solemn party on-screen. It reminded him why they were here. The Coalition feared his world. They were afraid of the Drakken wooing Earth, and so they beat the Horde to the punch by offering their most exquisite prize: Keira.

Jana and Cavin were wrong. The Coalition was bargaining from a position of weakness.

That's why they made a bid for you. Jared had too many years of real-estate negotiations behind him to let that advantage pass unexploited. *They* were the weak ones, not Earth. Oh, he'd let them have their betrothal ceremony mostly their way. After all, it was tied up in their religion—the queen was worshipped as a goddess, and he was fully prepared to respect the religion of his temporary fiancée—but the ball was in Earth's court.

Or—he thought with the slightest of smiles—the *balls.* His balls were on the auction block here; no one else's. And he was damn well going to use them. If there was to be protocol, then they could sure as hell adhere to Earth's. Even if he had to make it up as they went along.

"Jared?" Cavin murmured in his earpiece.

"Jared, you okay?" he heard his sister whisper a moment later.

He waved a hand without looking at them. *Relax. Everything's under control.* He took a breath and began: "Queen Keira, I bid you good day from planet Earth. Your loveliness takes my breath away…as it did the first time we met."

Keira's head jerked up, but he couldn't see her face through the dark veil. Her gloved hands formed fists in reaction to his breach in protocol. No, *change* in protocol. "Your memory is to be admired, Sir Prince, as my own recollection of the day seems to have faded."

She didn't remember him? *Bullshit.* "Perhaps I can help refresh your memory."

"Jared," Cavin snapped in his ear.

"Although our conversation was brief, my queen, it was quite powerful."

"How different views can be of the very same experience."

"You little brat," he muttered under his breath.

"I am pleased, however, that Earth has offered their prince in exchange for peace," she continued.

"The way I understand it, you're being offered to Earth in exchange for our loyalty."

Jana's hand landed on his shoulder. Good thing for the padding on the king of Denmark's jacket, or he'd have felt his sister's claws in his skin, he was sure.

Meanwhile, the queen's prime minister leaned over and whispered something in her ear.

Whatever she said back to him made the man flinch. There was the fire he remembered from their original meeting. The meeting she didn't remember. Ha. She remembered him. He'd bet the memory kept her up at night, too. *Like hers does to you?*

Silenced by their handlers, Jared and Keira glowered at each other.

"Present the betrothal gift now," Cavin urged.

Jared remembered the box. At this point in the script, he was supposed to offer it to the queen. He was so tense that the pressure from his thumbs had dented the lid. He pulled off the lid as everyone in the room held their collective breath. The pink diamond glittered, soft and warm—the opposite of the woman to whom it was being given. "An offering to the goddess-bride," he recited, trying not to sound sarcastic. "A gift from Earth."

The prime minister pushed the sullen woman toward him. She was supposed to accept the offering and acknowledge Earth's offer for her hand in marriage, and then this whole thing would be done and he could go home.

But instead she raised her veil. Her eyes were steely cold as the white-robed Jedi characters chanted what he figured was a prayer: "From the light we come, and to the light we return."

"She's deviated from the script," Cavin said. He sounded startled.

"Give her a break," Jared whispered back. "I started it."

The white-robed men and women were chanting: "From the light we come, and to the light we return." After they sang the line for the seventh time, they went silent. Softly, and, to his shock, almost shyly, Queen Keira sang: "Together the light burns brightest. Together we are one." She brought her outstretched hands together and dipped her head in a bow. "I accept your blessed offer. And now I give you mine. Do you accept, Prince Jared?" Did her voice crack, or was it his imagination?

None of this was part of the script so Jared just winged it. "Sure. Yes. I accept."

"Gods," Cavin said, pressing a finger to his mouth and squeezing his eyes shut.

Jared didn't know what had the man so worked up. "Yo, Cavin. We're fine. Don't worry about the script. I'm better off-road than on, anyway." Then he remembered getting his Bronco stuck in the mud and tried to put it out of his mind.

Keira turned to the people in the white robes. One handed her a small cup. She drank from it.

"None of this was briefed," Jana complained. "I'm just along for the ride."

He almost laughed out loud. "You and me both."

Finally, the queen stepped off the dais. Throwing the veil over her face, she walked away.

Jared crumpled up the script. "What did you think, Jana? I think she likes me."

"I think she holds you in utter contempt."

"So what? At least she's thinking of me."

Again the prime minister addressed them. "Prince Jared, representatives of Earth, I will contact you shortly regarding the details of the transfer." He crossed his arms over his chest as the screen faded to black.

"Transfer..." Jared glanced down at the box with the big-ass diamond. "I guess they mean they want this. How are we going to get it to her—FedEx?"

Cavin threw off his earpiece. *"Yenflarg,"* he muttered. It was a Coalition cussword.

"I'm sorry I went off script—the woman does that to me, infuriates me—but, hey, it went fine, right? We've got our shadow engagement. We're good to go." He tossed Cavin the box. "And her handlers want the diamond. Here you go. Since FedEx doesn't do interstellar yet, give it to the guys on the space station. Tell them to hand deliver it to Her Royal Diva with my regards." He pushed stiffly off the chair. His knee was killing him, and he was light-headed from food and sleep deprivation. Throw in beer deprivation, too.

He joined his father and Jana for a victory private huddle that the world's leaders somehow let them have.

"You did good, Jared." His father drew him into a hearty hug, pounding him on the back. Then he gripped Jared by the shoulders, moving him back to gaze at him with pride. "Your mother always said your mouth would get you in trouble someday, but it ended up getting us *out* of trouble."

"I just happened to be in the right place at the right time for once."

"Bull, son. You're a hero in my book."

"He's also a married man," Cavin said, walking up to them.

Jared laughed. "Just because I gave the woman a diamond doesn't mean I'm making a commitment."

"You *are* committed," Cavin said in a strange

voice. His fists were clenched and he looked sick at heart. "They performed the ceremony. I couldn't stop it once it was underway because to do so would have put this planet's freedom in jeopardy."

Jana looked panicked. "But it was just a betrothal ceremony."

"It began that way, yes. But then the priests chanted the wedding vows, and the queen took them. She asked if you'd accept, Jared, and you did."

He'd said *I do?* He raced over his memory of the last few minutes of the ceremony. Keira had brought her hands together and bowed. Then she'd said, *I accept your blessed offer. Do you accept mine?* "I thought she meant the diamond. She meant the diamond, right?"

"No. She meant you."

KEIRA WAILED AS SNOW swirled outside the palace windows. "We lost control of the ceremony! He did not adhere to the script. He ignored the holy words."

"The desired result was achieved, yes?" Rissallen pointed out. "You are married now. The treaty is completed."

"But Earth took control."

"At this point, they have control, my queen, whether we like it or not."

Keira hated that he was right. Hated that the Earth prince—*her husband*—had done things *his* way. Hated that his small, less powerful provincial world could make the mighty Coalition grovel. Well, it didn't matter. Once the prince landed on Sakka, control would be a thing of the past. *His* control.

With a satisfied little smile, Keira flounced off to her private bathing chambers. An oil massage, a glass of sparkling snowberry wine and some fun little fantasies as to how she'd put her arrogant little prince under her thumb, and she'd be feeling much better.

"WE'RE MARRIED?" Jared's heart bounced off his ribs. "Cavin, you're going to have to come up with something else because I'm not married to that woman."

"It cannot be undone."

"Then we just made a shadow marriage instead of a shadow engagement. Better yet, make it a shadow divorce." He started walking away, yanking open the royal uniform that was scratching his neck.

"Jared, please," Jana called.

He spun around, walking backward, hands up. "Just give me some space. I need…I need to think." He felt betrayed. Used. He was married. *Jesus.* "I was happy to help—hell, I *wanted* to help, but, damn it, you should have been straight with me. You didn't explain the risks."

Jana looked heartsick. "We didn't know."

"Did you really expect the Coalition would jump through every hoop we put out for them? They knew exactly what they were doing when they logged on today. They were determined to neutralize our threat, and they did. Did you really expect them to fight fair? You especially, Cavin. You know what they're like—you served as one of their highest-ranking officers. When they want something, they go after it, like Earth." He shoved a hand through his hair. "Like *me.*"

He strode away, shrugging off the medal-encrusted coat, shoving it into an assistant's hands, an "assistant" who was probably in reality the dictator or prime minister of a small country.

"Jared," his sister called out. "Where are you going?"

"Home. Tahoe. Somewhere." He needed to get away. He'd been dragged here against his will for what he'd thought was just supposed to be a little face time with Queen Sunshine, another part of the big ruse like the shadow fleet was. Now she was his wife? Screw that. "Get yourself another sacrificial lamb."

HORRIFIED, JANA WATCHED her brother cross the room, rebuffing attempts from dignitaries to congratulate him. It wouldn't do to have an emotional meltdown in front of the leaders of the world. She siphoned poise from a deep well that came hardwired to her Jasper genes.

Sure, her brother was as full of himself as ever, the consummate ladies' man and hotshot pilot, but as a national guard officer and businessman, he was as honest and loyal as they came. He was also one of the calmest, laid-back individuals she knew. Leaving the room in a snit was not typical Jared behavior.

But then she'd asked a lot of him. *Earth* had asked a lot of him—and much more than she'd ever anticipated. *Jared... Ah, God, poor Jared.*

"I'll talk to him," her father said. The congressman took off across the room, his red tie flailing over his shoulder. He caught up to Jared and laid a calming arm over his son's broad shoulders—shoulders that had borne more than anyone else's had today. It wasn't that Jared was incapable or even unwilling to assume risk and responsibility, but he'd been literally dragged here, doing as they asked of him without question—and without a lot of explanation.

"Squee…" Even Cavin's use of his childhood nickname for her failed to erase her frown. His hand found her back, rubbing in a slow circle.

"He trusted us," she whispered. "And we abused it." She started to run after Jared, but Cavin caught her hand.

"Let him go, Jana. Give him the time he needs. I know your brother. I consider him a friend. He's as good a man as they come. He will agree to this, but he has to make the decision his, not something I or anyone else rammed down his throat, intentionally or otherwise."

"That's the way he feels right now…like we forced him into this."

"In effect, we did. We forced him to face a risk none of us fully understood. What is your Earth expression—play with fire and you might get burned? Yet, what we can't forget is that we just bought Earth a safer, brighter future."

"But at what cost?"

"A terribly high cost to one man. One family. In exchange, over six billion souls get to resume their lives."

"That is, if the Coalition doesn't figure out the original trick." The fake fleet. As much of a triumph as that lie was, living with the fear of being found out was hell. "Something tells me they won't be too happy finding out they married off their precious queen to a poor, country commoner."

"I didn't say our work was over. The most difficult wars are won one battle at a time. For now, we have Earth back in our hands."

At the cost of her brother.

Until now, Jared had managed to steer clear of the blinding spotlight focused on their famous political family. But, boy, that sure had changed. Jared was center stage now, all eyes on him. He had to perform. He couldn't fail. Simply put, her big brother, Jared, self-proclaimed "regular dude," was possibly the one and last chance to lasting peace between the Coalition and Earth.

"He's a Jasper," Cavin reminded her. "He understands what he must do. Just as you do."

We're public servants first and foremost. Our duty to others comes before our own interests and ambition. There is no greater calling than to serve your fellow men and women. Never forget that. Never forget you're a Jasper. All her life those words had been recited to her—by her father, by her late grandfather—until the credo had become so ingrained in her psyche that it was part of her. A personal code of honor.

"Jared never dreamed of serving mankind," she said. "He just had the misfortune of being born into a family that's known for it."

Cavin's arm tightened around her shoulders. "And you had the misfortune of meeting me."

"What?" She pushed away to stare at him.

A wry smile softened his strong features, but the flicker of vulnerability in his eyes gave away his inner doubts. "If not for your involvement with me, you, Jared—and your sister, Evie, for that matter—would have lived normal lives."

"Until the Coalition invaded. My meeting you was the best thing that ever happened to Earth. And it was the best thing that ever happened *to me*." She poked him in the chest.

"If I hear you say anything different ever again, I'll… I'll…"

"Kiss me?" Cavin pulled her close, kissing her with slow, familiar heat until she'd practically melted into his body.

He cradled her against his chest. "Jared's strong. He will succeed in his marriage."

Her head popped up. "Hello. Are you kidding? She's the queen of the galaxy." Cavin knew better than anyone else the kind of woman Jana's brother had married. "Success is going to be the least of Jared's worries in that marriage. Let's just pray he *survives* it."

The past weeks had been chaotic, turbulent and emotionally draining. But if she traced the chain of events back to the very beginning, even before Cavin had descended into a secret hangar buried deep beneath a Nevada farmhouse to win Earth a reprieve, one person had caused problem after problem for her family. "The REEF. I blame him. It's his fault Jared got involved."

Cavin shook his head. "Blaming the REEF for Jared's situation is like blaming the symptom for the disease. You want someone to hold responsible? Then look to the cunning, diabolical person or persons who gave the order to have me killed. We may have bought your planet peace, Jana, but your brother's fate—the fate of us all, including his future wife—rests squarely on those conspirators' shoulders."

Jana shuddered. She knew he didn't mean to scare her, but the ice in his tone chilled her to the core.

CHAPTER NINE

JARED DID WHAT ANY MAN would do in his situation: he went back to work. Delta Development, known affectionately by him and his team as Double D, occupied several large and airy offices on the ground floor of an upscale Granite Bay building. But this morning the office was nearly empty of people. Most of the consultants he employed were either out in the field or wouldn't be in until late.

"Morning, Karen," he said to his receptionist, snatching a copy of the *Sacramento Sun* out of his in-box and a stack of mail.

"Hey…" she replied, appearing shocked that he was there.

"I bet you forgot I work here. I've got to start coming in more often." Things like saving the world kept getting in the way. He landed on his chair and spun to face the huge picture window.

Propping his feet on the ledge, he crossed one leg over the other.

"Jared?"

He turned in the chair. Karen was there, and Todd, one of his consultants. Terri, his office manager, stood half-hidden behind them. They simply stared at him. "What?" he asked.

"We heard about the marriage," Karen said hesitantly. "It was on the news. And in the paper. Everywhere."

"It kind of took us by surprise," Todd put in.

"It took *you* by surprise." Jared coughed out a slightly maniacal-sounding laugh. He went back to sorting through the mail. The trio didn't leave. He felt their eyes boring into his back. He turned. "What?"

"We were wondering," Todd began, "what's going to happen with Double D. You know, now that you're leaving." He cleared his throat. "Do you know who'll take over the company? Or if you're going to let us go? We were curious if there'd be a severance package, or… I mean, if you can't, I—we understand."

"Who said I'm going anywhere?" Jared had no intention of going anywhere—especially if it meant he'd be some spoiled diva's sex toy. He ruffled through the letters, separating legitimate mail from junk. Silence in the room had him glancing up again. He sighed. "Now, what?"

"But you married the queen," Karen pointed out.

"Oh, that. Well, I don't think it was legally binding. I haven't had time to look into it yet."

More uncomfortable silence. What had happened to his normally cheerful employees?

"But if you don't marry her," Karen persisted, "what happens to Earth?"

The fear in the woman's voice was unmistakable. Slowly, he looked up from the mail. It finally hit him that his employees were concerned about their basic welfare, their own situations; they weren't thinking of him other than they were glad he'd stepped up to the plate to save Earth. Except he'd never said he was going to save the planet. He'd never agreed he'd be the one to sacrifice everything to save everyone else. Maybe if someone had asked him, but no one had. It had been shoved down his throat.

He'd left Kentucky with the full intention of forgetting about the whole thing. Cavin and Jana would have to think of something else. They'd fool the Coalition the way they'd fooled them before, and that was that. Jared had done his part. The way he saw it, he was done. Now he was going to resume his life.

Was he in denial?

No, damn it. He just wanted to go on with his life.

"What will happen?" Karen prompted. Her fingers worried the hem of her sweater.

Jared opened his mouth to answer, but he didn't know what to say. His gaze fell down to the newspaper on his desk, and the screaming headline:

EARTH SAVED!

Washington (AP)—Jared Jasper weds queen of galaxy in a move claimed as a victory by both sides.

An emotional President Ramos today declared April 12th to be Jared Jasper Day, a national holiday celebrating Jasper's marriage to Queen Keira. "A more selfless, brave and amazing man does not exist on this planet," the president said. "Although it is difficult to do, we must let him go off to a faraway world where I have no doubt he will positively impact his new society with his unmatched heroism."

"Bite me," Jared said under his breath. Every paper in the world would be running the same headline. How could he not go through with the marriage now? If he walked away, he walked away from six billion people who were depending on him to save their sorry asses.

Outside the window, two mothers cruised by, wheeling their jogging strollers. Their babies kicked their legs, clearly having a good time. One, a little girl, shook a stuffed animal. She noticed Jared watching her from the window. Her blue eyes opened wide. Open and innocent. She held his gaze, even craning her neck as the stroller passed. The baby was utterly vulnerable, utterly at the mercy of the adults on this planet. Utterly at *his* mercy.

A suffocating, infuriating sense of inevitability swamped him. He didn't want this, he'd never wanted this.

But how could he refuse?

He flattened his hands on the desk. One by one, he looked into the concerned faces of his employees. "I'll talk to my attorney and discuss the options for Double D. I'll take care of you."

He grabbed his car keys and cell phone. He took a couple of steps and stopped. "And I'll take care of Earth, too." Making that promise was like running the final mile in a marathon— he had to do it, but it hurt like hell.

JARED DROVE HIS BRONCO the way he flew his F-16. Speeding, he careened around a bend on the highway. The tires skidded off the paved surface and onto the gravel. He recovered, fish-tailing back onto the road. How far could he push it? How far until he no longer skated along the edge of danger and plunged into it instead?

He had no destination in mind. He'd simply escape to the mountains the way he always did when he needed to unwind. But with no snow left on the mountains, he couldn't snowboard and burn off some of the frustrated energy pulsing off him in waves.

He took another turn, hard, and accelerated as the road straightened. An air horn and siren sounded above the thump-thump of his blaring stereo. Jared narrowed his eyes at the rearview mirror. It was a police car, racing to catch him. It was about time. He couldn't believe he'd made it this far into the Sierras without the feds trailing him.

Was Sarto on his ass again? He didn't really

care anymore. Somewhere between Kentucky and here, the fight had gone out of him. Somewhere between Kentucky and here, a little girl had looked into his eyes and asked him not to forsake her.

He slowed and pulled over. He killed the engine and got out his license and registration as he'd done any number of times before everyone on Earth knew his name. Before he was a married man. Before he was a goddamn prince.

Gripping the steering wheel, he sat still in the pocket of silence before the officers reached the Bronco. Ahead was the turnoff for Heavenly. He'd racked up a lot of hours there and at a number of other ski resorts this past winter. Did the planet he was going to have snow? He wasn't sure how he'd survive without snowboarding. Or sports. College basketball, March Madness. The Super Bowl. Where did people go when they wanted a drink? They obviously didn't celebrate Christmas or the Fourth of July. All were things he'd likely have to give up…so everyone on Earth could continue to have them.

"Sir?"

Jared rolled down the window. He had the

feeling the cop had tried to get his attention several times. "Yeah. Hey. Here."

The officer scrutinized him for a moment. Looking for signs of drunkenness? Or wondering at his marked sense of surrender? "So, how are we feeling today?"

"How am I feeling?" Jared rubbed a hand across his chin. "Like a fatally wounded fox evading the hounds, knowing the end is inevitable but you still want that end run." He glanced up at the cop. "You know what I mean?"

The officer gave him a slightly longer perusal before leaving with his license. "I guess not," Jared muttered, settling in to wait.

A few moments later, the officer returned with his partner and Jared's license. "Mr. Jasper. Sir. I didn't realize it was you." The cop handed back his license. "You ought to be a little more careful on the road. Maybe not so fast."

"How fast was I going?"

"Eighty-one," his partner said. "That's suicide in a truck. Please be more careful. Can we help you out with anything? Anything we can do?"

"You're not going to give me a ticket?"

"Are you kidding? I'd like your autograph." He thrust a notepad at him. "For my boy."

SOMETIME LATER, AFTER waving away offers of a police escort back down to the Sacramento Valley, Jared remained parked on the side of the road. He took out his cell and called Jana's private number. She and Cavin were "somewhere in Nevada."

"Jared," she said, emotion thickening her voice the moment she answered.

"I'm in," he cut in before she said anything that would get his own emotions going. Frankly, he wasn't sure what would come out, rage or grief, so it was better not to feel anything. "And I have a few requests." The cornered killer, making his last demands before the feds closed in on the standoff—that was what he felt like.

"Anything…"

"No brain implant." Cavin and the REEF and nearly every other Coalition person of high rank had a brain implant to assist with myriad tasks. He suspected they'd want to plant one in his head to speed his understanding of the Coalition language. "I'll learn the language on my own. I'm fluent in French, Spanish and German. It won't take long."

Cavin came on the phone. "I'll help you learn."

"Whatever it takes. Just no surgery."

"They requested what you know here on Earth as a DNA sample. It's needed to make a personalized medical composite."

"No body parts. I'm keeping everything I have."

"Just a cheek swipe. It's used to make a predictor of all the diseases you might develop over the course of your life, and to make the treatments to cure them, specifically tailored to you. Life spans on most Coalition worlds are two hundred years or more."

"Two hundred?" he coughed out. Two hundred years with the diva. Wonderful.

"In standard Coalition years. In Earth years, only approximately one-fifty."

Only? Not only would his compliance assure peace between the planets, Earth would benefit from the advanced technology. He'd make sure Earth got everything available. Knowing cancer patients might be cured and accident victims might walk again was something he could focus on when the reality of his personal sacrifice threatened to get to him. But how would they exchange medical and science technology without the Coalition finding out Earth had no spaceships and that the marriage of their queen to Jared was a total sham? One hundred and fifty years was going to be a long time to carry a lie. *No one said this was going to be easy.*

No, no one had.

JARED DROVE TO THE RANCH. He arrived at the front door with arms full of groceries to make dinner. His parents were in town for the weekend, but, inside, the house was as full of memories as it was empty of life. He dropped the bags on the counter and checked outside. The backyard was deserted. Jared turned to walk inside when the sight of his grandfather's vegetable garden stopped him. The dirt still held the tracks from where the old man would wheel his chair back and forth from the house. Jared stood there, unable to move. Weeds poked out in between the spring vegetables no one had touched since his grandfather had last tended them.

Jared crouched down and pulled out the weeds. "Kind of sucks, doesn't it? Once you're gone, no one looks after your pet projects quite the way you did." He plucked out dandelions and threw them aside. "My employees approached me today. They were worried about what would happen to them if I left. I told them they'd be fine. But I think I get it now."

They knew once he was gone, DD would change. It would lose the energy he brought to the company. The direction. Weeds would grow. He crushed a dandelion in his fist. "I'm going to sell the company. It's better for everyone that way. A clean break. I'll make sure everyone's compensated."

Jared glanced around to make sure no one was listening to his imaginary conversation with his dead grandfather. "I'm sorry I didn't follow in your footsteps. Or Dad's. I probably fought it a little harder than I had to. Sorry about that, too."

He could almost hear his grandfather praising his choice to go through with the marriage to the queen. *"Our duty to others comes before our own interests and ambition,"* he'd say, but Jared didn't want to hear it.

"My back was to the wall, Grandpa. I had to say yes. There's nothing about my decision to go through with this marriage that makes me proud. I agreed because I had no choice."

Jared left the garden to escape the conversation he was having in his head with his dead grandfather. *"They're at Evie's."*

Jared froze. The information had come in his grandfather's voice. This time it was almost as if the man had actually spoken. First he found out he was married to a queen. Now he could talk to dead people. What was next?

"Go to them, my boy. They need you as much as you need them."

A corner of Jared's mouth edged up. "Thanks, Grandpa," he said in a quiet voice. "I do need them."

JARED KNOCKED ON Evie's front door. His niece, Ellen, threw it open. "Uncle Jared's here!" Before he could open his mouth to say hi, she'd catapulted herself into his arms.

He closed his eyes briefly, holding her close, his hand cupping the back of her head. *I'll miss you,* he thought. *God, I'll miss you.*

Ellen bounced along next to him as they walked toward the kitchen. "Mom made your favorite."

"Crab enchiladas?"

"Yes!"

"How'd she know I was coming?"

"Aunt Jana told her."

"How did she…?" Jared caught himself and smiled. Of course, she'd predict he'd end up here.

They followed a trail of smells so good they didn't seem of this Earth. Bad choice of words, he thought, trying to stay positive. He had too few of these gatherings left to let thoughts of his future spoil them.

In seconds, he was surrounded by his niece and nephew, his sister and his parents. Evie jammed an icy bottle of Corona into one hand and her fingers into his other. With a silent, shuddering sigh, he loosened the vise gripping his gut, just a little, and let himself be swallowed by the warmth that was his family. He had one, maybe two more months' time left on Earth, and he was damn well going to savor every last second.

IT WAS LATE. EVERYONE HAD gone home. Jared, of course, was staying over. Evie wouldn't have it any other way. They sat in the family room together. Sweet-smelling candles were the only light. The table was littered with cans of Diet Coke and empty bottles of Corona. Sadie was sound asleep in Jared's lap.

"I wanted you to know something," Evie began. "You've always been after me to take my ability to cook and turn it into profit."

"Your *talent* to cook, Evie."

"Okay, my talent." Eyes shining, she smiled shyly.

"At least you have a talent. The rest of us poor slobs have to keep hunting until we find something we're reasonably good at. I've been on your case only because I know how much you want to be independent. You're no different from me in that."

"Here's the good news—I found out Grandpa earmarked some of the trust money for me to start my own business. Demanded it, actually. A candy business. I've already named it—'Evie's Eden: A Garden of Berries.' I'll start looking for someplace to lease with the equipment to make the candy and refrigerator space to store it."

"Very cool. You needed a break. Sounds like this is it."

"What I needed was a kick in the butt. Grandpa knew that."

"Even though he's gone, he's still making his presence known," Jared observed dryly.

"He talks to you, too?"

"At the most amazing times."

"Well, for the first time I'm feeling positive about the future." She winced and her face fell. "Sorry. That was a stupid and selfish thing to say."

"Just because my life's come to a screeching halt, it doesn't mean everyone else's has to."

She looked even worse, and he didn't know how to make it better. Hell, he wasn't sure he could. It was like dying of a disease and putting so much effort into making others feel better about it that you forgot to cheer yourself up. "Who says I'm not feeling positive about the future, anyway? It just so happens that I am."

"Yeah?" Evie looked relieved.

"Yeah."

It sounded good. Now all he had to do was believe it.

IT WAS PERFECT. Minister Vemekk had outdone herself. Smiling, Keira sauntered around the room, dragging an almost loving fingertip over the smooth walls. Metal cables for the restraints were anchored deep within the stone. No matter how hard her new husband pulled, he would not be able to free himself.

As she continued her inspection, trailed by Taye and several of the other eunuchs, she came up on her toes, bouncing slightly. Yes, the heated floor had just the right amount of give. Her prince would not suffer cold buns when sitting on this floor. It served the dual purpose of softening the prison she'd made for him. After all, this torture would be play, not the real thing, though she wondered if he'd feel the same after a night spent here. She smoothed a hand over a piece of cable designed as an ankle restraint. It was an intelligent cuff like the others. The harder one pulled, the tighter it squeezed. Same with the wrist restraints. The Earthling would learn very quickly that resistance was futile.

At her whim, he'd be spread-eagle. An image of his muscled body in that position aroused her, made her blood flow hotter and the curious pulse spring to life between her thighs. But as she closed her eyes and gave in to the fantasy, it was his arms around her she imagined. She reared away from the image. He must be restrained! Hands and feet! He must not be led to think he was in control until she was certain she could control him.

"What is this place, my queen?"

Tibor Frix had entered the chamber, appearing quite surprised. "It is a recreational chamber for my new husband," she informed him with a sniff.

The big guard made a small sound, which he quickly smothered. Eyes narrowed, he peered around the room, lifting a dark brow at the cuffs and shackles. "Are those for him or for you?"

Keira blushed deeply. And hated that she did so. "For him, you ignorant eunuch!"

"You did not tell me you were remodeling this area of your personal gymnasium."

"Ismae Vemekk arranged its construction."

"Ah. I did not realize the minister of Coalition intelligence's job responsibilities extended to the construction of personal torture chambers."

"I am the queen! I can have whatever I wish. And besides, she offered when I made the merest mention of my desire to have such a room." Keira wished she didn't sound so defensive. She could have a friend, could she not?

Tibor Frix inspected the chamber. Every once in a while he'd tap his sword against an instrument of play. It made a clanking noise. "And if his view of play differs from yours?"

"He does not have an opinion." She flounced

away to the opposite side of the room, where she turned, exhaling noisily. "Not one that matters, anyway. He is a frontiersman."

"Who happens to be the leader of a civilization powerful enough to cause parliament and the Coalition Army to take notice."

"He's a brute, as well. A barbarian!"

"Who, with a strong taste for freedom, will not take kindly to being—" Frix banged his sword against a cuff "—tied up."

"It won't be for always." She felt a blush coming on and stopped it as best she could. "It is for his arrival only."

"The mating night?"

"Why, yes."

Tibor's eyes gentled. "Tell me, my queen, would you seek to restrain your husband on this most meaningful of nights of a marriage? You have had a bad experience, but it is not always that way between a man and a woman—"

"How would you know?"

His expression was suddenly mysterious, revealing a glimpse of the man she realized she knew little about. He'd been with a woman before; she knew it then without a doubt. But when? He'd been a eunuch all her life.

The look in his eyes had passed and the circumspect guard was back. "It does not have to be that way," he repeated.

"Enough of this subject!" She paced restlessly, angrily, swearing under her breath. "I do not wish to discuss it."

"My queen…"

"What?" She whirled on him, seething.

"The mating must occur that first night," he reminded her quietly. "It must. No matter what your personal feelings on the subject. It is tradition. If you do not, if for any reason you hurt him, or repel him, the gods and goddesses will not bless this union."

She tried to keep her breathing from accelerating as fast as her heartbeat had. She refused to admit she was scared. Or to confess she wanted a chance to observe the Earthling prince as one would a captured animal before letting herself in the cage with it. With *him*.

"The mating will occur," she argued, unable to meet his knowing, penetrating stare that was also touched with compassion. *My father, the king, would have looked at me that way*, she thought. But then she'd have had her family to guide her into this…this unknown realm. To reassure her as she entered this marriage she didn't want. Now she was compelled to take matters into her own hands—by imprisoning the hands of the Earthling prince.

CHAPTER TEN

LEADERS, CELEBS ATTEND WORLD'S LARGEST BACHELOR PARTY

Reuters—one hour ago

LAS VEGAS, NEVADA (Reuters)—In what is surely the largest bachelor party in history, world leaders and celebrities kicked off a lavish celebration at the Bellagio on the Las Vegas strip honoring Jared Jasper's marriage to Queen Keira. Over ten thousand guests are expected at the event with millions more joining in around the world.

Jasper, the thirty-six-year-old newly-wed, seemed to take the attention in stride. "I've never seen a bachelor party like this before," he said.

On Friday, the former Sacramento real-estate developer and national guard fighter pilot will depart with his entourage for Edwards Air Force Base. There, he will be met by a special Coalition transport that will take him to the royal palace some 578 light-years away from home. After nearly seven weeks spent in near-total immersion learning the queen's language, Jasper approaches his new life with cautious optimism. "I expect it'll take some time getting used to."

So far, the team handpicked to accompany Jasper on his journey has not been approved by the Coalition government, citing security concerns. Despite last-minute wrangling, it is expected that Queen Keira's new husband will depart Earth on time, with or without his contingent.

This newspaper would like to take a moment to wish Prince Jared Jasper the very best. He has our deepest respect and gratitude.

JARED STOOD BY THE BELLAGIO'S famous fountains with his friends from the squadron, glad to have his buddies nearby. The night was still fairly young, but he'd grown restless. After a while, the stream of celebrities and succession of world-class entertainment, including performances by all his favorite bands, had a numbing effect. "You guys want to take off—get some drinks downtown somewhere?"

"Oh, stay, you guys," pleaded an actress hanging on Paco's arm. "This is the party of the millennium."

Jared had no such arm candy at the moment, though he'd gotten a goodly share of "Maybe I'll see you later?" hints. But then, he was married. Public displays of affection with anonymous or not-so-anonymous hot chicks probably wouldn't be a good idea.

"Yeah, for like an hour?" Paco said, reading Jared's thoughts accurately. "I'm up for that."

He untwined the woman's fingers from his arm. "I'll be back. Gonna entertain my good friend here."

The group made their way through security and wound up on the street out in front of the casino. Secret service called for transportation. Jared knew he wasn't going to be left unescorted tonight, and he didn't bother arguing, but he was surprised when a Ferrari glided up.

"This is my ride?" Jared asked.

"Yes. A gift from an anonymous private donor. And we have cars for your friends' use, as well."

"Yo, Prince. Don't argue," Gilligan said. "Get your ass in the seat. I'll drive."

Chuckling, Jared slid into the passenger seat and closed the door. Immediately, he smelled perfume and realized the driver hadn't gotten out. And realized she was drop-dead gorgeous and one of the supermodels from the Victoria's Secret catalog.

"Holy sh— Uh, hello."

"Hello," she crooned huskily in a Russian accent. Her manicured hands caressed the steering wheel. "Where to?"

"You're, ah, coming?"

"Not yet." She took his hand and slid it under her short, tight dress, over the ridge of her thigh-high stockings, over the silky, scorching-hot flesh between her legs. She wasn't wearing underwear. "But I can as soon as you want." She moved his hand over her crotch. She was hot, wet and very ready. All that kept his fingers from slipping inside her was his shock and his damn sense of propriety.

Fortunately, he hadn't lost his sense of opportunity. She moved over to kiss him on the mouth and he didn't stop her. He slipped his hand into her long, supermodel hair. It was as silky as it looked. He gave her the kind of kiss you gave a girl you didn't know after you'd just made the decision you were going to have sex with her. He got a hard-on immediately. He wanted to pull her uninhibited, no-underwear little self onto his lap and screw her right here in the just-off-the-showroom-floor Ferrari. No-holds-barred, no-commitment, animal sex.

Except that people were milling all around the car, and Gilligan was standing outside the driver's door, looking royally pissed. *Not to mention that you're married now.*

An image of Queen Keira's face flooded his mind: those huge, sad eyes and that little mouth that made her look all at once furious and lost. *She's a diva,* he thought. *She tricked me. This is all her fault.*

She's your wife.

Sighing through his nose, Jared broke off the kiss. "Want to join your friends?" the model asked. "Or, we can go right to the room."

"What room?"

"A private donor bought me, the car and the room." She circled her finger over his thigh. But he felt the touch right between his legs. "Top floor, best hotel in town."

"That's very generous. But whose tab is this going on?"

She seemed hesitant to say. "He didn't want thanks. He wanted to do it because of what you're doing for us. For all of us."

Jared got that uncomfortable feeling again, seeing the familiar gratitude in the supermodel's eyes. He didn't want accolades for something he didn't want to do. And he didn't want charity sex, either, no matter how good of a screw it'd be. "I don't want to thank him. I want to ask him a question."

"Sure." She lifted a thin, sleek cell phone out of a holder between the seats. There, he saw a key for the Apex, an ultraexclusive hotel funded by some movie stars. Saying it was the best place in town was an understatement. Why not go? His subconscious begged the question. A horny supermodel, all-night sex, the best penthouse in town, top-notch liquor and food, the whole banana without any obligation.

You're married. Yep. For whatever kind of sham it was, the fact remained. He was legally bound to this other woman, and it felt wrong cheating on her. *This just gives me one more reason to dislike you, Sunshine.*

"Dial six," the model said, pointing to the cell phone in his hand.

A familiar celebrity's voice answered.

"It's Jared Jasper."

Silence, then he asked, "Everything okay? Is there anything else you need? If Elsa doesn't do it for you, I can find you someone else. Or something else—"

"Elsa is awesome. The car is amazing. But..."

"What? Anything? Name it, and it's yours."

"Snowboards and snow. A mountain cabin and a fridge filled with beer." Jared waved at his confused-looking squadron-mates through the tinted glass. He'd known them for years, flown in combat with them, held their new babies, took them out drinking after the breakups and divorces, just as they'd done for him. When you distilled life down to what really mattered, a mindless fuck didn't top the list. Not his list, anyway. "The bachelor party was great. All of you who did stuff for me are great. But what I'd like is a real bachelor party. A weekend with the guys—my good buddies—some killer snow, food and drink."

"That's it?"

"That's all."

The man thought on that for a moment. "You're not going to find good snow this time of year. Not in the northern hemisphere. But I know a place in New Zealand with some pretty extreme runs. I board, too, so I know."

"Can you get me and my friends down there? No extras," he added, winking at the model, "just us. There's eight—eight guys."

"When?"

"Say, in about three hours. I gotta put in a little more face time at this shindig." Tabs put the event's cost at over eighty million. It was the least he could do.

"I'll have a helicopter on the roof of the Bellagio at 1:00 a.m. It'll get you to the airport. My personal jet will take you and your friends from there."

Jared thanked the "anonymous" Oscar-winning donor and hung up. Then he climbed out of the sports car to share the good news.

TWO DAYS LATER, JARED SANK his aching body deep in a leather recliner in front of a massive rock fireplace and held an ice pack on his knee. He didn't know whose ski chalet they'd borrowed, but it was damn nice. He brought a beer bottle to his lips. Only the Steinlager label reminded him he was in New Zealand. Everything else reminded him of a typical winter weekend spent boarding. Days he'd never have again.

Jared tipped more beer into his mouth. Wouldn't do to get too morbid. Time was fleeting. He'd been fighting that sense for the past two days. Every time he let down his guard or got sober enough, it came back.

Paco pondered him from the couch. He sat hunched forward, his arms propped on his legs, a Steinlager dangling from one hand. "I know leaving your family and everyone here has got you down, but look at the positives."

"Like?"

Paco searched for something to say. "Like your wife."

Jared winced. "Careful. We were going to avoid the *W* word, remember?"

"She's hot. If nothing else, at least you have that to look forward to."

Paco had a point. What often got lost in the shock of his impending life change was the fact that he'd be sleeping with a sexy, beautiful woman…and for the rest of his life. Not too bad, that aspect of it all. *"Revrokk sebah,"* he murmured. "Loosely translated—hot babe…in her language." By now he was speaking the Queen's tongue fluently—accented, but fluently. Soon he'd know her tongue pretty damn intimately, too. And every other part of her.

He imagined Keira as she'd appeared the first time he'd seen her, on-screen, whirling on him with that shock, outrage and delight in her eyes. He remembered the high color in her cheeks, her sleek grace, and a surge of sexual anticipation ran through him. Sleeping with Keira was something he looked forward to—on a basic, raw, male level. It wouldn't be lovemaking at first. He didn't know her, nor did he love her, but that was a situation of her design, not his. Sex with her would be based on mutual pleasure, not love. She needn't worry; he had every intention of giving as good of a time as he got.

"I didn't think I'd see you smiling after only one beer." Gilligan limped in to join them, leaving everyone else in the huge hot tub nursing aches and pains from a day on the slopes. They'd never been a bunch to hold anything back. They took the experience full-on, like flying, like everything else.

Gilligan had joked, but the relief in his friend's eyes at his smile shone bright. Jared shrugged. "Let's just say that I'm trying to focus on the, ah, more positive *personal* aspects of this situation."

Indeed he was. Keira may have forced him into this, but sooner or later, he was going to even up the game.

CHAPTER ELEVEN

"PRINCE JARED, THERE IS no need for you to remain awake at this time. We're well out of range of your planetary system—nothing more to see—and we still have a full standard day's journey ahead."

Standard Coalition days ran about twenty-five percent longer than an Earth day. With the light-years they were traveling, for the trip to be that quick was a miracle.

"We're about to enter the first of a series of wormholes—shortcuts through space," the pilot explained. "There will be three in total. The last drops us off a short distance, astronomically speaking, from the holy world of Sakka. The Goddess's Keep," he added with reverence.

The Goddess's Keep, huh? Jared hadn't heard anyone refer to the queen's planet that way, but this was his first interaction with regular, everyday people of the Coalition. They worshipped Keira as a deity. He hadn't realized how much so until now.

"That said, sir, this journey will be much more pleasant if you pass it in the sleeping pod."

Jared gave the ever-attentive pilot a polite smile. "No, thank you. I'll stay up. I'm fine."

"If there's anything I can do, anything at all, please do not hesitate to find me or anyone on the crew."

"Thanks." Jared went back to reading in the luxurious, dimly lit cabin. Soon the protocol attendant would visit him, asking the same questions and the cycle would start all over again. Hadn't they figured it out yet? He wasn't high maintenance. They must have him mixed up with his wife.

Although he *was* traveling with an entourage. A small one, but an entourage all the same. Karl was a veteran of the Secret Service and Han had worked in South Korea's version of the CIA. Both were borderline geniuses and martial-arts experts. Both were polished diplomats. Earth had wanted additional staff to come along with him—wardrobe experts, dietitians, personal trainers, scientists, soldiers, politicos, spies—

but the two men were all the Coalition would allow, citing weight limitations.

Jared cited bullshit. One look around the ship told him it could carry far more than his group of three and their crew of six. But it might have to do with a regulation not to have more bodies than cryopods—the compartments used for hibernation.

When it came to hibernating—no thanks. The trip wouldn't take more than a couple of days. However, Karl and Han, exhausted by traveling all over the world with their respective leaders, had grabbed the opportunity to pass the trip in peaceful sleep. The second the solar system had disappeared from the portholes, they were snoozing.

Maybe he should have done the same. He tried to concentrate on studying the *Agran Sakkara*, basically the bible that formed the basis of his new wife's religion. He wanted to have some understanding of it before he got there—to have some understanding of her. The gods and goddesses had formed all the stars and planets, and all the living things, more or less in Genesis fashion, but instead of ruling from heaven, they lived among the people in human form. They married, had babies, died, but were worshipped by trillions from their moment of birth until their last breath. He wondered what it was like, knowing you were a goddess.

But he knew life hadn't been a picnic for Keira. Orphaned at six or so, crowned at an early age, sheltered in a highly guarded palace, she was like a young queen in a hive of killer bees, sending soldiers out to pillage and gather riches while she lounged in decadent luxury, doted on by sterile male attendants in the innermost honeycombs of the palace. But she lacked the one thing he valued most: family.

"God, son, I'll miss you." Jared lowered the PDA as his father's words rang in his memory. Even now he could hear the thickness in his father's voice, could feel how tight he gripped him in his embrace. *"I'm sorry. I'm having a tough time of it."*

Jared let his head fall back against the headrest as his attention drifted outside. None of the stars looked familiar. *"As soon as I get settled, I'll arrange either for your visit to Sakka or mine back home,"* he'd told his father. *"Dad, this isn't going to be forever."*

Jared held strong to that promise. It was the only thing that had kept him from losing it during the emotional farewells with his family outside the ship just prior to departing Edwards Air Force Base late yesterday. Eight ships had landed that morning, not just this one. The others were unexpected gifts. Part of Queen Keira's dowry, Cavin had explained.

A simple "thank you" communicated Earth's receipt of the spaceships. They had to play it cool. No one wanted the Coalition to learn the truth: nobody knew how to fly the ships.

Jared fought a pang of jealousy. Had he not been the one tasked with marrying the queen, he'd have been one of the pilots selected to test-flight the shiny new toys. He fully intended to make that dream a reality once he settled in to his new life on Sakka.

As for other goals, he didn't know what to expect. He could stand many things, but the thing he feared most was loneliness. He valued his bonds with people; he was close to his family. He intended to be close with Keira, too.

If she lets you. All he saw in his mind was her throwing daggers.

Restless, he put down the *Agran* and went for a walk.

"Sir, do you need anything?"

"What can I get you?"

"Serve you?"

"Arrange for you?"

"Cook for you?"

"I'm fine. I don't need anything," Jared said. "Thank you." They were so eager to please.

They feel sorry for you.

Jared clenched his stomach muscles as the reality hit him. Yes, they do, he thought. They pitied him because he was marrying the queen. Oh, joy. It seemed Miss Sunshine lived up to her reputation.

He paused to peer inside one of the sleeping pods. There were ten. Six were occupied, Karl and Han in two of them. Suspended animation or bio-stasis, it was called, although technically your biological functions weren't completely suspended, only slowed down—a little for shorter flights like this, and a lot for long space journeys. As peaceful as the men looked, Jared began to wonder why he wasn't doing the same instead of wandering around the ship with his memories for company.

But in some small way, he needed to keep control of the situation. If he hibernated, he relinquished that control.

Suddenly, the protocol attendant was standing next to him. "Sir, you might want to sit down and fasten your seat harness if you're not going to enter stasis," he said. "It can get a little turbulent transiting the wormholes."

"Sure." Jared returned to his seat. *A little turbulent* was an understatement. Passing through the wormhole was like being shot out of a slingshot. The stars stretched into streamers, obscured by a rainbow of colors. The ship shook so hard that he couldn't focus on anything. Then, just as quickly as they'd entered, they came out the other side. "That was quite a ride," he said.

"In a little over six hours, we do it again."

"Cool." Jared put away his reading material and lowered his seat into a bed.

HE SLEPT THROUGH THE SECOND transit. But for the third and final pass, Jared was awake and alert.

"Strapped in, sir?" a pilot asked.

Jared gave her a thumbs-up. It baffled her. "Yes," he said. He was going to have to teach these space jockeys some fighter signals.

The shaking began. He folded his hands over his stomach and tried not to think of what his molecules were doing as they whipped through hyperspace, outside the rules of time and space. Then the ship came out the other side. Immediately, the ride smoothed out. Suddenly, fireworks exploded off the bow of the ship.

"We're under attack!" The pilot steered away from the ball of fire, but an ear-shattering boom told Jared they hadn't been so lucky.

Alarms sounded. The pilots were shouting to each other. If he'd thought the wormhole transit was turbulent, it was nothing compared to this. He was flopping around in his seat like a rag doll. He tried to get a grip on something, anything. Nothing worse than flying in combat and being nowhere near the flight controls.

One more explosion left the ship spinning. The alarm wailed. G-forces shoved him sideways. The stars whirled in a kaleidoscope. He smelled burning equipment. Wisps of smoke filled the cabin. They were going to have to evacuate, but no one had briefed that possibility. And they'd have to wake up the sleepers before getting out.

Then something hit, and it felt different than before, like a wave of warmer air, the flash of heat when you ignited the gas in the grill. The pilots had stopped yelling.

Smoke burned his eyes. The alarm warbled, but the shouting had stopped. "Are you okay?" He'd used the English word. There was no equivalent in their language. "Are you well?" he yelled.

Jared tore off his harness and crawled to the cockpit. Both pilots were slumped over the control panel. He grabbed the shoulder of the female pilot first and pulled her off the narrow desk. She flopped backward into the seat, her hand slipping off the control stick. The spinning slowed. Jared grabbed the stick and leveled the ship. The shaking continued, rattling his teeth.

He felt for a pulse. Nothing. Hurriedly, he tipped her head back and gave CPR. Dragging her limp body to the floor, he tried to get her heart started. "Damn it." He pumped, swearing, until he finally gave up. Her counterpart's lips were already turning blue. What killed them? Some kind of energy pulse?

Whoomph.

Ears popping, Jared spun around at the sound. *Whoomph.* There it went again, making his ears plug.

Whoomph.

It was coming from the area of the sleeping pods. He staggered to where the rest of the crew and his escorts slept, blissfully unaware of what had happened.

Whoomph.

Jared had one quick glimpse of Karl's relaxed face before the pod shot out the bottom of the ship. The breach to open space sealed almost instantly, awash in a white mist, but not fast enough to keep the pressure equalized. It explained Jared's popping ears. The pods were being ejected, one at a time. It must be an emergency evacuation feature.

Whoomph.

Outside, the pods floated away from the ship like tiny, glowing dust motes.

Whoomph. Another pod shot out of the ship.

The shaking was getting worse. How long before the ship came apart?

Jared figured he'd better be getting his ass into one of those pods. It was his life raft out.

Whoomph.

He climbed into an empty pod. A burst of light dragged his attention outside the ship. Glowing debris faded like sparklers. He stared, confused. Then there was another burst of light. One of the little pods exploded. *Good God.* Someone was shooting at the sleepers.

Whoomph. He jerked his gaze to the last remaining occupied pod. It was Han's. He had to stop it from ejecting. A light blinked red. Maybe that was it. He reached for it—

Whoomph. The pod disappeared.

"No!" Jared shouted, wrenching his body around to look outside. Han's pod floated away from the ship. A heartbeat later, a stream of light hit it and it blew up.

Jared's was the last remaining pod. He felt a buzzing run up his arms from his hands, which were propped on the rim of the sleeping pod. His legs were buried inside, and he was about to go for a ride. "Oh, shit."

He ripped out his legs and vaulted over the top of the pod. *Whoomph.* Tremendous suction almost dragged him back inside the pod. Crashing to the floor, he rolled away, pulling up to look outside as he got free. His empty pod tracked smoothly across the bow of the ship, heading for assumed safety. But it, too, vanished in a brief, intense explosion.

Jared stayed low on the floor. He didn't want anyone seeing him walking around if he wasn't supposed to be alive. He waited for the explosion that would blow up the ship, him along with it. There'd be no escaping this time. No lucky breaks.

But nothing happened. The transport continued to shake. A powerful vibration ran from bow to stern. It didn't sound good.

If the attackers had wanted to blow up the ship, why would they have destroyed the pods so methodically?

He didn't understand what kind of game was being played here, but he was going to find this puppy a place to land if it killed him—which was, he decided, a definite possibility.

He jumped in the pilot seat and took hold of the controls. Shaking and rocking, the damaged transport hurtled onward. Cavin had told him so much was automated on these ships, there was little the pilot needed to do. But this one seemed to be so damaged that whenever Jared let go of the stick, it wanted to pitch over. A huge, misted planet loomed ahead. How was he going to land there? He was an F-16 pilot, damn it, not Han Solo. He knew nothing about reentry procedures, other than stuff burned up if it came in too fast and bounced off the atmosphere if it came in too slow. Neither of those sounded too good.

In the midst of the shaking, a trail of lights appeared. The ship's nose jerked, aligning with the lights that floated down toward the planet like a trail of fireflies.

Lead-in lights for an approach.

"Oh, crap," Jared muttered, reaching for the seat harness and strapping in. No matter how good the approach lights were, the landing was not going to be pretty. Hell, he didn't know if he was supposed to lower landing gear or land on the belly. And if he did have to put down wheels manually, it wasn't going to happen at all because he had no freaking idea what button to press or lever to pull.

His bones rattled as the ship lunged toward the swirling clouds. It was beautiful, he thought, this alien world, all covered in white. Goddess's Keep.

And here comes Earth's prince in what was going to be a spectacularly memorable, if not-so-grand, entrance.

Ground details were visible now. He was accelerating, not slowing, it seemed. He looked for something resembling a brake and found nothing likely to stop him. The shaking grew stronger, but he fought to keep the stubby wings level. Just as he thought the ship was about to break apart, it jerked and decelerated. It looked as if he was coming in to a runway. It was dark against the ice, lined with magenta lights. At the far end was a tunnel. Were they crazy? He might be able to crash-land this thing on the runway, but no way was he going to shoot it through that tunnel.

He gritted his teeth, gripping the control stick. The runway came up fast. He broke the descent at the last minute. The ship hit, scraping with a hideous noise. Blinding sparks roared on both sides of the fuselage. He thought he'd stop before reaching the tunnel, but he'd come in way too fast. The ship screamed and shrieked over the runway. The tunnel entrance flew up so fast that he didn't have time to brace himself.

The ship roared through the entrance, decelerating rapidly, until it finally came to a stop. At the end there, he must have squeezed his eyes shut, because he was opening them, his breath ragged, to see if he was still alive.

It was silent except for his wheezing. His lungs burned; his throat was on fire. Toxic fumes, he thought. He'd figured adrenaline had made him light-headed, but now he knew that wasn't it.

People in dark uniforms were running toward the ship from all directions. He had the impression of having stepped on an anthill. Off to one side was a small group dressed differently from the rest—long, gray, thigh-length suits belted at the waist and riding boots. Inside the half circle of openly shocked men was a small, slender woman wearing a sparkly gown and an expression of disbelief. Keira.

The strangest sensation hit him—possession, the need to protect her, pride and pleasure in seeing her. She was his—his wife. His woman.

Jared jumped down from the hatch and into the grand hall as the nearly destroyed ship sizzled and hissed behind him. His head was spinning. His lungs hurt. He took a few staggering steps forward. "Hi, honey, I'm home," he said. Then the ground spun up to meet him.

CHAPTER TWELVE

IT MUST HAVE BEEN ONE KILLER martini, Jared thought as he came to. Or ten killer martinis. He was lying on his back in bed—not his—and a demolition crew had taken up residence in his head with a wrecking ball that slammed in time with his pulse.

"Jared…"

And if a wicked hangover wasn't bad enough, whoever he'd ended up in bed with sounded more like a dude than a woman.

"Your Highness, how do you feel?"

Your Highness? Jared groaned. He'd forgotten—he was royalty now. "Yo, I'm fine." Sort of. "It's cool."

"Sir?"

He'd spoken English. He switched to the queen's tongue and peeled open an eye. A tall, silver-haired man sat ramrod straight in a chair next to the bed. "Prime Minister Rissallen," Jared said. "I remember you from the ceremony."

"It is good to be able to meet you. I wish it were under better circumstances."

Jared winced. "Me, too."

"It was a terrible accident."

"It was no accident, Prime Minister. We were attacked."

"You breathed in a large amount of toxins," he said as if he hadn't heard Jared's remark. "How do you feel?"

"The light in here's too bright, but otherwise—" he took an internal audit "—I feel like *yenflarg.*" It was the only word in his new language that fit. "It feels like I drank too much alcohol—" how did you say hangover? "—but I'm fine."

Medical staff fussed around him. One lifted his arm and stuck a disc on the inside of his elbow. It made a faint hiss and almost instantly Jared's headache was gone. "Incredible," he said, bringing a hand to the side of his head.

"We would have done it sooner but didn't know your level of discomfort until you awoke."

Jared sat up and swung his legs over the side of the bed. No one tried to stop him. He liked that they didn't try to baby him. "Did everyone die? Am I the only survivor?"

"Yes. It was a great tragedy. A terrible accident."

"I'm telling you—it wasn't an accident. I watched every one of those pods blow up. Someone shot at them—deliberately." He thought of Han and Karl and the crew. Sadness formed an ache in his chest that no medicine would take away. "Eight people. Lost." To settle himself, he pressed a fist to his forehead. In Iraq, they'd lost a pilot in the squadron. It had sucked. The incident had worn on everyone. But one thing he'd learned from his time in the service was that you had to go on; you couldn't let the crap distract you. He drew on that now and shoved his grief to the back of his mind.

"It must be difficult for you, Prince Jared. I thank the gods and goddesses of Sakkara that you miraculously survived—and saved one of our transports in the process."

Speaking of goddesses…where was his wife? He didn't want to admit it, but he was kind of hurt she wasn't there, waiting for him to wake up. He'd never pictured a spouse being anything less than a best friend. While he and Keira weren't there yet, he'd think she'd be concerned about his health, or at the very least his state of mind as the sole survivor of an accident. Damn it, wasn't she as anxious to meet him in the flesh as he was to meet her? Or maybe she had been at his bedside and official duties called her away. "I would like to see Queen Keira."

"That is impossible at this time."

"Impossible? How's that?"

"She is in her exercise chambers. No one interrupts Her Highness when she is there."

"I can't see my wife because she's working out? Give me a break." He realized he'd spoken English again and switched back. "Tell Her Majesty that her husband wishes to see her."

The prime minister looked distinctly uncomfortable. "But the queen has already made arrangements for your meeting." He handed Jared a glowing cylinder.

It was a flexible computer screen that was as thin and as pliable as paper. Jared unrolled it. It was a formal invitation to join Keira for dinner, which was hours away. "How nice of her," he said dryly. "I suppose I have no choice but to wait, do I? I wouldn't want to inconvenience Her Royal Sunshine."

"Beg your pardon?"

"Nothing. Just a little pet name I've coined for my dearest wife."

The man's mouth twitched, but he said nothing. "Since you're well on your way to full recovery, I'll be going."

"Hold on, Rissallen. I haven't debriefed you and your staff on what happened outside the wormhole."

"Our accident investigation team is already studying the ship. A shame that with all the safety features, this sort of accident can still happen."

What part about "this was no accident" didn't the man understand? Jared spoke slowly to make sure he used the right words. "It was an ambush. It had to be. When we came out of the last wormhole, someone, a ship, was waiting for us. They attacked. It was as if they knew we were coming through. If that's true, you've got a major breach of intelligence on your hands."

"If what you say is true, why not destroy the ship? It seems odd to fire on the individual ejecting pods when simply vaporizing the transport would have solved the issue."

Jared started to argue but stopped. The prime minister had a point. Could it have been an accident? A malfunction with the ship or the pods? Possibly. His gut, however, told him otherwise. "I think it's wise to assume the worst. Your intelligence people need to be working on this. I'd like to debrief them as soon as possible. And Earth needs to be told, the men's families informed."

"Of course. My staff will see to all the details."

But the man acted unimpressed. If anything, he seemed mildly annoyed by Jared's accusations. Jared decided to drop it—for now. He'd find out who the minister of intelligence and military commanders were and make his own arrangements to meet with them. Was the Coalition so secure in their power that they could ignore an overt attack like this? They couldn't be that comfortable or they never would have married off their precious queen to neutralize Earth's threat.

Jared gave the departing prime minister a halfhearted wave. Contact intelligence, arrange a meeting with the military leaders—he had a lot on his to-do list. For now, a more immediate problem needed to be solved: that of his wife's apparent total lack of interest in her new husband.

THE REST OF THE AFTERNOON was spent settling in to his new quarters. His apartment was probably six thousand square feet. If he ignored the mind-boggling integration of nanotechnology in the decor—walls that changed color at a whim, floors and bedding that altered temperature according to personal preference, sound and smells that could be customized to fit his current mood—the suite of rooms resembled one in a first-class hotel, only five times as big and opulent. Wealth and good taste infused every fixture in the room, including many works of art in their own right. Describing it as *luxurious* did the place an injustice. Yet, as fancy as it was, as richly appointed, it was just as distinctly impersonal. There was no stamp of individuality anywhere, not even a scarf thrown over a chair or a pair of shoes left by the door. No signs of human habitation.

He remembered the warm, rich colors in the room where he'd first met Keira: the big pillows, the plush carpets. None of that was here. These rooms were a blank slate, ready for personalization. "This is my apartment only?" he confirmed with his escort. "Not the queen's?"

"The queen has her own chambers. This is where you will live."

"I see." Jared wasn't an expert in protocol, but when he pictured married life, it was sharing the same room as his wife. In fact, he expected to be in the same bed, too. But separate apartments? Not a chance. It was just one more thing he and Keira would have to discuss.

Another young man came in. Like the first escort, this one was slight of build and feminine. His voice was high and he had no facial hair. Eunuchs, Jared realized. In fact, he hadn't seen a single normal male since leaving the hospital, and that was well outside the royal chambers. They'd been "fixed," like Evie's cats. If done at puberty, castration all but guaranteed a man wouldn't develop most typical male traits. Cavin had told him that only eunuchs were allowed to attend the queen to ensure she stayed in unspoiled condition. The same was probably true with him—she might think beautiful slave girls serving him might be too much temptation. If only she'd seen him with the supermodel. He'd been a model of restraint.

"Your Highness, can I be of any further assistance?"

Jared interrupted him. "Don't call me that."

"What is the manner of address you prefer?"

Good question. His staff would need to feel they were using respect. "How about *sir?* Just plain old *sir.* Call me that. Not *Your Highness.*" He added, "We're more casual on Earth."

"Yes, sir."

"Very good," Jared said. Apparently these eunuchs were quick studies.

Another young eunuch entered the room. How many were there? He was losing count. "Sir, your bath is ready."

"I prefer a shower."

"There is no shower."

Great. He'd have to put in a request for one to be installed. While he enjoyed a good soak in a hot tub, he didn't intend to spend the rest of his life taking bubble baths.

"Shall I show you to the bathing chamber, Your Highness?"

"*Sir.* Just call me *sir.*"

"Yes…sir." The attendant's mouth seemed to have a tough time adjusting to the word. He carried several folded towels in his arms, almost reverently, as he preceded Jared into the bathroom.

Bathroom, hell. It *was* a chamber. "Holy…"

Jared stared, stunned at the enormous room. In the center was a huge tub. Perfumed steam thickened the air, blurring the outer edges of the room. Exotic plants and flowers twined around metallic statues of nudes. The ceiling was so high that he had a hard time focusing on the paintings. Cavorting gods and goddesses seemed to be the theme. And they were buck naked like the statues.

If this was a device to get him in the mood for his night with Keira, they didn't have to worry. His desire to get a little closer with the woman—hell, *a lot* closer—had only strengthened as the day wore on. Too much buildup over the past months, and too little contact; it made for an explosive feeling of anticipation.

"Your clothes, Your High…er, your clothes, sir." The eunuch held out his arms to take them.

Jared paused with one hand on his shirt. Did he ask the guy to turn around? Well, no. Technically, the eunuchs weren't interested in him sexually. But their feminine ways made him uncomfortable. *Just pretend you're in the locker room at the gym.*

He pulled off his clothes, shoved the pile in the eunuch's arms and dove into the tub. He broke through the surface at the opposite side, shoving fingers through his hair. Leaning on the edge of the tub, he watched dozens of busy eunuchs going here and there. Privacy, he thought, was going to be a commodity.

He pushed off the wall and swam back to where the first attendant crouched next to a basket of bath supplies. Jared plucked one of the soaps and a scrubber out of the basket. Sliding back on one of the steps, he got to work cleaning up while the eunuch silently waited with nothing to do. It felt a little weird having company, but hey, what could he do? Once he settled in to palace life, he'd make changes. Taking solitary showers and baths went on the mental list he was compiling. That was, unless Keira wanted to join him.

But the silence of his attendant was unnerving. "What's your name?" Jared asked to make conversation.

The young man glanced up. "My name is Taye."

"Do you like working here, Taye?"

"I am blessed to be so."

"But do you like it? Do they treat you well?"

"Yes, sir. I am blessed to be deserving of their attention."

The eunuch seemed shocked that Jared would care to ask the question. "Did you...choose this life?" What he really wanted to ask was if he'd wanted to be neutered. If Jared was going to live in this palace, there'd be no lopping off of testicles without the owner's express permission. Period. "Is it something you request as a boy? Or does the palace decide?"

"One must express interest, and many do. It is a great honor to serve the goddess and live in the Keep on Sakka. Many wanted to be similarly blessed but were not chosen."

"But it requires you to be castrated."

The eunuch blushed almost prettily. "It was done when I was a boy. There was no pain. Now I can serve the goddess without the distraction of baser urges."

Jared frowned as he scrubbed shampoo through his hair. Having eunuchs as attendants seemed barbaric, a relic of Earth's Dark Ages. At least the surgery was done painlessly and while the attendants were still boys. Any later in life would cause a hormonal uproar, he imagined.

After rinsing, Jared rose, dripping wet, and reached for a towel. Out of the corner of his eye, he caught the eunuch aiming a silvery object at his balls. Jared jerked his hips away and grabbed the eunuch's slender wrist. "Drop it," he said, squeezing hard.

The eunuch made a breathy yelp and the object splashed into the water.

"What was that? What were you trying to do?" Jared wasn't sure he wanted to hear the answer. "Speak!"

"I was preparing to shave you."

"Shave me? Shave me where?"

"Why, everywhere, sir."

Jared was speechless. "I don't think so, buddy."

"But the queen requested it."

"That I shave my body?" What kind of weird issues did his new wife have? If she wanted him to look like one of these eunuchs, she'd married the wrong guy. "Give me the shaver." He stuck out his hand.

The relieved-looking eunuch fished the shaver out of the tub and handed it over. It didn't look like any razor Jared was familiar with. It was a stick with a disc on one end. Where was the blade? "How do I use this thing?" He felt like a primitive islander studying an explorer's wristwatch.

"Sir, you press it against the skin. Nano-blades remove the hairs."

Microscopic blades. Jared brought it to his jaw and hesitated. "Tell me it's not like waxing."

"Waxing? I do not know what this is."

"Good. That's the answer I wanted." Clearly, on Sakka, they'd evolved beyond smearing melted wax on skin and ripping out body hair by the roots. Jared pressed the device against his cheek and began to shave the way he did every day—no more, no less. He'd come to his wife clean-shaven tonight, all right, but not in the way she expected.

KEIRA STOOD QUIETLY as her attendants prepped and primped her. One brushed out her hair, another braided gemstones into the strands, while still another massaged scented oils into her skin. Her skin was gleaming, completely smooth. Her private parts had been laced with flavored lotions. It seemed odd to be working so hard to attract the prince when all she wanted was for him to stay away.

Liar. She swallowed, lifting her chin. No! She would not admit to her curiosity about the barbarian. Soon enough she'd see him naked. *As he will soon see you.*

Arousal trilled through her, but she blocked it. She would not touch him—she would not let him touch her—until she was assured of his docility. *He is not a docile man.* Not on-screen, he wasn't, she thought angrily, but in person it would be different. He was the reigning Goddess of Sakka's consort, the dutiful mate of the queen of the galaxy. The sooner he learned his manners, the better.

The sword is the best teacher.

True. But now that she was married to the man, she needed the primitive for producing heirs. He must remain intact.

An attendant pulled her arm away from her side, turned her hand palm up, and began the tedious work of imprinting an intricate pattern of nano-dye on her wrist. It was the famous holy Sakkaran symbol of a married woman. The pattern was created from a special shimmering red-orange dye and would stay with her all the years of her life. Only a true goddess was marked in this way. She remembered her mother's imprints.

An attendant lifted her other arm. She winced, her eyes watering. The pricks stung.

"A numbing agent?" an attendant queried.

"No!" Keira wanted to feel the prick of the needle just as the ancients had in a ceremony that had remained virtually unchanged over millennia. Every stinging invasion of her flesh reminded her that she was alive and not spinning out of control in a life orchestrated by others. She didn't want this marriage; she didn't want this husband. She didn't want the assured monotony and predictability of the years to come, trapped in this palace, unable to leave due to the danger the Drakken posed. Everyone, it seemed, had a say in her destiny but her.

An attendant tugged on her arm. Her wrists burned. It was silent; no one spoke to her, and she had nothing to say to them. This should be a happy night, but she hadn't felt this lonely since losing her family. Her mother should be here with her for the tattooing, her younger sister, too. They'd be laughing and joking, teasing her. Happiness would be shared. She wouldn't have the worries and fears she secretly harbored because the women in her family would have been there to answer her questions and reassure her.

Keira felt an uncomfortable thickening in her throat. Deep down, she knew the reason they weren't here, why anyone close to her died. The gods and goddesses had cursed her. She was bad luck. Even the Earthling prince had barely arrived in one piece. He'd almost been killed! The transport had malfunctioned, Rissallen had told her. How the prince had made it out alive no one knew.

Least of all Keira. He should have succumbed to the bad luck that all her other potential consorts had. She hadn't even been able to bring herself to see him in the hospital because it would have been too much of a reminder of her role in his accident. She hadn't asked after his condition, either. She'd locked herself away and had done something productive—working out and practicing with her weapons. Guilt was an emotion she steered clear of. It was second only to fear on her list of feelings to avoid.

Or did love top the list?

She gave her head a shake. Bejeweled braids clicked and rang. She would not love the Earthling prince. Her unwanted mate. *But he's not like the other ill-fated consorts paraded before you. None fascinated you like this one does.*

No, she admitted, this one was different.

All the more reason to make sure he was put

in his place from the start. Marriages occurred for a reason—to procreate. Once she was with child, she'd have her own life, and he his. They would not have to see each other at all.

JARED STOOD IN FRONT of the mirror in his apartment, smoothing a hand over the sleek lines of his charcoal Armani dinner suit. The fit was superb. It felt even better. He was lucky to have it. Many of the other clothes he'd brought with him from Earth, most of it donated designer wear and custom-made royal uniforms, had been ruined in the crash. The rest were being repaired.

His room chime sounded. "Enter," he called, running a comb over his hair one last time. He'd glossed it with a light gel, giving the short strands a bit of a spike. *Not bad.* He rubbed his smooth chin. He knew one thing—thanks to that futuristic razor, he wouldn't be giving his girl beard burn tonight—no matter where he kissed her, which he intended to be everywhere she let him put his mouth.

He was getting turned on just thinking about her.

A bouquet of flowers lay on the dressing

table. They were a little strange-looking but colorful. Roses they weren't, but you had to work with what you had. He'd asked for the flowers to everyone's confusion. This was a planet locked in the depths of winter, he knew, but surely there were palace gardens or a greenhouse. When they were finally delivered according to his instructions, it was with continued confusion on the part of the attendants as to why in the world he wanted to give flowers to their queen. "Every woman likes flowers," he'd explained.

Their pinched expressions didn't make him feel too confident about that statement, but he'd give them to her anyway.

Deep down, he wanted to make a good impression on Keira, no matter how pissed he was at the entire situation. He was here now, and he'd make the best of it. It was his nature to do so.

The door chimed again. "Enter," he called out. He heard nothing, no greeting. A moment later he smelled perfume.

A woman had slipped through the door. Palace staff, Jared decided, because the eunuch "manning" the door had allowed her to enter.

"Greetings, Prince Jared." Like an exotic dancer, she spun and rotated her hips as she came closer. She was beautiful, perfection, and he felt the definite signs of attraction. Or was it her perfume, musky, exotic?

He stared, completely taken off guard by her presence and his reaction to her. "Who are you?" he asked lamely.

"I am your dreams, your desires..." She let a scarf brush across his open mouth as she glided past. "And your lover," she breathed in his ear.

Lover? "Hey, I don't think—"

She twirled around to face him. Then she stepped back and opened the scarves. She was nude—well, sort of. She wore body jewelry— nipple rings and a gemstone in her navel. Her skin glowed with a light sheen, and her scent nearly did him in as she came back a second time, smiling a knowing little grin. She slid her fingers around his wrist and pulled him away from the mirror. "Use me," she whispered. "Use me hard and now. Use me any way you like."

He couldn't believe it. Another incredibly sexy woman throwing herself at him. Twice in a week. Had he been in his twenties and single, he'd have said bring 'em on. But ever since he'd tied the knot, it seemed he'd been given the green light to getting laid by every woman except the one he was supposed to be having sex with. Fate had played a cruel joke on him in more ways than one.

He pulled his hand from her grip. "Thanks but no thanks."

"Not even one little taste?" She brushed long fingers over her pink nipples, squeezing her full breasts and lifting them as if offering succulent fruit fresh off the vine.

Blinking, he swallowed, ridding his mind of the analogy as he tried not to stare. "Who sent you here?"

"My heart brought me to you."

Sure it did. Who thought he'd be open to this kind of entertainment? Was it the staff? Rissallen or the others? It was an insult if they thought he, as a representative of Earth, had morals so nonexistent he'd be interested in screwing a palace whore on what was basically his wedding night. "Cover up. It's time for you to go."

"I will come back another time, my lord prince. I am yours. Tonight and for always."

"No, you won't—and no, you aren't." He took her by the elbow and urged her toward the door. He opened the door and placed the woman outside. "I appreciate your interest, miss, but I'm married to your queen. On my world, Earth, sex outside marriage isn't cool. From what I understand, it isn't here, either. Go, and don't come back."

He turned to the wide-eyed eunuch at the door. "Did you know anything about this?"

The young man shook his head. "No, sir."

Jared returned to the mirror to make sure his suit wasn't suspiciously wrinkled. It wasn't, but he was coated in the woman's perfume.

The door chime rang again. Now what? "Unless it's my escort to the queen's quarters, send them away."

"Yes, sir." The eunuch allowed a man to enter.

The newest arrival wore the pale blue robes of a eunuch, but the man couldn't have been more different from the others Jared had seen so far. He entered the room, eyes downcast, but he was older than the others, who weren't much more than teens. Strange, too, was that he had the faint shadow of a beard and musculature not so different from any normal male. Immediately, Jared had his suspicions.

He thought of the ambush and the prime

minister's dismissive reaction to his opinion and put himself on alert. Was this a security breach? A terrorist disguised as a eunuch? He had yet to see the weapons he'd brought along from home, most of them gifts. Yet, the attendant had let geisha girl waltz in only minutes earlier. That was a dumb move—a mistake. She'd turned out to be harmless, but it could have gone the other way. He could be lying in a pool of blood right now. His personal bodyguards had died in the attack. With no one watching his six guards, he'd damn well better do it himself.

"Your Highness, I am to escort you to the queen's chambers," the attendant announced, his eyes downcast.

"Get scanned, then we'll talk."

The man bowed submissively, his hands brought together as he bowed. He walked over to the security box and submitted to a retina scan. His identity flashed on-screen as okay.

Jared let out a breath he didn't realize he'd been holding. "You look different from the others."

The eunuch lifted his eyes. In them, anger and shame burned strong. "Unlike them, it was not my choice to be this way."

"To be a eunuch?"

"Yes, my prince."

The younger servant stood by the door and cleared his throat.

"But I am blessed to be here," the man finished as if worried he'd be in trouble for revealing his opinion on his physical state.

"Are there others like you?" If he had to become an advocate for Coalition men to be allowed to keep their balls, he would. "Have others been forced into your condition?"

"Only me. This is the result of my own despicable actions," he recited almost robotically. "I am blessed to have been shown such mercy by our goddess, the queen."

Something Cavin had told him rushed back. About a rumor that the queen had defended herself against a man by what amounted to castration by plasma sword. In the ultimate punishment, she'd kept him alive and forced him to serve with the other eunuchs in the palace. "God. That was you?"

The man nodded and waved a hand at the door. "Her Highness wishes me to escort you to her chambers."

"To humiliate you or to send me a warning?"

The man flinched at the anger in Jared's voice. "To remind me of my crime, I believe, by asking me to escort her new husband to her on her mating night."

Mating night, eh? Jared liked the sound of that. He hadn't been sure if tonight would be dinner only, or more. He wasn't going to force anything; he wanted her to feel comfortable with him first. But at least he and Keira were on the same wavelength; only he wished she hadn't felt it necessary to mete out punishments while making the arrangements.

Flowers in hand, he followed the gloomy eunuch from his apartment through the halls of the palace. The man brought him to a huge set of double doors. "I am to go no farther." He started to leave and stopped. "My prince, I wish you...good luck," he added and left.

Good luck? Who needed luck? He could handle Keira—he could handle her offscreen as well as on.

He adjusted his tie one last time and pushed through the set of heavy doors.

He caught a glimpse of a large, nearly empty room before the doors slammed shut behind him with a thunderous bang.

"Keira?" He turned, looking for her. What was this place? The room smelled fresh and faintly floral, a scent that inexplicably attracted him. It was also silent, as if soundproofed. There was no furniture, and the walls and floor were padded like a gym. And were those handcuffs hanging from the walls? Was this Keira's idea of a joke? It looked like the den of a dominatrix. He half expected her to appear dressed in black leather. With the body she had, who'd mind? As long as she left her daggers behind. He didn't trust his new wife with sharp objects.

A whirring noise dragged his attention to the opposite wall. Four silvery cables writhed on the wall as they came alive. He couldn't believe what he was seeing. The cables hunted, as if searching for something.

Time to leave, he thought and took a step backward. *Mistake.* All four writhing cables turned in his direction. Then they rushed at him at high speed.

Jared threw his body at the door. He fumbled for a way to unlock it. When that failed, he pounded on it. "Someone open the freaking door!" he shouted, panic making him resort to English.

The cables flew around him like hungry

snakes, whirring and clicking. Flowers spilled everywhere. He tried to pull the cables off, but they spun around his arms and legs. Snaking around his wrists and ankles, they cinched tight and yanked him backward.

Arms over his head, he was whipped across the floor on his ass. He slammed back-first into the padded wall. It knocked the wind from him. The cables on his ankles tugged him onto his back and spread his legs wide.

Gasping to catch his breath, there was nothing he could do but watch as a new cable on the wall came alive and slithered across the floor.

What was this one going to do?

Take a guess, buddy. He was spread-eagle and this thing was rushing for his balls. Instinctively, he tried to bring his knees together, but the cuffs wouldn't budge.

Tell me this isn't an involuntary castration device.

He twisted around and tried to wrench free. On any normal day, he was a pretty calm guy. Faced with the prospect of losing his manhood, however, that all changed.

The cable slowed as it reached him. It seemed to sniff around, whirring softly. Jared froze. He barely breathed as the cable sniffed gently at his jaw and neck then stopped where the collar of his suit began. He wasn't sure what the thing was searching for, but he wasn't going to help it out. As long as it stayed in the northern hemisphere, fine. The second it headed south, he'd be making some noise. A lot of noise. He wasn't going to take castration lying down.

The cable slipped under his collar. Jared gritted his teeth against the feel of the cold metal tip hunting around his neck. Then the robotic snake hooked around his collar and tore open his shirt. Buttons flew. The Armani suit shredded as it was ripped away from his skin.

The thing pulled off his clothes, tearing open his suit and underwear like a kid ripping into gifts on Christmas morning. In seconds, all he wore were scraps of fabric and his wristwatch. The metallic cable hissed across the padded floor and snicked into the wall, leaving him spread-eagle and just about buck naked sprawled on the floor.

CHAPTER THIRTEEN

THE ROOM WAS SILENT EXCEPT for Jared's ragged breaths and the soft whirring noises as the cuffs made minute adjustments on his ankles and wrists. Maybe he'd been right about the manly eunuch, and now he'd been led into a trap. Were these conspirators part of the same group that had ambushed the transport no one in the Coalition government wanted to admit was ambushed? The biggest threat to the Coalition was the Drakken. If the Horde had infiltrated the palace, he had to get Keira out now. He had to protect her.

Jared struggled against the restraints. They seemed to be robotic; the harder he struggled, the tighter they became. If he went still, they released some of the throbbing pressure, but as soon as he tried to wriggle a hand free, they cinched tight.

He forced himself not to fight the restraints. Carefully, he rotated his wrists. The cuffs whirred and tightened. He paused, the pressure eased and he was able to slip his hand out a millimeter more. Moving his hand a tiny amount at a time, he worked at getting free. Pause, slide, pause. Finally the cuff held to his fingers only. He yanked hard and his hand was free.

The cuff whipped around like an angry snake whose dinner had been pulled from its mouth. Jared fought to keep his arm out of the cable's reach. With three limbs pinned, it wasn't easy. After a brief struggle, the cable found his wrist and coiled around it, tighter than before.

"Ah." He grimaced in defeat. But at least he knew he could free himself. Now he had to get smarter about it. If he could give the cable something else to grab—his other wrist, or a leg; in other words, make a swap—he could get a limb free.

He was in the middle of starting the process all over again when the doors behind him opened and someone slipped into the room. Light steps padded on the soft floor.

A white-robed woman walked in front of him. A veil covered her face and reached all the way to her ankles. She was barefoot with rings on all her toes peeking out from under fabric that looked fluid. It reminded him of water, but he couldn't see through it. A trick of the microscopic computers embedded in the fabric, he knew. Liquid, it clung to every curve of her body as she followed the trail of crushed and mangled flowers. The cuffs had let up on their pressure. He inched his right hand out, stopping when the cuff whirred.

The woman paused to regard him before bending over to pick up the flowers until her hands were filled with the blooms, or what was left of them. "What is this?"

It was Keira; he recognized her voice. Heat exploded inside him. He wasn't sure if it was anger, insult or desire. Probably all three. "They were flowers. *Were.* Until I was bound and cuffed and dragged across the room. What the hell is going on, Keira? I thought we were under attack."

Her head jerked around at that. Her flower-filled hands gave the slightest tremble.

"I thought the Drakken had infiltrated the palace."

She cried out, throwing the flowers at him.

"The palace is safe! To worry about your security here is to insult me!"

"I wasn't worried about my security. I was worried about *yours*," he shouted back. He'd never thought of himself as having a temper. Keira had changed all that. God, the woman could make him furious.

"I am safe here! To say otherwise is to insult me."

"And to send a woman to my room for sex is insulting to me."

Her voice changed tone. "Did you like her?"

"I didn't touch her."

"You…didn't?"

"No. I have no intention of being unfaithful to my wife on our first night together. Or any night."

She simply stared at him. He wished he could see her face behind the veil. "Keira," he said, quieter. "If your idea was to tempt me or to get me to break the rules, you wouldn't be the first. People were trying that on Earth even before I left. If I didn't fall for it hundreds of light-years away, I won't fall for it here. One man, one woman. That's the way we Earthlings do it. Or, at least that's the way I do it."

He moved his legs. The cuffs whirred, tightening. "Take these off, Keira. Now."

"And set the barbarian free?"

"I'm the barbarian? I show up dressed in my best clothes—with flowers—prepared to dine with you, to get to know you over dinner and conversation. To get to know my wife. The person she is. What she likes or doesn't. What her hopes and dreams are—what makes her mad, what makes her laugh—and somehow I end up trussed like an animal." Her gaze tracked down his partially clothed body before she averted her eyes. Was his Sunshine shy? No, it couldn't be. But the contradiction in character intrigued him. Aroused him, too.

He worked his right hand lower. Now the cable was wrapped around his fingers. One tug and he was free.

She circled him, seeming unwilling—or afraid—to come closer. Did she cover fear or uncertainty with anger? Jared narrowed his eyes and studied her. Maybe so. And if so, more about her made sense.

"Why are you looking at me like that?" she demanded.

"I think you're afraid of me."

She sucked in a breath, sputtering. "Hardly!"

"Oh, I think so."

"I'm not afraid of a primitive, Earthling barbarian!"

He rolled his eyes. "Here we go again. First you tried to have me shaved. Why? Do you prefer eunuchs to men? They're not, after all, as scary."

"Your insinuation is a lie!"

"Is it? Why did you tie me up if you weren't afraid of me loose?"

Her chin shot straight up. "It was important that you know your place."

"My place is as your husband and at your side. I defer to your higher rank in public. However, in private, we're equals. No argument. No compromises. Equals."

"I would think you'd want to be the dominant one, Earthling."

"Trust me, there will be plenty of times I'll be dominant. Then we can switch. The goddess and the barbarian—there are a lot more fun ways to play that game than this, and all the variations are voluntary. Unlike this—chained in a dungeon."

"It is a play room."

"You wanted to play? To fool around? Why

didn't you say so? If you wanted to see me naked, all you had to do was ask," he drawled.

"By the gods!" she blurted out in fury. White robes flowing around her curves, she stormed toward the doors.

"Going already?" He hoped not for her daggers or plasma sword. "Too scared to hang around and fight? I'm disappointed. I thought you were braver. Goddess of Sakkara and all that." His hand moved out of the cuff another sliver. "Must be a weak bloodline."

That did it. Hot button. She was back so fast his head spun. She didn't have a clue that his hand was almost free as she crouched next to him in a whoosh of fluid robes. She tinkled faintly—jewelry inside her outer wrapping of robes—and the scent he'd smelled before radiated from her skin. He liked her scent, he realized. A combination of her personal scent and perfume, something he'd never smelled before, it was unique and exotic, like her. "My bloodlines are second to none. They are uninterrupted all the way back to the beginning of time."

"So why are we wasting time talking about your bloodlines when I could be helping you extend them? You know, the old-fashioned way."

She gave a little gasp of outrage. "Your accent is too thick—I cannot understand you," she claimed, even though he was sure she knew exactly what he'd meant.

"Maybe I'd better talk with my hands." He whipped his arm out of the cuff.

The cable whipped around. He kept his arm clear. In a frenzy of whirring, it hunted for purchase and found Keira. The cable, it seemed, didn't care whose wrist it grabbed, only that it had one.

It snaked around her wrist and tugged her down, crossways, over his body. What luck! He couldn't have arranged something this good if he'd tried. Wiggling her cute little butt, she twisted and bucked, struggling unsuccessfully to get up. He was rock-hard immediately. No surprise there. He was pretty much naked with a beautiful woman lying on top of him, writhing and wiggling—a woman who was his wife. How could he not react? He felt every warm curve of her firm, athletic body. Her breasts were crushed against his chest. She squirmed as he laughed at the craziness of the situation and her indignation at it, and it only made his raging hard-on worse.

"Well, I didn't realize you wanted to work on your bloodlines so fast. I was hoping to get to know you a little better first. But here I am—barbarian at your service, Goddess. Where shall we start?" His hand landed on the small of her back. She was sprawled on top of him, one thigh wedged between his legs. A bolt of arousal went straight to his groin. He ran his hand over her butt and down her thigh.

She yelled and yanked off her veil. Her eyes were wild with humiliation and fear. Anger had turned her cheeks bright pink. "Get your hands off me!"

"Hand," he corrected. "The other one is tied up." But he did as she asked, laying his arm across his forehead. There was nowhere else to put it. "So. Let's talk. We haven't had a chance to yet. Where'd you grow up?"

"Where do you think?" she yelled, her teeth clenched.

"Getting sassy are we?" He took a strand of her amazing hair and wrapped it around his finger. "Women handcuffed to barbarians probably shouldn't be too sassy." He rubbed the tips of the strands across her plump, pouty lower lip. She tried to bite him and got a mouthful of hair instead.

He laughed as she spit it out. "Now see? That was sassy. That's what happens."

She arched her back and swung a punch at him. He caught her fist but her knee shoved up between his legs. "Ooph." Eyes watering, he coughed out a groan of pain. With a full hard-on, that was not fun. He slammed his eyes shut and took deep breaths.

"Jared..." He felt inquiring fingers brush across his face. "Did I hurt you?"

He opened an eye to her worried face. "You actually care?"

Instantly, her expression darkened. A wall came over her expressive brown eyes and she closed him off. But for a minute, he'd peeked inside her. It was a glorious sensation, and one he might not repeat for a long time if her angry expression was any indication. "Not about you," she snapped. "I was worried I'd hurt your..." She blushed, her cheeks filling with pink.

So, she was shy. He'd assumed she was experienced, having made out or made love to one or more men over the years, but maybe the near-rape was all she'd known.

"My what?" he asked, gentler and with a slightly playful tone.

"Tonight we must mate," she told him, answering without really answering.

"Ah, so you thought you needed to handcuff me to do it? You didn't think I'd make love to you voluntarily?"

Her gaze slid to the side.

"Or were you worried I'd try to do it before you were ready?"

Her wide eyes snapped back to his. He stopped her tirade with a finger pressed to her opening mouth. So, she had been scared of him. He saw it in her face but didn't humiliate her with the knowledge. He didn't know much about this passionate stranger who was his wife, but he'd already started to figure out she didn't like being frightened—maybe even less than admitting it. "I didn't want this marriage," she said.

"I didn't want it, either."

Hurt flashed in her eyes. "Just mate and go then. Get me with child and you never have to see me again."

"That's not how I see it, Keira. I don't 'mate and go.' We're married. You have a husband now whether you like it or not. I may have entered this marriage as a treaty to keep the peace, but it's just as real to me as any marriage I'd have committed to." He paused to take in the sight of her hair, dark, thick and wild. Her face was oval shaped with that little mouth he wanted to kiss and those huge eyes, golden brown and slightly almond shaped with amber specks that glowed like copper.

Of all the women in the galaxy, this one was his. It was a staggering thought. He'd grow old with Keira. He wanted to soak her in, to commit her to memory. Her chest was rising and falling rapidly, and her brows were slanted over furious eyes, but he could imagine her smiling. Sort of. In time, he'd grow to love her.

"It's okay to be nervous," he said quietly with an overwhelming urge to kiss her. "I'm nervous, too. About being with you, wondering if you'll like making love with me. Hoping I can satisfy you." *You're a queen,* he wanted to say. *And I'm just a regular dude. A commoner.* "However, it is the first time for us. It'll get better. I promise you that. We'll learn what pleases each other."

Her lips compressed and her blush deepened.

"Keira, we don't have to do anything tonight, no matter what your tradition says. Let's take our time to get to know each other. I'm fine with that."

She shook her head, on the verge of getting angry again. "No. It must be tonight."

"Why? Is someone going to check the sheets? Is someone going to watch?" He hoped not. The cuffs were kinky enough without an audience. He glanced around, checking for cameras.

"The gods are watching. If we do not mate, our union will be cursed, the marriage will be damned and any future children we have will not grow to see adulthood."

He'd heard of wedding-night pressure, but this was ridiculous. "Keira, have you done this before? Or is this your first time?" he asked tenderly.

"If you mean consensual sex, yes."

"Or course I mean consensual." How many times was he going to have to reassure her? *If she was raped, maybe a lot of times.* "What happened, Keira? I need to know."

"There was a suitor," she said in a voice that told him she didn't want to talk about it. "He was a mayor of one of our largest worlds. He'd come to the palace so we could spend time getting to know each other. I was young. Very young. I didn't think he would want more if we only kissed, but one of the times we were together it went too far. I let it go too far."

"It wasn't anything you did, Keira. No man has to cross that line, no matter how turned on he is. Not if the woman says no."

At first she seemed amazed that he'd said so. Then her expression soured and she made a fist. "It was a single penetration, only for a few seconds. That's all. But enough to hurt. I wasn't ready."

She was also a virgin. Anger swelled in him when he remembered how the eunuch had gained his brief sympathy. Now he felt like picking up a plasma sword and finishing the job.

"I fought him off," Keira said. "And then I finished him from ever doing the same again to any other woman."

"Why did you send him to me tonight to escort me here? Why?"

"Many reasons! I wanted to punish him for taking what I could never give you. I also wanted you to know I was not weak, that I would not tolerate being forced. I—" She sighed. "It happened a long time ago, but sometimes it's hard to forget. I have let no man get close to me since."

"Until me."

"You are my husband. We have to mate."

"We don't *have to* do anything. We don't do anything you don't want to. Period." He pulled her close. No wonder she was nervous. She was as inexperienced as a virgin even though technically she wasn't. He'd never thought much about a partner's sexual experience, preferring more of it as opposed to less, if he'd had to be honest. But knowing he'd be the first man to *make love* to her brought feelings of distinct pride, protectiveness and pleasure.

With a rush of unaccustomed feeling, he buried his mouth in the warm place under her ear and inhaled her scent. He felt her stiffen, then, almost fractionally, relax, breathlessly waiting to see what he was going to do. He kissed her there, slowly pulling away. She turned her head and it was all that was needed to brush their lips together.

Hungrily, she started kissing him. After a second or two of total shock, he kissed her back. His free hand fisted in her thick hair, holding her close. She made a soft little groan, her hand closing around his upper arm as she opened her mouth fully to him. He crushed her close, or was it she who gripped him close? It was a crazy kiss, uninhibited as hell and way too hot for two people who only moments ago had been ready to kill each other. They separated, if only to drag air into their lungs. And then they came back for more.

Finally, a breathless Keira rested her warm cheek against his. "Gods," she whispered. "Gods."

His fingers fanned out on the side of her throat to feel her pounding pulse as he kissed his way lower. But he couldn't go any lower than her shoulder without pulling his arm out of his socket. He remembered her magnificent breasts. He wanted to hold them, to touch them. He wanted to hear her beg for his mouth on her. "We've got to get these cuffs off," he breathed.

"I know," she breathed back, her voice thick with arousal. Her eyes were dark, her mouth wet from their kiss.

He slid his hand up and over her knee and up the long, smooth expanse of her thigh. He locked eyes with her so there was no mistake as to where he wanted to touch her next. His fingers stopped where her warm inner thigh curved. God, she was hot—on fire. His hand trembled as he fought going any farther without a green light.

To his shock, Keira's hand came over his and

lifted it, placing it exactly where he wanted to touch her. Watching her reaction, he slid his fingers between her legs. She sucked in a breath, her eyelids drooping. But her body was tight, rigid. She was nervous. He decided not to say anything to call attention to that fact. Better to see if he could distract her.

His pressed his fingers where she was so slick and hot. He was so aroused by now, he ached. He wanted to be there where his fingers explored, deep in her body. He stroked her, his fingers slipping in and out, circling until he found the small bud he hoped would shove her nerves to the back of her mind.

She made a soft cry and rose up on her knees, but her outstretched, cuffed arm kept her close. He smiled at the look of surprise and pleasure on her face, and the way her body slowly melted. He stroked her until she pressed into his hand, then he backed off. She protested and he resumed, harder this time, withdrawing when it seemed she was about to come. "Please," she said.

Was she begging the barbarian? The Earthling? The queen of the galaxy was at his mercy. He sank his fingers deep, moving the heel of his palm where she was most sensitive. She made a cry through clenched teeth. She arched her back and ground her hips against his hand. He felt the surge of wetness as she pulsated around his fingers still embedded deep inside her. The contractions seemed to go on for a long time until, slowly, she went limp against him.

"Gods," she whispered as he stroked her hair, wishing he was holding her in his arms. He'd come a step closer to truly making her his wife. Somehow, he knew that to give and not to demand was the way to her heart—and her trust. It was important to him, having that trust. The relationship wouldn't go anywhere without it.

You want her trust when everything you are is a lie? You're a commoner. She thinks you're a prince.

He hated the deception, knowing he'd have to live with it for the rest of his days. *Everything about this marriage is a lie, including the ceremony itself.* He'd never agreed to it—the Coalition had forced it on him without his permission. If he was a commoner, well, she deserved what she got.

Yet, having left everything that mattered to him—his home, his family, his careers—he was damn well going to get something in return, and empty sex wasn't going to cut it. No matter what had got him into this mess of a marriage, his goal was to make Keira his, body and soul. But that wasn't going to happen with him bound and trussed like a steer.

He rubbed her back with his free hand. "I've lost the feeling in my left arm. We need to get these cuffs off."

Keira lifted her head to look at him. "The release is on the wall and we can't reach it." She bit her lip. His heart swelled at her hesitation. How could he go from intense dislike to a major crush this fast? "I will have to summon my guard to set us free."

Like sex-rescue 911, he thought. Keira was a lot of things, but "a proud woman" had to be near the top of the list. It would be embarrassing for her, having her staff find her like this. One look at their queen straddling him, her robes shoved up to her knees, and him, spread-eagle and wearing nothing but an expression of total arousal on his face, and they'd know they'd been fooling around.

"Well, on the positive side, it would smash any doubts as to whether we're going to consummate our marriage. No one will have to worry about curses. There might a few rumors floating around to our sexual preferences, though. Or perversions? Kinky games in any case." He started to laugh, thinking of what the staff would think. "Whatever you do, don't call Rissallen. Please." He imagined the expression of shock on the acerbic prime minister's face and laughed harder.

Keira's eyes shone with held-in laughter. "He's the last person I will summon here. No. Supreme Commander Neppal is."

"Don't worry. We're not calling anyone. There are a lot of secrets in this palace and I intend to keep the details of our wedding night one of them."

She tried to pull her arm from the cuff. It whirred, cinching down. "What are we going to do then?"

"Let your arm go limp."

"I don't understand."

"Your arm—hold it still and watch what happens to the cuff."

She hesitated then did as he said. The cuff loosened slightly. "Now, pull your hand out—very slowly." She got farther than he had the first try.

Her eyes narrowed. "This is not good that one can escape the cuffs so easily."

"I beg to differ. I thought it was very good."

"But we use these to hold prisoners. No one escapes."

"Maybe I've made some friends amongst the eunuchs. They adjusted the cuffs so I could."

She reacted with a disdainful huff. "My servants are always making mistakes."

He wasn't so sure. "All the ones I've met seem intensely loyal, intelligent and efficient. When they make their so-called mistakes, they may be doing it deliberately."

"So they wanted you to escape?"

"Or at least give me a head start."

After a few more moments of concentration, she freed herself from the cuff. The cable whirred wildly. "Go!" he yelled at her. Keira rolled out of the way. The cable whirled around Jared's wrist. Back to square one.

Keira crawled back to him, her hair wild and tangled. "You set me free," she said. "You could have trapped me, captured my other arm, but instead you let me go."

"Of course I did. Now go release the cuffs, please?"

"You don't understand. My life is not my own. Every last detail is orchestrated by others. No one has ever given me a choice before." She lifted her robes and straddled him. "No one until you."

For the first time, the full force of the passion she exuded like hot lava was directed at him. Her thighs were hot and soft. Her wetness was almost too much to take. "Keira," he warned. He strained against the urge to raise his hips and plunge into her. "I can't take much more of this. I'm just being honest here—" He caught a glimpse of slender, sleekly muscled thighs before she tilted her hips and took him inside her.

Her snug, wet heat came as a shock. If she was a goddess then he'd just had a religious experience. It was definitely transcendent, being inside her, and he almost exploded with the sensation. "Keira…" He groaned, lifting his hips to meet hers.

Her head hung low. Her hair swept over his face, tickling him and filling his nostrils with her floral scent, now sharp with musk. "There," she whispered. "It's done."

"Baby, it's not close to being done. In the gods' viewpoint, maybe, but not mine." He throbbed, aching to pump into her. Spread-eagle, there was little he could about it. "I can hardly move. You have to." He lifted his hips, urging her. "Please," he rasped. He was a take-charge kind of guy in bed, but there was something erotically charged about leaving the whole show up to Keira. If she didn't start moving, he was going to explode. He probably was, anyway, but he was desperate for the friction.

She arched over him with catlike grace as she lifted up. He met her halfway on the way down, driving deep, almost to her womb.

"Again," he begged her. "Keep moving." His fists clenched in the cuffs, the cables whirring. "Yes, like that," he whispered as she rocked, finding a rhythm with his guidance. She was so snug around him, so wet.

He put pressure against the leg restraints, needing to move his legs, but unable to do it. He thrust upward, groaning. She rotated her hips, grinding against him. She was incredible. The way she felt, the way she smelled. She was his—his wife. His woman. He'd never dreamed marriage would be such a turn-on.

His hips lifted off the floor even though it was killing his arms. She sank her fingers into his shoulders. The soft sounds she made drove him closer to the edge.

Keira's eyes grew darker and wilder the longer they made love. There was something in them he hadn't seen before. She held his stare as she circled her hips, lifting and plunging, making him groan. It was control, he realized. She felt in control. And as she took that control fully, he lost it.

"Keira!" Her name came out in an explosive burst of air. He rode a peak so powerful that it almost hurt. And then his release swept over him like a tidal wave, rocking him. Keira clung to him, grinding against him until the last of the convulsions eased.

Her tangled hair sifted across his face as she raised her head. She was smiling, a tired, satisfied smile. But she hadn't had an orgasm that he could tell. It didn't surprise him. She was inexperienced and he hadn't been able to touch her the way he'd wanted. "Next time when you have a climax, it'll be when I'm inside you," he promised.

"Why?"

"Because you won't believe how good it will feel."

She shook her head. "Why do you care? You

have me now. Why do you work so hard to make it better?"

"You're my wife, Keira. That means something to me."

She regarded him intently, seeming to really see him, for the first time. She didn't have to say a thing; he knew what the woman was thinking. She'd expected him to be a first-rate jerk, and now she realized he wasn't half-bad. Call them even. He'd expected her to be a bitch and a high-maintenance diva. But he'd gotten a peek inside her, a glimpse that told him some of that was an act. Or so he hoped. At least they got along when they made love. That was as good of a start as any for an arranged marriage. They could work on getting along out of bed later. He'd make sure of it.

CHAPTER FOURTEEN

AFTER BRINGING THE Earthling to her bathing hall for a long bath together, during which he made good on his delicious sexual promise, Keira retreated to her private chambers to dress for dinner. Not *Earthling,* she mentally corrected as a eunuch styled her hair. Husband. Jared. Jared, Prince of Earth. Sitting in front of the mirror, she felt fluttery as she murmured his name. Not too long ago, those flutters had had her crying out as he'd moved deep inside her. She'd been so wildly aroused by his magic touch that all her inhibitions had fallen away.

She hadn't always been sure what to do, where to touch, how to move, but he'd shown her with patience and laughter. The mere memory of their playfulness conjured a warm, thick feeling low in her belly all over again. The mating had been so far beyond her expectations that it had seemed a different experience entirely. Perhaps it was the spontaneity of it; she'd expected the evening would go very differently. To think she'd intended to make the Earthling grovel for her, to admit his inferiority. In the end it had been her begging him.

Magic fingers…

It was more than that, Keira. He asked, he didn't demand. He let you give, he didn't take.

She waved away the attendant and stood, anxious to meet her husband in the dining chamber. But as she slipped through the door, fluffing her skirts around her, she practically collided with Tibor Frix. He grabbed her shoulders to keep her from falling, staring in obvious amazement at her good mood. "Hello, Tibor," she said.

"Your Highness." The big guard cleared his throat. "Are you all right?"

"I am wonderful."

"And the prince? How is he, ah, faring?"

Tibor Frix of all people knew what she'd set out to do to Jared. Now he couldn't help but know how spectacularly it had failed. The mating had taken place regardless of the barriers she'd set up to delay it. After many tries, the Sakkaran queen finally had a full consort. A

royal mate. It would change many things in the
queendom—her, the most.

"The prince could not be doing better, Tibor.
You are kind to ask after him. In fact, he awaits
me now in the dining chamber."

She slipped past the guard. He followed. "No,
Tibor," she said, turning. "You may take your
post *outside* the chamber doors."

"As you wish, my queen." But he seemed reluctant to leave her side. It must have been ex-
ceedingly difficult for him this evening, staying
out of sight, and now she'd asked the same of
him for the dinner. He'd been her shadow all her
life. Leaving her in the care of a husband would
not be easy.

She swept into the dining chamber, striding
across the room to meet her husband. Jared was
dressed in his traditional Earthling clothes, a coat
that reached to the waist, trousers and a dangling
strip of silken fabric he'd tied around his neck.

"You're gorgeous in that gown, Keira." He
brought her hand to his mouth and kissed her
knuckles, his eyes hot. A curious custom, that.
But she liked it. Then, taking her hand, he
escorted her to her seat, pulling it out for her
even though it was a smart-chair and would

know her custom settings. She adored his provincial manners.

"You may bring the meal," she called to the attendants. "My husband is hungry."

"I am," he whispered in her ear as he took his seat next to her. "Very hungry."

She shivered. She knew what he was hungry for—and so was she.

He took his seat at her side as eunuchs brought out dish after dish. She'd long taken the feasts for granted, but experiencing it through his appreciative eyes helped her see the richness of the presentation. Maybe long, lonely meals would be a thing of the past now that she had the prince at her side.

In a choreographed move she'd seen countless times, the attendants lifted the lids off the platters and pots all at once, releasing geysers of steam. The serving eunuchs remained behind as others whisked the lids away to the kitchens. The servers waited serenely for Keira and Jared to indicate their choices of food.

"They can go," Jared said in her ear. "We don't need them."

"Why, they must remain to serve us."

"We can serve ourselves."

"But—but that's…"

"Barbaric?"

She frowned at the twinkle of challenge in his eyes. How would she prove to the Earthling that *his* civilization was comprised of barbarians and not hers? However, dismissing the staff would afford her some privacy, and she wouldn't mind that. She waved a hand at the eunuchs. "You are dismissed."

They appeared confused as they began clearing the table.

"Please leave the food," Jared instructed them. "But you're free to go, as the queen requested. Go on, take the night off."

The gaggle of eunuchs bowed as they backed out of the dining room and closed the doors behind them. Keira caught a glimpse of Tibor, standing just outside the doors, peeking in with curiosity and disbelief. Let him wonder! For the first time, it seemed, she'd achieved some measure of independence. Who would have dreamed she'd have done it by marrying, a move she'd been certain would have stolen what little freedom she had.

She waved a hand at the globes of smoked meat in spiced sauce. "I will start with the lake-beast and gravy."

To her shock, he took her hand and wrapped it around a serving spoon. "Have you ever served yourself a meal?"

"Please. Of course I haven't."

"Never once in all your life?"

"No! Have you? Does the prince of Earth wait on himself? Does your royal family do the work of servants?"

A funny look crossed his face then. She couldn't make sense of it. During their love-making, the Earthling had seemed an open book to her, and it was delightfully refreshing, but it was obvious he had his secrets. Since he seemed more apt to reveal himself when they were intimate, why then, she'd simply have to continue to make love with him to find out what his secrets were. What could he possibly be trying to hide?

"You have to learn, Keira," he said, shattering her delicious little fantasy of him taking her right here at the dining-room table. "And to cook, as well."

"Cook?" She recoiled. Now he'd gone too far. "Why do I need to learn these things if I have no desire to do so, and if they are things I'll never need to know?"

"Nothing is set in stone, Keira. Nothing. One day we're sitting here being served. The next we may be going hungry and searching for food."

She reared back, her heart pounding. "What do you mean?"

"I've upset you, and I'm sorry. Chances are nothing that bad will ever happen, but you have to know how to survive in the event it does. You have to know how to survive on your own. Being dependent on others for everything isn't just naive, it's dangerous."

She grabbed the bowl and spoon from Jared's hands and slopped lakebeast onto her plate. Her hand shook. The sauce splashed onto her dress. "Nothing will happen." *Nothing.* If she willed it to be so, then it would be.

"Keira, you're very much protected here, but don't let your guard down. There are things I've seen that worry me. Danger signs the Coalition seems to want to ignore. Whether intentionally or not, I don't know, but first thing tomorrow, I will find out."

The food she'd just swallowed went down like a rock. She thought of everything she didn't know, that she never knew. She thought of Rissallen, Neppal and the others coming to inform her of increased Drakken aggression and the death of the minister of intelligence right here in the palace. And she thought of what Jared had insinuated earlier about the eunuchs' complicity. Her anger boiled up. "We will change the subject of this conversation or I will leave this dinner," she snapped, her stomach burning.

"You're right. Tonight's not the night for this kind of subject." He took her face in his warm hands. His earnest gaze and tender touch steadied her and muted her fear. "If it helps you to understand where I am coming from, I see one of my duties as your husband as protecting you. You're a strong woman, Keira. Smart, capable— okay, maybe not too smart about locking me in handcuffs," he put in with a cocky smile, "but we'll overlook that for now. One way I can start protecting you is by making sure you would know how to take care of yourself if you ever lost your caregivers. Does that make sense?"

She nodded, trying to control her anger. She didn't want to ruin this special night.

He drew her close and kissed her. She closed her eyes, letting his unexpected gentleness soothe her.

Sullenly at first, she began to serve herself

more food. Jared chose other bowls and did likewise. They filled their plates. It wasn't so bad a task, but certainly it felt strange not to have the servers do it.

"This is great," Jared said as he tried the baked grains. "What's your favorite?"

Did he really care, or was it only polite conversation? Her life had been filled with polite conversation. It seemed he did care about her answer, judging by his intent expression. *He wants to know you.* A small rush of exhalation buoyed her. "My favorite is actually a sweet. Snowberry ice. It is made from snowberries that appear as winter ends. They are bright lavender. When they peek out of the ice and snow, I know that the warm weeks are coming. It is winter for most of the year on Sakka. We are far from our star. If not for a very unusual orbit, we would not receive any warm weeks at all."

"I read about that before I came here. I was happy to see there was so much snow."

"Why would that make you happy? You have to stay inside all the time. I have not been outside for so long I have lost track of when I last breathed in unfiltered fresh air." She inhaled, remembering. "I cannot wait for the warm weeks to arrive so that I can go outdoors again. It is so beautiful, but only for that brief time. I will take you. I only wish it was not so far off."

"You haven't been outside since summer ended? Sorry, Sunshine, but we're going to have to correct that."

"But there is snow everywhere."

"Exactly." A look of pure anticipation lit up his handsome face. "I snowboard. It's my favorite sport. When I first learned I was coming here to live, I thought I'd have to give it up. Then I found out about the snow. Yeah, baby. Powder, powder everywhere. And no crowds!" He laughed, saw her expression of confusion and brushed his thumb over her chin. "Don't you know what snowboarding is?"

She hated for her ignorance on a subject to be exposed. "No. It must be a barbarian Earth sport."

"Yes, it is. And I'm going to show you how to do it. You're so athletic. You'll love it. But there are no runs here, I take it. I'll meet with your staff on constructing some. One advantage of being royalty, I guess." He stopped himself on that last sentence as if he'd blurted out something he hadn't intended. He dipped a spoon into a cloud-soft mountain of snowberry ice.

"It is a dessert," she explained.

"Who says we can't have dessert first? No one's here to tell us what to do." Jared piled some on her plate, paused and spooned some into her mouth. The crisp, sweet taste burst over her tongue. As she dabbed at her lips with a finger, his gaze lingered on her mouth.

Now she would feed some to him, she thought. They reached for the spoon at the same time. Their knuckles collided. She flushed and smiled. "God, you're beautiful when you smile, Keira," he said.

Her cheeks warmed some more.

"And you're even more beautiful when you blush."

"Ah! I am always blushing now. I cannot seem to be able to stop it. I don't think I have ever blushed so much as I have with you."

"Do I embarrass you?"

"You arouse me. You make me think of things that make me blush." The air thickened with their attraction. He moved to kiss her. She reached for him and pulled him to her the rest of the way. She did not want to think about what he had said about the danger. She wanted to forget it.

She kept kissing him. She could not get enough. "I want you," she pleaded, tugging open his shirt and smoothing her hands over his muscled chest and stomach. His skin was so warm and smooth.

"We've made love all day. You'll be sore in the morning...."

"I have billions of nanomed computers in my bloodstream that will ensure I will not be." The same computers that would choose the most hardy and promising of Jared's sperm to deliver to her egg when she ovulated. "I promise you," she said, tugging on his belt, "we can make love all night and I will feel nothing but pleasure."

Jared cleared the table with a sweep of his hand, moving the plates aside. Some cutlery fell to the floor. Lifting her, he sat her on the table-cloth, kissing her as he lowered her onto her back. He shoved up her skirts and dropped his pants.

Keira shrieked in surprise as the cool air hit her bare bottom. Jared's voice was hot and it tickled her ear. "Barbaric of me, I know, but I figured there was no time to waste."

One of his hands disappeared under her skirts. *Magic fingers.* Her head landed on the table. The laser-sharp lights of the chandelier turned into stars as he teased and caressed between her legs until she throbbed for him.

He seemed to know the exact moment to thrust into her. She opened her mouth as a cry of pleasure slipped out. Her toes curled and she arched her back. "How does that feel, sweet Keira? Is it good?"

There was nothing to compare with that first plunge, nothing. He had her pinned to the table, her entire body focused on the blazing, pulsing, luscious ache where they were joined. She wanted him to move. To move! But could do little but make small, mewling sounds. The art of language seemed to have escaped her.

He gripped her hips, holding her, kneading her flesh as he began to thrust. His delicious swaying was slow and deep, and it rocked her to the core.

It didn't take her long to come apart in his arms.

It was even stronger than the first time. She wrapped her legs around him, clinging to him as he drove into her. When he reached his climax as hers subsided, the pleasure was so sharp she thought she was going to die of it.

"You have me now. Why are you working so hard to make it better?"

"You're my wife, Keira. That means something to me."

A strange and wonderful sensation filled her, then, and not only because of the sex. It took some moments of thinking, but she finally realized what it was. For the first time since she was orphaned, she knew what it felt to be happy.

LATER, SPRAWLED KEIRA LAY atop the tangled bedding in her darkened sleep chamber, sated from the meal and more lovemaking. She waited until her husband had fallen asleep, and then rolled to her side of the bed they would share for the night. She wanted so much to snuggle closer but she was afraid it would become a habit and soon she would need him too much. And unlike the rings on her fingers or any of the other objects that surrounded her, people could not so easily be replaced.

CHAPTER FIFTEEN

"Huh! Huh!"

Awakened by a female voice, Jared felt blindly for Keira's warm body. The indentation where she'd slept next to him last night was cool.

"Huh!"

He opened his eyes and pushed up to a sitting position. The sheets slipped to his waist. Keira was gone.

"Huh! Huh!"

What was that noise? Keira yelling? More like grunting. He slid out of bed and pulled on his boxers, scratching a hand through his hair as he followed her voice. He felt a little stiff. He smiled. He'd definitely used a few muscles last night that hadn't been worked lately.

"Huh!" It sounded like she was in the middle of a workout. Didn't the woman ever relax?

He found her in the gym. He paused by the entrance to watch her. She wore practically nothing—what amounted to a few black strips of fabric over her breasts and butt. Her incredibly hot, tight little butt. His hand twitched, remembering how she'd felt as he'd gripped her, pressing her close as he'd made love to her. His boxers got a little snugger.

"Huh! Huh!" Grunting, Keira released two daggers, one at a time. The weapons flew across the room, sinking into a target on the opposite wall. The woman was good, he thought, folding his arms over his chest. Real good. She turned to choose two new daggers. Her hair was tangled and wild. It looked as if it hadn't seen a brush since they'd last tumbled over the bed. Her face was flushed, as it had been last night, but her eyes were dark and angry. Now what? They hadn't even had a chance to fight yet.

He entered the room just as she hefted two more knives. For a moment, it was like looking into the eyes of a cornered fox. Her gaze was wild and frightened, and she looked capable of doing anything with those knives, including sinking one into his chest.

He lifted two hands in surrender. "Hey,

Sunshine. I thought you wanted me around a little longer."

She swallowed, closing her eyes for a fraction of a second, closing him off from the flurry of emotions he saw there. Then she spun away and threw the daggers. One went astray and skidded across the floor.

Jared heard the clanking of body armor. He turned to follow the sound and a huge man blocked him from going any closer—blocked him with a sword. Jared glanced from his half-naked wife to the muscled warrior and demanded, "Who the hell are you?"

"Tibor, let him pass."

At Keira's order, the man dropped his sword. "I am Tibor Frix," he said, coming to attention. "The queen's guard."

She doesn't need a guard, he wanted to say, but where had Jared been while Keira was up? Sleeping. And where was his body armor? Or weapons? He had none. He was standing there in his boxers, which only out of sheer luck had he thought to pull on at all. He made a mental note to be better prepared from now on. What right did he have to lecture Keira on complacency when he wasn't any better?

She took the last two daggers and sank them into the wall. "Bath," she said and spun on her heel. She swept a towel off a table and breezed out of the room.

Jared turned to Tibor. Peeking out from his body armor was the light blue tunic of a eunuch. *No way.* The big man must have caught the surprise in Jared's expression because his lips compressed and his dark eyes became unreadable.

Hmm. Jared made yet another mental note: find out more about this man who looked more like a pro wrestler than the neutered boys wandering around. Yet, the guard didn't seem to show any interest in Keira in a sexual sense that Jared could tell, and that would take some discipline, seeing what she was wearing—or, more accurately, not wearing. "How long have you been my wife's guard?"

"Since she was ten cycles."

Since Keira was six or seven, Jared calculated. About the time she lost her family. "My pleasure to meet you, Tibor Frix. We'll be getting to know each other well, I suspect." He gave the man a nod. It wasn't Coalition custom to shake hands. Jared turned to follow Keira and stopped. "Tibor, I know you're used to coming and going in the queen's chambers, but in the future it might be a good idea to make sure you let us know—that you let *me know*—before you enter. The queen needs more privacy now that she's married."

The guard's mouth twitched. Was he embarrassed? "Yes, Your Highness."

"Sir," Jared said. "You can call me *sir.*"

He'd rather the staff called him Jared but he'd left informality behind the day he'd left Earth.

He made his way to Keira's bathing chamber. Taye and the other eunuchs milled about, tidying up and generally appearing busy although it was hard to tell exactly what they were doing. Completely nude, Keira stood in the pool under a waterfall gushing from a rock wall. Water streamed over her skin as she lifted her arms over her head to shampoo her hair. Water sluiced over her breasts. She turned, lifting her face to the waterfall as water streamed over her bare ass and thighs. Jared was hard before his eyes ever got that far.

"A refreshment, sir?" Taye offered him a tray loaded with glasses of fruit juice and breads.

Jared glanced from the young man to his naked wife and back again. It was wrong, damn wrong: no less than a half-dozen boys milling around while his bride bathed and he battled a raging hard-on that was difficult to hide standing in a pair of boxers. Jared took two glasses of juice off the tray. "You may leave. You and the others."

"But the queen is bathing."

"Exactly my point," he told the baffled attendant. "Go on, take the others with you. I'll call you when it's all right to come back in."

The eunuch's pale blue loincloth flapped as he hurried to gather up the others. The herd of young men turned to bow in unison before they disappeared out the door.

Jared downed a glass of juice. Breakfast juice contained nano-computers that refreshed the mouth and cleaned the teeth. The shortcut to toothbrushing was one more Coalition creation he was fast growing attached to. His wife was another.

He stripped and dove into the pool, breaking through the surface behind Keira. "I didn't have a chance to say good-morning."

She went rigid in surprise but only for a second. Nuzzling her neck, he slid his hands up her wet belly to hold her breasts. Her nipples puckered at his touch. *She* might not be overly eager to see him, but her body was.

He turned her around to face him. Water gushed down. Her drenched hair streamed over her bare breasts, making her look like a sultry mermaid. "You didn't look very happy in the gym. Last night left me in good spirits. Why not you?"

He expected a defensive response. He expected an argument that would somehow place the blame on him. He expected anything but the reaction he got.

She threw her arms around him and kissed him full on the mouth. He staggered backward as she practically climbed up his body, wrapping her legs around him. He'd expected they'd talk first, work out her anger; then they'd make love. But she'd reversed it. A guy's dream. He'd take sex over talking, any day.

She moaned in his mouth, writhing against him, trying to push him inside her before he got his balance. He supported her weight with both hands cupping her cheeks, swinging her around to the closest rocks. He sat her down and thrust into her.

She was so hot that he nearly came right

there. Shuddering, he steadied himself and rammed into her, urged on by her cries. She gripped him tightly, inside and out. Clawing at his biceps, hard with the tension of his holding her in place, she dragged him down for a kiss. He couldn't believe she wasn't sore. God bless nanomeds.

He felt her orgasm begin before he had a chance to touch her and bring her there. Hard and fast, he plunged into her until she arched her back and cried out, a husky, soft sound.

"Jared," he said harshly in her ear as she shivered in his arms. "Say my name." He wanted her to know who made her feel this way. He wanted her to know whom she belonged to. Somehow it was important, deeply important, and it was becoming even more so as time passed. He didn't want her to see him as an interchangeable part. She could have married any one of a number of men, including Cavin, but Jared wanted her to believe that not one of them would have made her feel this good.

But as he exploded inside her, pleasure ripping through him, she turned her head to pant against his jaw. "Jared," she gasped for the first time. "Ah, Jared…"

Her hands clenched in his wet hair as she clung to him. Until now, she'd moaned, gasped and sighed as they'd made love. She'd uttered every sound but his name, as if she'd stubbornly held back from doing it. Something had changed. He wasn't sure what but he'd sure as hell try not to screw it up.

He remained inside her, kissing her, holding her, until they'd both settled down.

They sank into the warm pool, half floating, arms wrapped around each other. He sensed she needed this part as much as she'd needed the sex. He'd learned something else about his goddess. She chose physical contact over talking. In that respect, she was more of a guy than any woman he'd ever met. The craziest mix of helpless femininity and kick-ass brutality. Predictability wasn't in the equation. "I liked our good-morning," he said, nuzzling her.

"I liked it, too. And now I'm hungry."

She took his hand and led him out of the pool. They slipped into robes. A buffet was set up with a variety of food and fruit. Her longing gaze went to the door, where the eunuchs had exited. She picked up a plate, pouting. "Will I ever be able to be served when dining with you?"

"Of course. That wasn't my issue this morning." He whispered in her ear, "Privacy was."

She smiled and shrugged. "As you wish."

"Though I see you had no problem being naked in front of them."

"They are eunuchs. Besides, I'm not ashamed of my body."

"And you have no reason to be...but would you have been as comfortable with the eunuchs watching as we made love?"

"They wouldn't have watched."

"Keira." He sighed. She was so very sheltered, he realized. How many here were taking advantage of that naiveté? He needed her strong because he needed the Coalition strong, because it was how he'd keep Earth safe. Mind-blowing sex aside, *that* was the reason he was here. He couldn't lose sight of that. "I doubt they would let you know they watched, but they would have. Everyone in this palace sees and hears more than you think they do, because their queen has her head stuck in the sand."

She put down a serving spoon with a bang. "I told Tibor what you said about the security threat to the palace. He said there is nothing wrong!"

"Does he know what happened the day I arrived? Why I crash-landed?" He followed her to the table.

She sat and stabbed at her breakfast. He watched as she mangled a piece of bright yellow fruit. Shoving a piece in her mouth, she chewed angrily. "There was a malfunction on the transport that brought you here. Your men were killed, as was the crew. It was a terrible accident."

"That's what they'd like you to believe. The crew said we were under attack. We were attacked because I was onboard. Keira, someone feels very strongly about keeping the goddess of Sakkara unmarried. My near death on the transport proves it."

Keira went pale. "How dare you make such an irresponsible accusation? First you insult the security of this palace. Now you say one of our transports was attacked while carrying a very important passenger? You insult me, Earthling." She threw down her napkin.

He covered her hand with his, holding tight.

"Is that to soothe me or to keep me from escaping?"

"Both," he admitted. He used a low and

private tone even though no one remained in the room. Who knew who eavesdropped on the queen? Man, he was sounding more and more paranoid, but something in his gut told him he'd better be. "Tell me, then, where are your former suitors? Any of them still around?"

"I don't know or care, Earthling!"

"Do you know what happened to your most recent husband-to-be?"

She put on her haughty expression, the one he'd learned she used as a shield when she felt uncertain. "No one in the palace knows. The coward heard the rumor about my skill with a sword, perhaps, and ran away."

"I know for a fact that isn't true. I met him when he escaped to Earth, looking for a hiding place," he fudged.

She lowered the piece of fruit she'd brought to her mouth. "What? He ran off to a non-Coalition world to escape me?"

"He was running for his life—not from you, but from a REEF assassin. His name was Cavin of Far Star and he was one of the highest ranking military officers in your space force. Prime-major Far Star believed the assassin's kill order came from someone high in the Coalition government because they didn't want you marrying him."

"That's what he tells you. REEFs aren't sent after just anyone. It may be that he was involved with some illegal activities in the military. Good officers go bad. I don't know—or care. The games of soldiers do not interest me."

"Keira…" The woman was in major denial. She was blind to everything going on around her. The more he illuminated, the angrier she got. "When my transport exited the last wormhole, something hit us. The pilots shouted that we were under attack. Something came through their control console—an energy pulse, I think—and killed them both. Then all the biopods started ejecting."

"They're supposed to do that. I remember the briefings from when I used to travel with my family."

The way her voice hitched on the word *family* really got to him. It wasn't hard to imagine her as a lost little orphan in this huge palace. In some ways, she still was. He wasn't sure what passed for grief counseling in this alien society, but whatever it was, he wondered if she'd had enough. Fifteen or so Earth years after the accident, and she still found it difficult to discuss.

"Vacations?" he asked gently.

"Sometimes. We'd combine official duties with pleasure, yes, but the main purpose was to visit other worlds to give worshippers the chance to pay homage to us." It drove home how different their backgrounds were. While he'd been kicking around a soccer ball, Keira had been prayed to. "I have not left the planet since, but I'm sure evacuation procedures haven't changed much. When all systems fail or are in danger of failing, the pods eject."

"I realize that. Then how do you explain those pods getting fired on, one by one?"

Her hand tensed. Fury simmered dangerously in her eyes. Her voice was tight, reflecting just how hard she was trying to hold on to her temper. "It must have been something else related to the malfunction. Not deliberate. No one in the Coalition would do such a despicable thing."

"But what if they were trying to kill me and wanted to make the whole thing look like an accident? Blowing up the whole ship would look too suspicious, so assuming I was sleeping in one of the pods, they destroyed them. When rescuers came looking for the ship, they'd think the pods were lost in space." He imitated Rissallen's nasal tone, "A terrible accident," and frowned. "It was no accident. Why Rissallen wants it to be so badly, I don't know."

Keira didn't, either. She shut her eyes to combat a bolt of fear. Jared had her tied in knots. He had her questioning everything that she thought she knew. It magnified her sense of vulnerability and the almost constant ache of loneliness, something Jared's presence had blessedly begun to assuage—until he'd decided to persist with his insane accusations.

"Keira." She jumped, startled by the feel of Jared's warm hand sweeping over her cheek. "Open those eyes. I won't let you close yourself off, Sunshine. Not from me. Not from life."

She was so weary of being alone. "I don't want to close myself off from you," she confessed and let him take her into his arms.

Softening, he said, "Regarding the transport, I'm going to launch an investigation. I hope I'm proved wrong. I pray I am. But the questions have to be asked. I have a lot invested in the Coalition remaining strong."

He touched a finger to the underside of her chin and tilted her face up. "My home planet's welfare depends on it as much as your well-being does."

Jared's eyes were so intensely green, so alive, like the summer meadow grass that sprouted for such a short time each year. *With him in your life you'll have the green of summertime all year round.* The thought was more soothing than it should have been. He could be taken from her in an instant. Didn't he know how quickly it happened? He was so determined to do good, so forthright in his crusade for honest answers, thinking he could make their worlds safer, but this was the Coalition and the Drakken Horde was clawing at the gates. She envied her husband's apparent innocence of that fact as much as she knew he despaired of hers.

"THE QUEEN'S CONSORT IS ALIVE, my lord. He is at the palace."

At the messenger's shocking news, the young man slammed a fist on the wall. "He was supposed to have been killed before his arrival! You failed. All of you. Again."

"I am sorry—"

"Of course you are, you stupid twit! But that doesn't help me. I'd kill you now but I need every one of you fools in place."

"I know, my lord."

"Has he mated with her?" The question was asked through gritted, perfect teeth. Genetic engineering could make even a monster look good. A young monster, he was. Little more than a boy.

"Yes. Many times, apparently. The two, it seems, have become inseparable." And quite openly attached, despite a rocky start. No one could believe it.

"We have miscalculated, then. We assumed our little goddess would consent just once before ovulation to appease the gods on the mating night. Is she not as frigid as her home world?"

Certainly, everything possible had been done to assure that, the messenger thought bleakly. "It does not matter. She has ingested the required nanomeds, my lord. I have made sure of it. No matter how many times the prince mates with her, he will not be able to impregnate her."

"That is *my* task—and one I will complete very soon," he said with a teenage boy's hormone-infused bravado. "Barring no other disasters. Do not err on this. Do not. The only babe to grow in her belly will be mine. It is my father's wish. At all cost I will make it so."

The messenger had no intention of fouling up. The queen was a goddess. Anyone she took as her mate would likewise command that adoration. Divine rule—it was the purest of all powers. It would bring anyone who controlled that power superiority over the entire galaxy. It had taken some doing to convince the Drakken *not* to repeat their attempt to exterminate the young princess whom they'd missed during their sloppy massacre. After all, the Drakken home world was the original cradle of the goddesses before their ancestors had fled to the icy worlds of the Coalition. To keep the young goddess alive, they'd convinced the warlords of the merits of returning Sakkaran blood to its rightful owner.

The young royal clasped his hands behind his back and turned to gaze out at a storm-darkened sky. Lightning flashed, lending an epic eeriness to the moment. "I, Rorkk, Lord-General Rakkuu's firstborn and a warlord of the Drakken Horde have come of age. It is time to retrieve my bride."

CHAPTER SIXTEEN

JARED STRODE INTO THE GYM where Keira had been working out with a plasma sword, perfecting the ancient moves. Although he often joined her for exercise sessions to practice his martial arts while she worked with weaponry, the sight of the sword seemed to bring him up short. She lowered the glowing tip to the floor. It made a small sizzle. "Don't worry, dear husband. You are not in any danger of losing your male parts. I don't think I'd be able to survive without them."

"That makes two of us." He kissed her and walked across the room to a refreshment bar where Taye served the disgusting hot drink Jared loved so much. Coffee. Ugh. But then her husband felt similarly about the pungent hot and sour beverage that was a staple at any Coalition breakfast table. As he sipped the concoction, his

Earth-jeans stretched deliciously tight across toned, muscular buttocks. He was so marvelously alien.

And visibly unhappy. "What is wrong?" she asked.

"Vemekk, your intelligence minister, denied my claim that the transport was attacked."

Keira's good cheer faltered. Many weeks had gone by without mention of the issue. She'd secretly hoped he'd forgotten it and they could concentrate on each other.

"I asked if they'd pulled the onboard flight camera and analyzed the destruction of the cryopods, and your military leaders freaked."

"Freaked?"

"That's English for shocked and upset. Apparently no one had told Supreme Commander Neppal anything about the pods. Can you believe it? He promised a full investigation by a military tribunal now that Vemekk's office concluded that the whole thing was nothing but a *tragic accident.*" Sarcasm gave Jared's tone a hard edge. "Both he and Fair Cirrus are angry they were left out of the loop during the investigation. Vemekk and Rissallen claim it's a civilian matter. The commanders, of course, disagree."

"Infighting. How tedious. I feel sorry for Ismae Vemekk having to deal with Neppal. He's an ape."

"He's also the leader of your military. Why do you hate him so much?"

"Because he thinks he's better than me. His disrespect shines like a laser in his eyes."

Jared pondered her as he sipped his wretched drink. "What have you done lately to earn his respect?"

"I am a goddess of the Sakkara! Respect is not something I have to earn like a common servant. It is given freely."

Her husband did not appear impressed. "Neppal may sense your utter disinterest in government affairs and dislike it—not because he dislikes you, but because he feels you're putting yourself in danger by hiding from the facts. Yet, he can't say anything to you because he'll anger you. After all, you are the queen."

Was that really what Neppal thought? She'd always thought the man despised her, and so she despised him back. He was so silent and intense that it was possible Jared's take on the matter was true. Bah! She had not become desperate enough to befriend the ape. Not now, nor anytime soon.

She shoved her sword at an attendant who carried it away to storage. "Sit in on the next session of parliament," Jared said. "Your throne is there. Always empty. It seems wrong. Your presence would make a difference to Neppal—to all of them. We'll go together. What do you say? Is it a date?"

She recoiled. The very idea of setting foot inside that horrible chamber made her insides twist. "I have a massage scheduled."

"That's days away. Reschedule it."

She unfastened her arm guards and threw them to a waiting eunuch. "I do not move my massages or any activity to watch the playtime of government cronies."

"Ignorance isn't bliss, Keira, it's dangerous. It's my duty to protect you. That's why I want you to be more involved."

"It's your duty to impregnate me," she blurted out, furious that he was pursuing this. "Anything more is entirely optional and infinitely unnecessary."

She tore off her boots and braces. Turning, she gasped as an angry Jared swung her off her feet and carried her into her bedchamber and away from the curious stares of her attendants.

He threw her on the bed, pinning her there with his body. "So, I'm your boy toy, huh?" He pushed against her. "Just a sex slave. Good for nothing but my sperm."

"Yes," she said, her chin coming up in defiance.

"Liar," he said and kissed her hard, kissing her until she answered with soft, mewling sounds of desire. But the moment she slid her arms over his broad shoulders, he pushed away, leaving her alone and hungering for him on the bed.

"Our marriage is more than that, Keira. It's more than either of us expected. You know it and I know it."

She turned her gaze away so he wouldn't see the truth of his statement in her eyes. Already he'd become an indispensable part of her life. When he was away from her side—meeting with the leaders of the government and the palace staff, poring over data in the library, studying the holy *Agran Sakkara* or practicing the Sakkaran language to polish away his thick accent—it was as if part of her were missing. Only with her family had she felt anything similar. She hated to admit to that kind of vulnerability and *would not!*

"Keira, it's important that you attend the parliament sessions. It will reinforce your position as leader."

"I lead nothing but eunuchs."

"By whose choice?"

She fiddled with a fingernail.

"Your status as a goddess notwithstanding, respect is earned. It can be earned through fear and intimidation, or it can be earned through admiration. Think on it. Which would you rather have?"

"The fear. As long as I frighten them, I maintain my power over them—they who seek to control me, they who take away my choices." She flounced off the bed.

Jared caught her arm as she passed, pulling her close. "Then come to the next session. Strike a little of that fear into the hearts of Neppal and the others. Someone's lying to us. Let's flush out the rats."

The challenge in her husband's eyes almost caused her to say yes. "I cannot go inside those chambers. I have not been there since the day I was summoned to appear and learned I'd lost my entire family."

"That's how you found out?" He appeared shaken, as if her anguish was his. "You didn't know?"

She remembered standing in the vast chamber, feeling so small, all eyes upon her. "No," she said tightly. "I thought my family was in the hospital. I didn't know they'd died. I learned it only then in the halls of parliament. Jared, my heart was ripped in half before an audience of strangers. Please don't make me go. I can't do it."

Emotions surged inside her, her fear and anger chief among them. Scowling, she glanced around the room. "I need something to throw. There's never a good weapon around when you need it."

Jared followed her, snatching her arms and pulling her back. "You don't need a weapon," he said.

"Yes, I do!" How could she explain that the weapons, the workouts, were the only thing that kept her sane?

He gripped her shoulders, forcing her to meet his eyes. The green of summer grass. She focused on that and it anchored her. That sense of security was all she needed to spill what had been bottled up inside her for so long. "I grew up alone," she blurted out. "Always at someone else's command. I was so afraid all the time. I didn't understand what they wanted me to do, how to be the queen, so I retreated, choosing nothing. No one thought to comfort me, not in the way I wanted—the way I needed. It wouldn't have taken much. A hug…" Her voice broke.

A simple hug would have meant the world to her. Knowing she wasn't alone. She'd never admitted her weakness to anyone, not even to herself. But in the face of Jared's quiet strength, his accepting, nonjudgmental gaze, she was finally able to unburden herself. "Anger protected me from the fear," she continued. "Working with weaponry channeled my anger and gave me a sense of control."

"That's why you didn't come to the hospital to see me after the crash." His face shone with relief and revelation. "You were afraid I'd die."

"Yes…" Her head dipped, her hair sweeping over her face. "I threw daggers until my muscles trembled so much I could no longer raise my arm. Then I switched hands and kept going."

Jared hauled her to his chest, squeezing the breath out of her. His voice rumbled under her ear. "You don't need the daggers, Keira," he repeated. "You have me."

You have me. The three simple words could assuage her fear and all the long years of loneliness. But were they to be believed?

In his arms, she knew the answer. Jared didn't retreat when she pushed him away, something she did far too often. He came right back even stronger than before. She couldn't scare him off, no matter how hard she tried.

His embrace told her the truth: this marriage mattered to him. *She* mattered to him, not only in a physical sense, but for who she was on the inside. The realization filled a place inside her that had been empty for as long as she could remember. She tipped her head back, gazing up at him. "I have you," she whispered shyly.

"Hook, line and sinker," he murmured in his native tongue, and brushed his knuckles across her cheek with obvious emotion.

She shook her head, not understanding the words, but he didn't explain. Instead he told her, "As for the halls of parliament, someday you will walk into that room, Queen Keira. And when you do, it will be because you *want to.*"

He sounded so certain that she believed him.

And it was exactly why she'd fallen in love with him.

THAT NIGHT DOZENS OF CANDLES flickered all around the tub where they soaked together. Jared slipped his arms around her waist and turned her until she sat facing him, straddling his lap, her breasts peeking out of the water.

"Mmm." She smoothed her hands over his biceps and rounded shoulders, over his chest and the ridges of his stomach as he nibbled lazily on her neck. They knew they'd soon make love. They knew how good it would be. There was no need to rush. "It is my fertile time. Perhaps I have already begun to ovulate."

"You know for sure?"

She laughed softly. "Every one of my cycles is tracked and monitored—menstruation, ovulation. I take nanomeds that keep me in perfect, functioning order. I am, after all, a breeding machine."

"No, baby, you're a sex machine." He took one of her nipples into his mouth, tugging gently as his hands circled over her hips. Water lapped around their waists. The next thing she knew, she was on her back on the side of the pool and he was kissing her all over. Gods, she spun on a magical cloud of pleasure. He pressed a hand to the side of her face, forcing her to look at him. His smiling gaze twinkled darkly as he pulled her thigh to his back. "Maybe that's why the sex is so good with you. It's the computers."

She giggled. "Sorry, that's all natural—helped along by the Sakkaran blood. It runs infamously hot. All my computers do is assure pregnancy or prevent it. In our case, it's turned on full force."

"You turn me on full force. Who needs computers?" He was fully aroused, hard as he pressed against her belly. A tilt of her hips and he'd be inside her.

"If I have ovulated, the nano-computers will choose the strongest of your seed to bring to my egg."

"So the guys get a police escort, huh? Technology. Gotta love it." He buried his mouth in the hollow between her shoulder and neck. "I hope a rogue gets through without permission. That's how the best babies are made."

"I could get pregnant tonight or the next."

He lifted his head. "If that's what you want. I have no problem waiting until your cycle's done. We have a lot of time, Sunshine. You shouldn't feel pressured or rushed to get pregnant."

You have the freedom of choice. No one had

given her that before. It was her decision to be made. No, *their* decision. Their decision as a couple. "And you, my husband, what do you want?"

Many emotions crossed his face. Again, she glimpsed his secrets; and once again she made the decision not to uncover them. "I've always wanted to be a father," he said.

She'd have a family once again. "Then let us make you one." She slipped her hands behind his head and pulled him back to her mouth.

KEIRA STOOD PERCHED in blinding sunshine on the summit of a mountain she'd never visited in summer, much less in the dead of winter. She wasn't sure if she'd ever been outside the palace in winter. There was a snatch of a memory of throwing balls of snow with her father, the king, but it was so faint she couldn't be sure. She decided to think of this as her first visit outdoors in winter. The wind was light, which was why her husband—her crazy, adorable, maddening, deliciously barbaric husband—had chosen this day. But the air was frigid and stung the exposed skin around her sun goggles. She watched with wary anticipation as Jared fastened her boot to the thing he called a snowboard. Palace engineers had fashioned several of them just as they had these "runs," and a chair lift designed to her husband's specifications. He had been amazed at the swiftness of the construction, but then he was used to his primitive world that inexplicably maintained a vast fleet of battleships and yet operated day to day without the benefit of advanced technology. An odd, old-fashioned place, Earth was. Old-fashioned and powerful, like its prince.

Jared stood behind his wife, keeping her from sliding by pressing two hands to her hips. "You ready, Sunshine?"

She peered over his shoulder. "It's steep."

"Nah. It's a bunny slope."

A bunny was an Earth creature with long ears and a twitchy nose, as well as an insulting—but humorous, Jared assured her—term for a shallow slope. "It doesn't look shallow to me."

He lowered his goggles over his eyes. "That's because the elevation is so high." Together they paused to peer at the palace in the distance, built into the mountainside like a frozen waterfall. "Just do as we practiced in the gym. Remember to lean into the turns. Like this." He took her elbows, guiding her. The board slipped a bit under her and she whooped half in fright, half in exhilaration. But Jared caught her. "If you have to, just fall. You can always get back up."

She caught his face in her gloved hands and kissed him—a deep, lingering, carnal kiss instead of the peck he may have expected. How she hated to do things halfway. She couldn't help thinking of some of the erotic things she'd learned to do to him with her mouth and grew aroused with the memory. Jared was a good teacher, but thanks to her hot Sakkaran blood, she was a fast learner and the teacher was at risk of becoming the student.

Adjusting her goggles, she readied herself for her inaugural run. They'd be going down the backside of the mountain first, in blessed privacy, out of sight of the palace. It was too far away to see, but she was certain Tibor was standing at the windows in her chambers, frowning about being left behind and worried sick.

Jared followed her to the crest of the hill. "Me first, or you?"

"Me!" She threw her body forward. Powdery snow sprayed, and she almost fell, but miraculously she stayed upright and aimed the tip of her board downhill. Walls of ice sped by in a blur. The wind whistled in her ears. "By the gods— woo!"

"Turn!" she heard Jared yelling from behind her.

She used her arms for balance, managing to carve a couple of *S* turns. On the third one she fell, spinning backward on her behind until her board caught on a bump and came off, flipping her onto her belly. She ended her spectacular run by plowing chin-first to a stop.

All was silent. She pushed up to her knees, clumps of snow dropping from her face and hair.

Jared skidded to a stop next to her. Concern tightened his mouth. "Keira, are you okay?" he shouted, using the Earth word she'd grown used to. He raised his goggles. "That was at least a nine from the Russian judge."

"The who?"

He grinned. "Never mind. Are you hurt?"

She flopped onto her rear end, threw her head back and cried out, "I am wonderful!" She laughed out loud. The sound carried, echoing in the frozen trees. "Now, help me up, Earthling. I wish to resume my run."

"You got it, Sunshine."

And so they did. Jared was a strong, athletic skier. Her first runs were rather awkward at first. Then, with increasing confidence, she understood why he wanted her to experience this. It was like flying. No, better than flying, it was as if she'd soared skyward and become part of the wind itself. She whooped in joy. The rush of air drowned out her voice as she sped down the slope with Jared.

It was beautiful up here, she realized. Cold, yes, but majestic and pristine and fresh. Why hadn't she ever considered coming outside in winter before? Somewhere along the way, she'd been convinced not to. Concentrating, she tried to remember who on the staff had told her, but she couldn't remember a specific instance. Her entire life was a blur of don'ts and can'ts, which had all but dissolved in the sheer joy of this glorious day.

They skied from top to bottom on all the runs except the most advanced and repeated the venture many times, taking the lift to the summit. The silver ball of Sakka's little sun, never high in the sky this time of year, sank lower. Soon it would disappear below the edge of the world and the air would turn dangerously cold.

There was dampness in the air, too, as wisps of silver clouds laced together over the sky.

"One more," she urged Jared at the end of what should have been their last run.

He gauged the amount of daylight left. "Why not?" They climbed onto the lift. The chair swung dizzily above the ground as it soared upward. "And then a hot bath in the pool, drinks, dinner and you."

Their snowboards collided as she leaned over to kiss him. "No bath, drinks, dinner. Just *you*."

She felt his lips form a smile as he came back for a longer kiss. Her pulse sped up, this time because of their physical closeness rather than the exhilaration of the day.

As the lift descended toward the debarkation point, Jared frowned at the sky. "I thought the palace forecasters predicted clear weather."

"Predicted?" His archaic Earthling terms amused her. "There is no prediction involved. What they say the weather will be is what the weather will be."

The first flurry of snow trickled out of the suddenly leaden sky. It landed on Keira's heated pants and melted. Jared laughed.

"Off with the chief meteorologist's head!"

she cried. She lowered her goggles and prepared to ski off the lift. "I must practice my queenly rages lest you make me too soft," she explained and hopped off the chair.

Jared met her at the base of the landing. He whipped an arm around her waist and pulled her close. "I like you soft, I like you hard. But I especially like you naked."

She giggled against his mouth and he kissed her. Silver sunshine filtered through the lowest branches of the trees. More snow was falling now. The distant palace was almost invisible.

"We're doing this run together," Jared said, putting his arms around her waist.

"How can we snowboard together? It will never work."

"That's what they said about our marriage. Now, come on. It's snowing harder and I want to get back." He pushed off, taking her with him.

Keira yelped and gripped his arms when he took a turn much faster than she would have liked. They sped downhill. Snow piled up on her goggles. She turned up the heater. Slush streamed off her goggles and froze in her hair. "You are crazy."

"I thought that's what you liked about me."

She was almost completely blinded by the heavy snow hitting her face. "How can you see?" She shrieked when they narrowly missed a stand of icy trees. "My gods, you can't see!"

"Who says I need to? I can tell by how hard you squeeze my arms whether I'm going to crash into something."

She half screamed, half laughed as Jared expertly steered them down the hill. Laughing, they coasted to a stop where the slope finally leveled.

Boards in hand, they trudged through the snow to their rover.

The snow was falling heavily now and the wind had picked up. Keira sensed the change in the air. The temperature had plunged. Even the heating computers in their clothing couldn't keep the cold out for long. Despite such technology, she and Jared would be dead by morning if they were to remain outdoors.

She shivered, grateful to see the rover, sitting where they'd left it, half submerged in snow. She waited under a sheltering stand of trees while Jared used his gloved hands to push snow off the hood and windscreen. "Let me get it started before I do any more digging and I'll get the heaters online."

Standing in the snow, he leaned over the edge of the door and punched in the code for the ignition. There was a flash of light from the dash and Jared jerked back with a curse.

"Jared!" She bolted toward him.

"No," he bellowed hoarsely. "Keira, stay back."

She skidded to a stop. His jacket was caught on the rover. He tore it off and stumbled backward, hugging an arm to his chest. Blood stained the snow.

The terror that had been a constant companion for most of her life plunged like a shard of ice into her chest. "Jared…" Her voice was low and guttural. "Gods, what happened? Is it bad?"

"No. Just a graze."

She swerved her gaze to the rover. Several metal spikes were embedded in the seat back of the driver's chair. If Jared had sat on the seat the spikes would have shot right through his chest and stomach, impaling him. Perhaps the nanomeds in his blood would have kept him from bleeding to death, if no major organs were destroyed, but how would she have gotten him to the palace? She didn't know how to drive a rover. She didn't know how to drive anything. Because of her, he would have died.

Keira, someone feels very strongly about keeping the Goddess of Sakkara unmarried. My near death on the transport proves it. Now he'd almost died again because she'd done nothing to support him in his quest to find out who was responsible for the first "tragic accident."

A deep sense of shame at her helplessness and ignorance filled her. Jared had tried to get the transport incident discussed in parliament, but to no avail. She should have been the one to demand it the moment he'd arrived. She was the queen and his wife. Yet she had chosen silence. What would the goddesses of Sakkara think of such a cowardly girl?

His jacket was nailed to the seat and the temperature was dropping rapidly. "Jared, we've got to get out of the cold." She fumbled with gloved hands to dig out her communicator. Her breath formed clouds in the chilled air as she opened the small unit to call the palace. *He almost died. He almost died.* When Jared reached her, she grabbed him, dragging him close. Incredibly, his presence soothed her, and so did that of the gods. *They are with you, Keira.*

Her ancestors were fearsome. Their blood flowed in her veins. *You are strong. A warrior.* She took control, quelled her fear. "I do not know who is responsible for this atrocious act, but I have to call for a rover. We have to take the risk. We will not make it back to the palace on foot."

"The workers that built our ski slope made a shelter out of the interior of the base of the lift for when they took breaks. When they were done with the project, I asked them not to dismantle the structure. I thought it could be used in an emergency."

"You are brilliant, my husband."

"Remind me of that when we get inside." They hiked through deep snow toward the base of the lift. The shelter was unlocked. They stumbled inside and shoved the door closed behind them. The room looked barren and frigid.

"I want to see your wound."

"Let's get some heat going first."

Jared skillfully arranged wood in a hollowed-out bowl and used a laser stick to light a fire. Shivering, she watched in awe as the blaze quickly roared to life. "There's more wood piled deeper in the shelter. I made sure it was stocked for survival," he said, rooting around for more supplies. "Food, water, blankets."

The shelter was already warming up as the blizzard raged outside. While it had seemed barren when they'd entered, the glow of the fire and the heat gave an impression of coziness.

He sat next to her on the couch and pulled up his sleeve, grimacing. His muscles flexed, sinewy and strong. Where his skin was torn, blood welled up. His sleeve was soaked with it.

"Your nanomeds will knit the wound," she assured him. He wasn't yet used to having foreign bodies in his circulatory system. Even as they watched, the blood flow began to slow.

"Cool. I feel like Superman." He kept his wounded arm in his lap and draped the other one over her shoulders, pulling her close. They were both still shocked by what had happened.

"Someone tried to assassinate you, Jared."

"Tell me about it."

"It wasn't an accident."

"Tell me about that, too."

She sighed. "What happened to the transport was just as obvious. It wasn't an accident any more than this was. I've kept my eyes shut for too long.

No more. There have been other accidents, too."
She told him of the deaths of the two intelligence
ministers and of the other suitors who'd mysteri-
ously disappeared before they'd ever gotten close.
A tremor shivered through her, and not from the
cold. "I think I have a rebellion on my hands."

"Our hands," Jared said. "Who on your staff
knew of our plans today?"

"I wanted to sneak away with you. Only Tibor
knew." Her heart sank. "Tibor Frix. The head of
my guards. It can't be his doing. He is like a
father to me."

"A father is right. He's no eunuch."

"He wears the blue robes of one."

"He can wear anything he likes, but one look
in his eyes and I don't see a man missing his balls."

"It can't be Tibor. I trust him the most out of
all the people in the palace. I trust him as much
as I do you."

A shadow crossed Jared's face. His jaw
clenched. Why he'd seem so unhappy about
having her trust, she didn't know. "Tell me about
Tibor. How long have you known him?"

"Since the day I returned to the palace after
losing my family."

"How did they die, Keira?" he asked, softening his tone. "I heard it was in a crash. I want to understand what happened."

"I would like to understand, too." She got up to pace. She couldn't sit still. If she'd been in her gym, she'd have been hurling her daggers. "We were traveling home from a pilgrimage on a distant world. I was sleeping. My mother woke me. She said that there was a problem with the ship and that we had to find a safe place. She brought me to an air pipe and told me to crawl inside."

"A pipe?" Jared shook his head. "An evacuation pod, maybe?"

"No. It was a pipe. I remember it was dark and tight. I couldn't move and I couldn't see." *Stay here, Keira.* Her mother's fear-filled voice rang in her mind as if it were yesterday. "'Do not move,' she told me. 'Do you understand? No matter what you hear, do not come out.' She held my baby brother in her arms. She said she'd bring Narekk to a safe place, too. She told me we'd be all right. The ship would shake but the pipe would keep me safe. So I waited. I heard loud noises, like explosions. The ship rocked after each one, violently so. I heard my brother crying. Then I heard my mother scream, and my father yell. I wanted to go to them, oh, how I did. But I promised my mother I would stay put. After that, it was silent. Cold and silent." She hugged her arms to her ribs. "I passed out, I think, because I don't remember anything else until I opened my eyes in my bedroom in the nursery."

She turned and Jared was there, sweeping a hand over her hair. She wanted to drown in his compassionate gaze. "Rissallen was there when I woke, but not to comfort me, because I didn't yet know of my family's fate. He introduced Tibor Frix. To me, Tibor looked fearsome, like a Drakken soldier. But Rissallen told me Tibor was my very own guard and that I shouldn't be scared of him. Then he asked me to tell him what I remembered about the voyage. I lied. I told him I remembered nothing because I didn't want to relive the frightening things I'd seen and heard. I asked to see my parents. He told me they wanted me to get well first. I heard nothing else until I was summoned to parliament and learned I was a queen. 'A tragic accident,' they said." She stopped herself, her heart slamming against her ribs.

Suddenly the truth glowed bright. It blazed down the long, dark years of her life and forced her to see what she couldn't before. Keira went still as a calm certainty stole over her. "Jared, my family was assassinated."

CHAPTER SEVENTEEN

JARED'S LIFE HAD TURNED into a speeding freight train with no place to jump off. He was on for the duration and he had the feeling it was going to be one hell of a ride.

"Tragic accident" was the excuse du jour around here, but something wasn't adding up. "In the *Agran Sakkara,* it says anyone who kills a god or goddess is cursed for all eternity. Rissallen and the others may be bastards, but your people are extremely pious. Why would they do something with such hefty consequences?"

"We're religious, yes. The Drakken aren't."

The Drakken...

The freight train had just jumped the track.

"The Drakken are operating from inside the palace to destabilize the Coalition," Keira began. "Every aspect of our security has been compromised. Anyone who insists otherwise is suspect in my opinion."

"Rissallen… Vemekk…"

"Yes. Of course, this does seem to vindicate Neppal, unless nothing is as it seems."

She whipped her hair over her shoulder as she turned to pace in the opposite direction, her fists clenching. He'd bet his bottom dollar that if she were in her gym, she'd be throwing daggers.

"You won't like the question, but what stopped them from killing you years ago? Why go through all this trouble to keep you alive, isolating you, knocking off your boyfriends and curious intelligence officers?"

She turned, her eyes ablaze. "The leader of the Horde, Lord-General Rakkuu, had a son."

"And…" He tried hard to follow along. Palace intrigue wasn't his thing.

"The might of Sakkaran blood in its purest form is passed from firstborn daughter to firstborn daughter and so on, through direct female descendants of the original goddesses. There is only one, true matriarchal line. The priests have kept records from the beginning of time. Modern genetics supports these records—it can prove or discredit any claim of holy blood. To have control of the Sakkara is to have control over trillions of worshippers. To marry a true goddess into their dynasty would bring them the power they've always lusted after. They have battled us for years, but victory has eluded them. This is why. They don't have me. They don't have the power of the goddess."

Jared dragged a hand over his face. And here he'd thought California politics was convoluted. "Then why haven't they kidnapped you yet?"

"They have been waiting for the son to come of age, because the plan would be to impregnate me with his seed immediately."

The idea of Keira forced to be with another man made his blood boil. "He must be grown by now. They're going to make a move—and soon."

"I think so, too." Fear tightened her mouth and it was just as quickly extinguished.

Jared gripped her upper arms. "They'll have to get past me first."

"They almost did," she whispered sadly.

Sudden pounding at the door startled them. Jared hefted a piece of wood. It was their only weapon. The door flew open and Coalition Army troops piled in, followed by Supreme-second Fair Cirrus. Snow swirled over the floor. "Thank the gods," the senior officer muttered. He turned and called over his shoulder, "The queen is alive!" In the distance she heard the muffled shouts of soldiers.

Fair Cirrus dipped his head, slamming a fisted arm across his heart. "We have come to bring you home, my queen."

"Who told you we were here?" Keira asked.

"Tibor Frix reported you missing."

Of course. Tibor knew Keira didn't know important skills like driving and that without Jared, she'd be in need of rescue. How would the conspirators have explained away his death?

An accident. A tragic accident.

More didn't add up. He thought of Earth and the Coalition's offer of marriage for peace. But if the Drakken warlord wanted Keira as his daughter-in-law, why let the Coalition broker that kind of deal? That it had occurred at all meant Coalition loyalists still ran the show—a good thing—but with Drakken loyalists undermining every move. Not good.

With its royal family exterminated and a queen shoved off to the sidelines, the Coalition government was in shambles. Who was who? It was like playing chess when all the pieces were the same color.

Jared accepted the offer of a heated blanket from the soldiers. With his arm around Keira's waist, their heads lowered into the stinging wind, he ran with her to the waiting rovers. As they lifted off, his wife scrutinized Fair Cirrus with narrowed eyes and frowned as she scanned the other soldiers' faces. Jared knew what she was thinking because it mirrored his own thoughts: whom could she trust, and whom couldn't she?

Only one course of action made sense: trust no one. *Including you.*

Jared winced. His wife was surrounded by liars. Damn it, he couldn't stand knowing he was one of them. It was time to come clean.

CHAPTER EIGHTEEN

THE GROUP ARRIVED at the palace to much interest and speculation. As Keira and Jared strode inside surrounded by soldiers on all sides, palace workers peeked at them, whispering behind hands. Keira knew it was because she was so rarely seen outside her quarters. That was about to change. She was ready to take on the role she had shunned out of fear—fear that had been instilled in her by the traitors who wished to sell her to their leader's spawn.

She saw Rissallen approach. If he was shocked to see Jared alive, he hid it well. "Call an emergency session of parliament," she ordered. "Now."

"Now?" Was that the slightest of trembles she heard in the official's voice?

"Yes. Now. Someone tried to kill my husband."

His startled gaze swung to Jared. The man's

shock was so genuine, she felt a twinge of doubt. *What if Rissallen isn't one of them?*

"As you wish," he said, bringing a fisted hand across his chest.

"I will add extra security," Minister Vemekk put in, seeming to come out of nowhere. Keira glanced around. Every high-level official in the Coalition was here. Word must have spread quickly she was in danger, trapped outside the palace walls at nightfall. How could she tell her enemies from her friends when they shared the same goal—to keep her alive at all cost?

"Ismae, give my husband weapons. I want him armed when he enters the halls of parliament. He needs to be able to properly defend himself if need be."

"But weapons are illegal in the great hall, my queen."

"Assassination is illegal, too. We don't want another *tragic accident,* do we?" In disgust, Keira turned away from the woman she'd thought was a friend. Certainly, she hadn't seen her much since the marriage, but there had always been some sort of bond between them—strong women operating in the male-dominated arena of higher-echelon politics. But Vemekk was either part of the conspiracy or ignorant of it. Neither was acceptable. Keira could trust no one—no one but her husband.

She waved a hand at the flock of attendants hurrying along on the sidelines. "Go to my chambers, bring me a gown and my husband a suit—I don't want to waste time.

"I also don't want to encounter Tibor alone," she whispered to Jared. *Oh, Tibor. Why you?* Betrayal cut deeper than any other evil. "I can bear many things—not deceit."

Jared's jaw clenched.

All over the queendom, politicians were being wrested from their activities, from sports, from dinner and perhaps from lovers' beds. There was a feeling of excitement. The queen herself had summoned them. When had that last occurred? Probably not since none but the oldest of them were in office.

Hustled into a private room, she shrugged off her snow coat. Underneath she wore a skin-tight tank top. She kept it on out of respect for Jared. He simply abhorred her being nude or even partially nude in front of others. But that was his custom, however quaint, and she'd abide by it.

He grabbed her arm. "This is fast, Sunshine. Are you sure you want to do this tonight?"

"You told me the day I finally walked into that room it would be because I wanted to. I do. Oh, how I do." It promised to be a session of parliament no one would soon forget. "By the blood of warriors and the power of the gods, I am ready."

Since the day her family had been taken, she'd been rushing toward an unknown destiny with her eyes closed. Now, for the first time, her eyes were open wide. It was time to rid the palace of its traitors and keep the Horde in the infested corner of the galaxy where it belonged. "I'm going to tell them what happened today, and that it was the second time someone has tried to take my beloved husband from me. I will give that person or persons the chance to confess and avoid the worst of punishments. If they don't—and I doubt they will—they will soon wish they were dead."

Keira shed her clothes quickly. It was difficult to summon patience as the eunuchs slipped on her dress and adorned her hair and wrists with rubies to match a ceremonial gown of bloodred. An infinitely appropriate choice: it was the color of love, and the color of war.

With attendants milling around them, she walked up to Jared and worriedly smoothed his Earth tie. He wore the dark suit she liked best. It emphasized his broad shoulders and narrow waist. Too bad it did little to show off his rear end and muscular thighs, but he would not be pleased about appearing in public in a loincloth. He would not even do it for her in private—and she'd asked. In the midst of the chaos, she had her adorable, sexy, maddening, deliciously barbaric Earthling to depend on. "In the dark, you are my light," she told him. "Your arms are my safe haven, your heart is my strength. With you at my side I feel as if I can fly. I love you, Jared."

He looked so shocked by her poetic profession that she laughed as she came up on her toes to kiss him. "I love you, I love you," she murmured against his parted lips. "You see, I cannot stop saying it, so you will have to get used to it."

She took a step back, a little unsure of his expression. She had no doubt that he loved her back; he showed it in so many ways. But he had never told her in words. She realized now on this important evening how much she wanted to hear those words.

She pouted. "You do not feel the same?"

Shaking his head, he captured her face in his hands. "Of course, I do. But, Keira, I—"

"Supreme-second Fair Cirrus sent me, Your Highness," a security officer called out. "Your weapons, Prince Jared."

He seemed to wince at the officer's use of his official title. Her husband was acting strangely.

She pondered him as he armed himself: a laser pistol, a dagger, shock-grenades to temporarily disable an attacker. She tamped down on a surge of the old fear. If she wanted to save his life, she had to be strong.

Jared shrugged his suit over the weapons, hiding them. "Armed and ready," he said. Together they returned to the corridor.

JARED FELT LIKE THE BIGGEST jerk in the galaxy as he walked next to his wife. The biggest jerk and the biggest fake. She said she loved him. He loved her with everything he had, but he hadn't wanted to say it until she was fully aware of his identity. He rehearsed in his mind how he'd break the news. But not now. She'd need all her focus to address her government. As soon as the session was over and they were in their private quarters, he'd tell her everything.

People had come from all over the palace to glimpse the queen. As Keira assumed her royal stance and moved through the crowd, some touched her, some simply stared; still others dropped down on one knee, hands clasped under their chins.

She touched those who dropped in supplication. "Rise and go with the gods," she told them. Still more bowed, paying homage.

Within seconds, they were surrounded by the pale blue robes of her attendants, who formed a protective barrier between her and her subjects. But hands slipped through the bodies to touch Keira's sleeves or some other part of her. Serene, she smiled. Now he knew why the traitors had raised her to be afraid of appearing in public— it was so she wouldn't venture out and discover her power. *This power.* These people loved her. They'd do anything for her.

Outside the parliamentary chambers, an enormous view screen displayed a crowd that was swiftly gathering to get a peek of the goddess. The screen's image faded and a new locale was displayed where a similar scene was taking place.

"Wave, Sunshine," he told her. "They like you."

Hesitantly at first, then with increasing confidence, she lifted her hand in greeting. In a simultaneous wave of motion, thousands of worshippers went down on one knee.

They left the giant screen behind and entered the halls of parliament. Though he'd been here twice, he could understand why it could be intimidating, especially for a little child called to face a group of strangers and learn that her family was gone forever. Keira, however, was doing fine. She seemed distant somehow, connected to a higher source of power, maybe?

He lingered with her before they parted, holding her hands in his. "Look at you," he said in a private voice. "You're here."

"I am." Her eyes sparkled with as much pride in herself as amazement.

"Give them hell, Sunshine." He gave her hands one last squeeze.

"I love you," she mouthed.

"I love you, too," he said, hoping he didn't look too pained thinking about what he had to say once they got back to their room later. A flicker of uncertainty flashed in her eyes. It made him feel worse. She sensed something was up.

Not now. As soon as this was over, they'd talk.

He sat in his designated seat in the front row along with the leaders of the Coalition, sandwiched between Rissallen and Vemekk, a pair he was sure were up to no good. He watched Keira ascend steps leading up to the podium to the throne, which for her entire reign had gone empty. No more. She sat down, looking perfectly regal.

The crowd hushed as Keira lifted an arm in a signal she was about to speak. "Greetings," she began. He could hear the nervousness in her voice, but she covered it well. He certainly wouldn't want to be up there, preparing to kick verbal butt with betrayers sitting in the audience and not knowing who was who. Keira's eyes were on fire as she began to speak. It was the passion he remembered from the day he'd first seen her. "I have come to order an investigation into a series of assassinations and attempted assassinations that have been dismissed as tragic accidents."

Gasps and murmurs rose. Rissallen made a sound in his throat. Neppal leaned forward to glare at Jared. Vemekk looked as though she was plotting his demise—or, rather, his next accident.

Jared caught sight of Tibor standing at attention close to an exit door. Jared's adrenaline kicked up a notch. The guard's full focus was on the queen. His expression was unreadable, but then it always was. Tibor was an enigma. He'd won his wife's trust, yet the chain of events today put him under suspicion. *All the chess pieces are the same color.*

Jared sat back in his seat, folding his arms over his chest. First thing on the agenda after this was to tell Keira whom she'd married and why. Number two was to slam Tibor up against the wall and shake out some answers.

"I will find out those responsible and, by the gods and goddesses, I will rid the queendom of these collaborators!"

Uneasy mumbling and hearty applause met the end of Keira's short speech. It wasn't her preference being on public display, her fear of it was too ingrained, but she'd done it and done well. He hoped she'd still want to celebrate her triumph after he revealed his secret.

He rose to meet his wife. Neppal stopped him. "I will have a military security detail guarding your safety at all times, Prince Jared. It may impact on your privacy, but I see no other choice."

"If it keeps me and my wife safe until we make the arrests in this case, I'm fine with it." As long as the soldiers weren't sharing the bed with him and Keira.

"Security of royals is a civilian responsibility, Commander," Vemekk cut in. "My office will take care of it."

"Your office handles intelligence, Ismae, which has been as sorely lacking of late as security around this palace. This is a defense matter. My office will handle it."

Vemekk's eyes narrowed. "Maybe you and your soldiers are behind the recent rash of accidents, because it seems to me you are making a brazen grab for power, stealing what should be my ministry's responsibility."

"Guarding the queen is the responsibility of the royal guard," Tibor declared in his deep voice as he joined their growing group.

Jared made a derisive sound in his throat. "Where were you today when someone booby-trapped my rover? It could have killed me. Worse, it could have killed Queen Keira."

Everyone within earshot sucked in a breath. "She's been interested in learning to drive. What if I had coaxed her into the driver's seat? That's the risk the assassin takes every time he comes after me. He or she may kill me or your queen, or both of us. You don't know."

"It seems I do not know even my own husband."

Jared ripped his attention away from Tibor. Keira stood outside the circle, regarding him with hurt, disbelieving eyes. Rissallen stood at her side, his expression smug.

His stomach clenched. He'd waited too long. "You know?"

"Everyone did, apparently." Keira's chest rose and fell, her gown glittering with each breath, her hands in white-knuckled fists. "Everyone but me." She gave him a look of utter pain, grabbed her skirts and rushed from the room.

Rissallen's gaze was calm, almost pitying, as Jared took off after her.

CHAPTER NINETEEN

JARED CAUGHT KEIRA BEFORE SHE reached the exit. She tried to yank her arm from his grasp. "Unhand me, you beast."

"From barbarian to beast in six-point-two seconds," he muttered. "Don't I get a chance to explain?"

"What is there to explain? You've humiliated me, Jared. How could you? Everyone knew but me. You of all people know how much I hate being made to look a fool in public."

"We're not doing this in public." Jared snatched her hand and dragged her into one of the smaller, private parliamentary rooms off the main hall. She folded her arms over her chest and put on her most petulant expression.

"Okay, so I'm not a prince. I'm a regular guy. But I come from a family of famous politicians. I've lived my life in the public eye, much more so than you. Only I'm not a leader. I use my persuasion skills in a different way. I arrange the sale of large tracts of land for commercial projects—you probably don't even understand what that means—and I'm also a military officer, a pilot. I hold the rank of major in the national guard. I fly fighter craft in defense of Earth. In fact, that's how we met, me and you, Keira. I was in a spaceship your last suitor's would-be assassin crashed in my family's backyard—the screen came on and there you were."

Keira realized belatedly that she'd stopped breathing. She blinked, but couldn't think of a single thing to say in response. It didn't matter because he kept going.

"'Prince' is a nickname I used in the cockpit of my fighter. I said I was the prince—I didn't mean I was *the* prince. It was a lie that dug me deeper and deeper—the longer I played the game, the less I liked it. The closer we got, the more I hated knowing I hadn't been honest with you. But now with lies all around you, I didn't want to be another one. I wanted you to know before you went in those chambers and lobbied for my life at the risk of yours, but I didn't want to upset you before you had to make the speech of your life. I planned to tell you as soon as you were done, but that bastard Rissallen beat me to it."

He drove a hand through his hair. "We on Earth did what we had to do to survive, Keira, just like the Coalition does what it has to do. I won't apologize for that. Don't forget, your people called mine and demanded the treaty. I tried to get them to pick someone else. I didn't want any part of this marriage."

Neither had she, but hearing Jared say so stung. She gripped her skirts and wouldn't let go. The fabric flowed from her fingers like blood. His tone gentled. "Lying wasn't the best way to begin a marriage, sweetheart, but neither was your people's trick the day of the betrothal ceremony where I somehow ended up married when I thought an engagement was the only thing I had to worry about. What I think we should do is say we're even."

"But, Jared…"

"Look, I'm not sorry for what I did—I made a sacrifice to save my world—but I am sorry you think you fell in love with the wrong guy. I never intended to fall in love with you. I wanted to protect us both. It just happened." He looked exhausted. "I don't know what Rissallen told you, but now you've heard it from me, at least."

"But, what about your sterility?"

For a few seconds, he stared at her in total confusion. "My what?"

"Your sterility!" Her frustration reached its limit and heated her simmering temper. "Rissallen says you must have known of your condition."

"What *condition?* I don't have one, unless you're talking about a major case of confusion."

"Your inability to sire children."

Jared didn't seem to be listening to her at all. He rubbed the back of his hand across his mouth. Then he let out a quick, disbelieving laugh. "That's all he told you? Nothing about Earth? Just that I'm sterile?"

"Just?" She could not believe he wasn't upset. It showed just how unimportant continuing the Sakkaran line was to him. "Were you ever planning to tell me?"

"About my fake title, yes. Tonight, in fact. But, Keira, I'm not sterile. Not by a long shot. I had a complete physical before coming here and everything checked out fine. I don't know where they're getting this information."

"It's been two cycles and I've not gotten pregnant." She hated that her voice shook. "How do you explain that?"

"Think about it. Someone probably doesn't want you having the wrong man's kids. I bet your computerized sperm patrol is doing the opposite of what it's supposed to be doing."

"Gods…" What if he was right?

Of course he is right. Why would Jared lie to you?

But he had—about his title.

He lied to you.

What was true and what wasn't? She didn't know anymore. Keira covered her ears to block out her internal dialogue. Traitors in the palace had masterminded everything from her parents' death to her monthly cycle. All without her knowing. *Nobody tells you anything. You're always the last to know.* "To tamper with a goddess's fertility is sacrilegious enough without attempting to do so without permission."

"The conspirators are nonbelievers, remember? They killed your family."

Jared could state the obvious better than she ever could. "I will call their bluff by demanding a medical exam, right here, right now, in front of many witnesses." She turned. "Taye, fetch my personal physician!" The eunuch scurried off. "Now we shall see what the conspirators have flowing in my bloodstream. Let the damning evidence be revealed. Come, let us return to the hall!"

JARED FROWNED AS HE PACED in front of his wife's throne. He'd come here expecting *Star Wars*. This was Reproductive Wars!

Several members of the palace medical staff surrounded Keira. She offered her arm for bloodletting. Granted, only a pinprick was taken, but the entire thing struck him as barbaric. Or was it because the issue of his manhood was on the line?

Parliament had turned into a circus. The hall was packed to capacity with people watching the show.

Keira curled her arm on her lap. The procedure was done. The sample was brought to a computer. Results scrolled past. The physicians huddled together, conferring.

Jared couldn't stand it anymore. "What's in her blood?" He hoped to God it wasn't anything that had harmed her. It boosted his protective instincts. He wanted to put this whole bizarre episode behind them and retreat to their chambers where he could get her alone. They had some patching up to do and some preparations to make. With accusations of collusion flying, life was going to get a whole lot more dangerous. Secretly taking her to Earth for safekeeping wasn't out of the question. If the Coalition couldn't take care of their queen, he'd do it for them.

"The results are in," the chief physician announced. She played the suspense to the hilt, letting the anticipation in the audience build. "The queen's blood levels are…"

Jared braced himself, even though he knew all was well.

"Normal!"

Boos rumbled from the audience. Keira shut her eyes. She seemed to be fighting tears. Jared, on the other hand, was fighting disbelief. Normal meant that he wasn't. "Wait a second." He pushed his way to the readout. "Where does it say that?"

The physician acted with open contempt. "See, all her fertility levels are at proper levels."

"Could the results have been altered by some other means? Who's had access to your computer?"

The woman rolled up the computer screen and slipped it in her pocket. "Test *me,* then. Take a sample. Right here!" he shouted after her as she walked away. "Damn it." He slapped a hand on the table. "It's a lie, Keira. A damn lie."

She looked as if she were about to die of a broken heart. Gone was the fire in her eyes. Her stare was flat and cold. "That you are a prince or not isn't important to me," she said in a small voice. "I don't care what you are, only that you lied about it to me."

He crouched at her side and pulled her hands away from her gown, clasping them firmly. He turned a hand over and traced his finger over the inside of her wrist, following the intricate pattern of her marriage tattoos. She shivered. "I'm sorry I hurt you, Keira." He spoke softly so that only she could hear. "My title may have been a lie, but my feelings for you never were."

"You can shake me up like no one else," she whispered. "You can make me feel what no one else can, but does your true devotion lie with Earth or with me? To move forward in this fight, you must make a choice. Earth or me, your wife."

"I can't make that choice. It's like asking

me to choose between cutting off my right hand or my left."

Her stare didn't waver.

"Keira…" He wanted her. He loved her. Their marriage had come to mean something, and he wanted to see it through, to watch it grow into something fantastic. Then there was Earth. Six billion people trusted him not to reveal the fact they owned no space force. Doing otherwise would put them at risk of invasion by a society obsessed with remaining more powerful than its mortal enemy. After only two months living on Sakka, Jared knew they had a good reason to be worried, too. "I can't make that choice, Keira."

"Very well then." She grasped the armrests of the throne with slender, be-ringed fingers and pushed to standing.

He took her arm and pulled her close as her staff and the crowds looked on. She was still his, no matter what anyone said. To put a barbaric spin on it, he'd mated with her in every way a couple could mate. He'd imprinted himself on her soul, just as she'd branded him with hers. He knew it with one look in her eyes. It was exactly why hers were filled with such heartache now.

"I'm going to get to the bottom of this, Keira. I swear it. I'll be up to our rooms as soon as I can."

"Where are you going?" She fought a growing feeling of dread.

"I'm going to blow this sterility bombshell out of the water, starting with Rissallen. I'm going to have him pull the records of that sham of a blood test."

"Bring the security detail with you." Her eyes bored into him. "Promise me you will."

· He wasn't helpless, but he agreed so she'd feel better.

As she glided away, trailing streamers of bloodred silk, he turned toward the prime minister. "You and me—" he jerked his chin toward the suites of offices used by senior parliamentary officials "—we're going to talk. Now."

Both Rissallen and Jared stationed their security squads outside the office. It looked like a *Terminator* convention. "A private talk," Rissallen told them, moving to shut the doors.

Jared stuck out his arm. "Doors stay open."

"As you wish."

Jared checked for his weapons and took a seat at a meeting table. The smart-chair put him at a distinctly irritating distance from the table. This chair would have communicated with the ones in Keira's chambers but Jared had never bothered programming them to save his preferences. *Deep down you always considered your stay here temporary.*

He had a sinking feeling it was true. He'd taken the woman he loved, whom he'd never intended to love, and had blown her trust like a bunch of unneeded pocket change. That was wrong, and it was going to change. It *had changed.*

He flattened both hands on the table. "What the hell was the deal with that test? My sperm count is normal." He couldn't believe they were having this conversation. "I demand a retest, several tests by independent sources. And I'm going to do my own tests on myself and my wife."

"As you wish."

Jared leaned back in his chair. "No argument?"

"I am not your enemy. I know I may seem so. You are unhappy with decisions regarding the incident on the transport."

"Damn right."

"I can't have panic spread through the Coalition worlds."

"So you concoct lies to keep people from worrying?"

"The queen has a delicate disposition."

"Telling her lies won't help her. It puts her, you and the entire Coalition in danger."

"Coming from your isolated world, you can't understand my reasons."

"Try me," Jared said dryly.

"What you see as major happenings are but small incidents in what is an epic struggle between good and evil. My decisions are driven by my responsibility to my people. To the queen's people. Did you know that the line of Sakkara began on the Drakken worlds? They fled after being threatened with extermination by warlords who feared their power. Even after millennia of forced conversions, believers remain amongst the Horde." He lowered his voice. "Just as Drakken sympathizers live in our midst. If sometimes my actions do not make sense, then see what it's like trying to steer your society toward some semblance of a future while being dragged in opposite directions by the lusting of overaggressive militaries. Ours and theirs."

Grudgingly, Jared said, "That does clarify a

few things." *What color is his chess piece now, Jasper?* "But I want that blood test redone. Someone is lying about the results."

"Or someone is lying about their virility."

"Don't go there, Rissallen."

The man leaned across the table. "I know about Earth."

Jared hoped the flash of fear in his gut didn't appear in his eyes. "What's there to know?"

"Do not play the part of a fool. You have no space fleet. No battle force. You tricked us."

Tension thickened the air.

"Thus, it would be wise to give up this particular battle if you want to see your home world safe."

"Are you threatening me, Prime Minister?"

"I'm making a deal with you because I like you. Stop your push for investigations, cease digging around in business that isn't yours, and I'll keep our acquisition force away from your very defenseless planet Earth."

If Jared thought the freight train of his life had jumped the track, it was now speeding straight for a concrete wall. All he had to do was say yes and Earth would be safe. One simple word in exchange for six billion lives. But what about Keira and her people? Traitors had hijacked her government. If he turned away from the fight for truth, she'd remain a helpless pawn in a game played by those without scruples. Billions more could die if it came down to war. He couldn't abandon her out of fear.

Yet, the memory of his vow to Cavin haunted him. *"I won't let you down. I won't let Earth down."*

To whom did he owe his loyalty now? His home, his family? Or to the woman he loved yet had known for such a short time? Both.

In that moment, certainty steeled him. For the first time since arriving here, he saw the true measure of his sacrifice: to save Earth, he'd have to save the Coalition first.

"No deal," he told Rissallen. "The investigations must continue."

"Please, take your time with your decision."

"I've taken all the time I need."

Rissallen reached for a decanter of clear liquid. "Time is our friend. Impulsiveness is our enemy." He slid the decanter and two heavy crystal glasses between them, pouring two drinks. He offered Jared one and lifted the other. "A toast," he said. "To achieving a meeting of the minds."

With a fingertip, Jared glowered as he pushed the shot glass away. "No thanks."

Rissallen lifted a brow. "Please, it is our custom. Plus, a little bit of snowberry liqueur will relax you."

Snowberry liqueur was Keira's favorite. "At the risk of sounding paranoid—go on, you first."

Rissallen switched their glasses. Jared shook his head. "That's the oldest trick in the book."

Rissallen took a small taste of each glass, wiping both with a cloth before handing it back to him. "I'm still alive," he said. "Here. Choose one. I'm honestly not trying to poison you. I don't know why I would. Things are unstable enough in the Coalition without my adding to it."

"True…" Instability emboldened the Drakken and made it easier for them to plan to take Keira. Jared studied the "chess piece" sitting across the table, wondering where Rissallen's loyalty lay. Just because he'd threatened Earth didn't mean he was willing to cut a ruthless deal with the Horde. Or did it?

Jared chose a drink at random. Rissallen emptied his glass, exhaling in appreciation as he swallowed. Jared followed suit, tossing the liqueur into his mouth. He held it there, savoring the tart-sweet flavor before letting it burn its way down his throat. It warmed him almost immediately.

"Another?" Rissallen asked.

Jared shook his head. "No, go ahead."

The prime minister poured another drink. Jared had a vivid memory of tracing designs with the stuff over Keira's naked body and then following the trails with his tongue.

"Prince Jared, was there something else you wanted to discuss?"

There was, Jared thought. Something about investigations. But he kept seeing his finger making circles on the inside of her thighs and everywhere else. She was as smooth as a baby down there. Brazilian to the max. He'd traced the pink, swollen lips of her private parts with the sweet liqueur until she'd quivered, moaning in delight. Then he'd followed with his mouth and had taken her the rest of the way. It was the best damn shot of liquor he'd ever had. Then she'd reciprocated. It had ended up being one wild night.

"Prince Jared?"

Jared shook himself back to alertness. His entire body throbbed for his wife. He wanted to

go to her right now and make love to her all night.
She had the hot blood of a goddess, all right.

"Have you anything else you'd like to chat
about or would you like to go back to your apartment now?" Rissallen prompted.

"Nope. I think that covers it all."

"You will return to your apartment now." The
prime minister's eyes were so persuasive. "It is
important for a man to have some time alone."

"Yes, you've been very helpful. I thank you
for your time." Jared rose. He was feeling much
better about the prime minister. He was feeling
much better about life in general. He smiled.
"Enjoy your evening."

He turned on a heel and strode to the doors.
Nodding briefly at the security team, some of
whom broke off to escort him, he made his way
back to the area of the palace that housed the
queen's chambers. He started to go in the direction of her chambers and stopped, remembering
a reason he wasn't supposed to go there. Oh,
yeah. He needed some time alone. He couldn't
remember why, though.

He headed for his apartments. The guards
allowed him inside after searching the interior
and deeming it a Drakken-free zone.

Drakken-free zone. Jared chuckled. Funny joke. He helped himself to a glass of water and sat at the table in the empty dining room. For a long time he pondered the water glass in his hand. After a while, he grew thirsty. More time passed as he contemplated why he couldn't get the water glass from the table to his mouth. Finally he put his head down and gave up.

KEIRA FLUNG DAGGER AFTER dagger into the wall. Each time Taye retrieved them, she'd start all over again, pushing herself for hours, until she ached from sore muscles and dripped with perspiration. She was nearly ready to fall over from exhaustion. Where was her husband? By now her hurt from learning Jared's secrets was nearly spent. It was safe for him to return. "One more round," she ordered Taye, panting as she swung her heavy, damp hair over a shoulder.

A eunuch appeared in the gym doorway. "My queen, Minister Vemekk is here. And Dr. Parekka."

"What do they want?" It was odd having an ordinary attendant announce guests, but because of the rover incident she felt it was better to dismiss Tibor for the night. It made both of them sad, but the guard respected her desires. She refused to let that ape Neppal place his military security men outside the doors to her chambers, settling instead for the comfort of familiar palace guards.

"Minister Vemekk brings news regarding the prince."

Keira sighed. More news? Hadn't the staff given her enough news of him for one night, whether lies or otherwise? "Send them in," she said tiredly.

Ismae Vemekk and the doctor walked in, their eyes kind but worried. Seething, Keira gripped a dagger. "What is it?"

"My queen, I bring you news of the prince. I'm afraid there has been a terrible accident."

CHAPTER TWENTY

KEIRA STAGGERED AS IF SOMEONE had hit her in the stomach. Her lungs tightened. She couldn't seem to pull in enough air. Her fingers throbbed around the hilt of the dagger. "Is he badly hurt?"

"He is dead, my queen. So sorry. It seems he died by his own hand."

"*Suicide?*" Her voice tore painfully from her dry throat. "Jared would never kill himself." She shouldn't have let him go off alone. She should have made him return here with her. Gods, what had she done?

"He was very distraught over today's findings. But it remains under investigation. He was pronounced dead only a short time ago."

Dr. Parekka nodded gravely. "The body is in the morgue pending further instructions."

Jared was dead. Gone. An odd, wailing sound filled the room and she realized it was her own voice. "No," she gritted out. "I will not accept this on your word." *You are strong. A warrior.* She moved toward the doors. "I want to see him."

"My queen, I do not advise you view the body," her physician advised. "It will upset you."

"Do not shelter me!" Keira turned and hurled the dagger at the wall. "Do not keep me from the truth!" Emotion pushed up from her chest like lava. She spun toward Vemekk, stopped, went to her tray to grab a dagger only to find it empty. She stood for a moment, confused, not knowing where to turn or who to turn to. When Jared was there, she never hesitated.

Grief and remorse tore out of her in a sob. She turned on Vemekk, grasping her by the shoulders. "You said you were my friend. Prove it. Take me to see my husband."

The woman's arm moved slightly underneath her robes. Suddenly, Keira's bare stomach was ice-cold. She glanced down between their bodies to see the minister's hand pressed to her stomach. She gripped something, pressing it into Keira's flesh. The cold turned to warmth and spread. Keira opened her mouth to protest, but no sound came out.

"Hush, my queen. It will be all right."

As Keira's legs buckled beneath her, she heard Ismae shout to Taye. "Help us! She has passed out from the shock of the news."

The last thing she felt was Taye's slender arms sliding around her head and shoulders as she sagged to the floor.

THE MESSENGER STOOD BEFORE a screen displaying the young Drakken warlord's suite. Rorkk he expected to see, but not the teenager's sire. The elder man's presence was a shocking surprise. "Lord-General Rakkuu…"

"Just giving my son some fatherly advice on how to woo a shy, virgin bride."

"Father insists it's not the best approach to bend her over a chair and screw her from behind her very first time. Maybe the second."

The men laughed like field soldiers and common thugs, a throwback to their savage roots and proof that power could be won and maintained by sheer brutality. Still chuckling, the lord-general swirled his black cloak around his shoulders and swaggered close to the screen. "You have done well, Tibor. You have always done well for us. Riches await you, finally, after all these years. It has not been easy for your wives, I'm sure, but your rewards, I presume, will more than make up for their trouble."

Tibor answered with a nod. "They will."

"What is her condition?" Rorkk demanded. "Is she ready for me?"

The boy fairly trembled at the prospect of mating with the goddess. After all, Tibor had brought reports for years on the shy, frightened, biddable girl in his care. Certainly they didn't know of her marriage. The only intelligence the warlords received was what Tibor and the others were willing to release. "The goddess is being readied for her journey," he replied.

"I hope she rests well, then," Rorkk said. "She will not be getting much upon her arrival. And neither will I."

"I am sure you are right, my lord." To the sound of raucous laughter, Tibor closed the screen.

KEIRA WAS AWAKENED FROM A DEEP, drugged sleep by a familiar, low voice.

"My queen, wake up. We must hurry." She smelled Tibor's familiar scent before she peeled open her eyes. "Now," he ordered.

"Where?" He'd never spoken so abruptly to her. It confused her. "What?"

"Hush now," he told her, placing a warm, calming hand on her cheek. His eyes were the kind, fatherly eyes she'd known all her life. "I'm taking you to a place where you'll be safe."

Did she dare believe him? With Jared dead and the drugs swimming in her head, she hardly cared what happened to her.

"Vemekk drugged me," she said, her tongue thick. "And Parekka."

"I administered something to rouse you. You'll be feeling better shortly." Tibor helped her wedge her feet into slippers and wrapped the robes of a servant girl around her shoulders. "Tired," she complained.

"You'll sleep later." He dropped the veil over her face and hustled her out a little-used exit. They hurried through her gardens and then down to the palace underground. As she became more lucid, common sense sounded an alarm. It was late, dark, and she didn't know where she was going. Her husband had been killed and no one had let her see his body. *Another tragic accident.*

She dug in her heels in protest. "I want to see Jared."

"Not now." He pulled her half off her feet, lifting her to his face. He appeared angry and scared at the same time.

"Please."

"There is no time. We're going to a ship now. You are no longer safe here. Rissallen and Vemekk believe I'm handing you over to our enemy. They don't know my real plans. You will see and hear things you don't like, but say nothing. Heed my words, Goddess. No matter what happens, no matter what you hear, say nothing."

A violent memory ripped through her mind: the sound of another panicked voice. *Stay here, Keira. Do not move. Do you understand me? No matter what you hear, do not come out.*

"You are the last of your line, Goddess. By the gods, I will not have it end this way. I will save you."

If only he had been able to save Jared. Grief welled up as Tibor resumed his punishing pace.

"We'll take it from here, Tibor."

The guard jerked to a shocked halt at the sound of voices. Keira lifted her heavy head. Ismae Vemekk and Rissallen blocked their way. "What's he doing here, Ismae?"

"I could ask the same of you, Captain, but I'd long ago suspected your part in this. We all share the same end goal—delivering the goddess to them."

Them... The Drakken.

"The warlord himself asked that I do this, Kellen. You have not been part of the plan."

"Oh, I have. In more ways than you know, Tibor. Everything I have done was to bring us to this day."

Their apparent treachery tore her heart out. She started to protest. *No matter what you see, no matter what you hear, say nothing.*

Was she to simply stand and listen as they argued over her fate like scavengers over a carcass? All her life she'd been told to be silent, and where had it gotten her? All her life she'd remained silent as horrible events had unfolded around her. She may not have been able to change the course of those events, but doing nothing, saying nothing, had sentenced her to a life of frustration and vulnerability. A useless life. A life that had been meaningless until Jared had come into it. He'd encouraged her to speak up; he'd badgered her relentlessly to raise her voice and speak out.

If your voice was not important, would they ask you to stifle it?

No, her voice was powerful and that was why the man she loved had wanted her to raise it. For him, for her people, she would do so. *For you, Jared.* "Unhand me!" She struggled to free herself from Vemekk.

"Keira, no," Tibor warned.

"Give her something, Ismae!" Rissallen said urgently.

"Coward." Keira sneered at him. "Traitor." Her legs folded as the sickening hot-cold of the sleeping drug plunged down her spine. She looked up at Vemekk, who held the blunt tip of a med applicator in her hand.

Tibor shoved Vemekk. "Not this way," he commanded. The woman hit the ground with a thud, her robes swishing. The glint of a pistol showed through the layers of fabric.

Keira tried to shout a warning but no sound came out. A zap of light crossed the small distance and Tibor made a horrible sound, coming up on his toes. He collapsed in an immaculate heap, his long legs and polished boots sprawled over the floor.

Vemekk came to gather her up. "You will be

cursed, you and your family, for all eternity," Keira whispered.

"I'm not a believer."

"Hell is filled with nonbelievers, Ismae."

The woman's gaze faltered at the sight of Keira's certainty. Then she swore in disgust. "Enjoy your new husband," she whispered in her ear as Keira lay helpless. "I went through a lot of trouble to deliver you to him." The voice grew muffled and soon it didn't sound at all.

JARED SPUTTERED AND COUGHED as awareness rushed back in a torrent of cold air. His vision swam as he slid over the floor, facedown and paralyzed. He fought panic. It was like one of those dreams where you try to move but can't.

He was lifted next and carried, his legs dangling. Pale robes brushed across his face. Whispers. The swish of slippers. Then it grew dark, but warmer.

What had happened to him? The last thing he remembered was meeting with Rissallen in his office. Slowly it dawned on him that he must have been drugged. Keira! They'd parted with unfinished business. She was upset and so was he. She'd wonder where he'd disappeared to—

and why he didn't return. Guilt and worry gripped him. "Keira?" he croaked.

"Shush," said the whispers. "Wait. Must be quiet."

There was a sensation of depth to the air. They were deep beneath the palace. A warren of tunnels, his blurry vision told him. He was carried into a small room and deposited gently on a bed. Only then did a light come on.

Dozens of fretful eunuchs surrounded him, their faces various shades of pale against their blue robes and tunics. Jared still wore his Armani suit, but it had been through hell. His shirt was hanging out; buttons and a cuff link were missing. "Sir, the nanomeds have been administered. Soon the toxins will be gone and you'll feel better."

"I'm already feeling better." He pulled off his tie. "What happened?"

"Taye found you in your apartment," one young man said. "You were unconscious. He knew the poison you'd been given because you smelled like snowberry liqueur. He gave you a blood cleaner, which started the reversal of the toxin's effects."

"It was just in time," another said. "Your

breathing had slowed so much that your lips were turning blue."

"But security was outside my door. How did he do all that without their noticing?"

"They helped. They were so worried about losing their jobs for gross oversight, they let Taye talk them into it if he promised to say you died on the way to the doctor for emergency care."

"Nice of them."

"I borrowed the clothes of a security officer and delivered you to the morgue," Taye said. "The report went out that your body had arrived. No one bothered to double-check because you looked dead. I returned with the others and we pulled you out of cold storage."

"Question—what the hell were you doing in my quarters?"

"I came to find you, sir. To tell you about the queen."

Jared sat up so fast his head spun. "What happened to her? What!" After a brief struggle, the eunuchs pushed him back down. It wasn't hard to do. He was as weak as a baby.

"She fell ill upon learning of your death. She is sleeping now."

Sleeping. That didn't sound like Keira. "Send word I'm alive."

"Beware, she is not alone. Tibor is with her, but also Vemekk and the physician. If the wrong people discover you're alive…"

"Okay, scratch that idea." He owed his life to Taye's quick thinking. If anyone found out what he'd done for Jared, they'd both be executed. "Thank you." The phrase seemed monumentally insufficient. "You saved me at tremendous risk."

"We are believers and fear for the welfare of the goddess." At that, several bowed their heads, whispering silent prayers. "And you were kind to us, sir. Always. Even if it were only your welfare alone that we feared for, we'd have helped you."

The door slammed open, rattling plaster from the ceiling. Everyone's heads swerved at once to view the newcomer. Hefting his sword in one hand and a weapon that resembled a futuristic sawed-off shotgun in his other, Tibor Frix staggered into the room.

His face was contorted in pain, his eyes raw and wild. "They got her. They took her."

Jared swung his legs off the bed as his fear

for Kiera brought back his strength. He grabbed the material of Tibor's tunic in his fists and swept the man off his feet and into the wall. "Tell me where and who, or I'll kill you right here, right now. I swear it." Jared's head pounded with blood. He gave Tibor an extra shake.

"He's on our side!" Taye shouted. The eunuchs were trying to pull Jared away.

Tibor placed a hand over Jared's arm. To calm him or to keep from getting strangled? "Vemekk and Rissallen." The guard paused to pant. He was either drugged or in terrible pain. "They sent her to the warlord's command vessel. It is waiting in a secret location just over the border in Drakken space."

"Sound a warning. Come on. We have to warn the palace. Tell the military—Neppal and Fair Cirrus."

"No!" Tibor shouted harshly. "The entire Drakken fleet lies in wait. You will start a war with your wife trapped between sides."

Jared dropped his hands. They were taking Keira to the Horde. The pounding in his head thundered to a crescendo. "What do I have to do to get her back?" He turned his hands up, his

plea raw. "Whatever it is, I will do it. Tell me."
She was all that mattered.

Tibor answered with a curt nod. His face was
tight with pain. "Get him the proper clothing,"
he ordered the eunuchs then gripped Jared by
the shoulders, his big hands shaking. "You must
go alone. No one will notice you're missing
because they think you are dead. I've a vessel
programmed for the rendezvous point. It will
take you directly there—with the proper security codes for docking with the flagship. To
the Drakken, you will seem like one of their
own. I know…at one time I was one of their
own."

"You're Drakken?"

"I was. They don't know I've turned."

The eunuchs returned with black Drakken
body armor and boots. Jared threw off his
clothes to change into the uniform. "Keira said
you were with her since her parents died. She
said you were like a father to her."

Tibor winced—in pain or with emotion.
"Lord-General Rakkuu ordered the extermination. When the princess survived, I was put in
place in the palace during the reign of confusion
afterward. My job—keep the princess isolated

and under my watch until she could be killed with the least amount of suspicion generated. I was to be both her guard and her assassin."

"Jesus," Jared whispered. Tibor had been handpicked to murder a little girl. What kind of man had Tibor been back then for the Drakken warlord to choose him for such a sickening job? Jared tried instead to focus on the man Tibor Frix was now, apparently risking his life many times over to keep Keira safe and alive.

"But she had such pluck. Such spirit. She fought everyone off, including me. I grew attached to her. I grew to love her like a daughter. As time passed, I changed from her prison guard to her true protector. And from true protector, I became a true believer. It was I who convinced the warlord of the benefits of marrying Keira to his son. I figured it would buy her more time, and me more time to make arrangements for her sanctuary. And now I have failed."

Jared threw a eunuch's robes over the Drakken uniform to disguise it. "No, we haven't. I *will* see Queen Keira safe." He refused to consider failure. It wasn't an option. Keira's world was all that mattered now. And getting her back in his.

CHAPTER TWENTY-ONE

As she drifted in and out of consciousness, Keira lost count of the number of wormhole jumps the small ship made. Each passage was worse than the next, and she feared for the structural integrity of the vessel. By the time they reached their destination, she felt storm-tossed and space-sick but infinitely more alert. The drugs in her system had run their course and neither one of the traitorous pilots had thought to give her more.

An enormous Drakken vessel loomed outside her window. The thump of docking punctuated the end of the journey.

The heavy thuds of booted soldiers' feet thundered toward her. Keira, dressed as a servant girl, was pulled from the craft and shoved ahead of them.

The ship smelled of men—sweat and armor. A

barracks would smell this way, she thought. The soldiers marched her ahead of them to the bridge.

They approached two men sitting on chairs and stopped. The younger one sprawled insolently, a leg hooked over the armrest. He leaned his elbow on the other armrest, supporting his cheek with one finger. He looked like his sire— pale skin, dark eyes and hair—but Keira doubted if he was even shaving yet. He'd barely begun to develop his manly form. *He's only a boy.* "She needs a bath," he said. The older man barked out a laugh and slapped his hands on armored thighs.

Rakkuu and his spawn. Keira's nostrils flared. They mustn't see her fear, they mustn't. *You are strong. A warrior.*

They guffawed like drunken soldiers after a victory, laughing at her and categorizing her faults. "Take off your clothes," the boy bellowed. "I want to see what I'm going to fuck all night. Go on, show me your body, Goddess."

"You wouldn't know what to do with it," she muttered.

"What did she say?" The younger warlord Rorkk looked shocked. "I thought you said she was shy."

"Let us see how shy she is," the elder man said. Monster. Scourge of the galaxy. "Take off your clothes," he ordered her.

Keira glanced around the bridge. Other men lounged about. Not a female in the bunch. No allies. The thought of being naked and defenseless in front of them nearly dropped her to her knees. But she was a skilled actress; she'd acted all her life, rarely showing anyone who she really was. *Jared knew the real you.* Yes, these monsters would not. To reveal her true self was to reveal her vulnerability and fear.

Opening her robes to their hungry perusal, Keira lowered her eyes and prayed to get through this night with her dignity intact. Before Jared had come and flooded her life with happiness and light, dignity had been all she'd had. It had served her well as a protective wall, one as high and as wide as those surrounding the Goddess's Keep.

Rakkuu's spawn slid off his chair. His uniform hid his arousal but it blazed in his eyes. "To my bunk, virgin goddess. My blushing bride."

So they thought she was untouched, did they? The traitors on Sakka had done their jobs well.

As the men exchanged ideas on what could be done with her and how, she furtively searched the bridge, the corridor, and glimpsed into rooms visible from where she stood. Only a few guards remained, all of them rough-looking and mean. But there were many more on this, the flagship of the Drakken fleet. Were there believers among them? A ray of hope warmed her. The key was to see more of the ship. "I want to bathe first," she said.

"She wants to bathe," the boy said in a high voice, mimicking her regal tone. The men broke into more laughter.

Rorkk picked up a stick of some kind and gestured down a corridor leading from the bridge. Closing her robes, Keira walked ahead of him. Periodically, he'd jab the stick in her lower back and murmur what he planned to do with it once he got her alone. "Shall the stick take your virginity, Goddess, or shall I?"

She gritted her teeth, but somehow kept her temper under control. The vessel was far larger than she'd realized. She began to despair of ever escaping this ship. Her cycle was ripe for becoming pregnant. If the Drakken had altered anything in her blood to refuse Jared's sperm and accept this creature's, she'd conceive. She'd be raped and humiliated and made to bear children whose mixed Hordish and Sakkaran blood would change the course of the galaxy. If she'd thought her life was stifling before, it didn't come close to what her future would be like.

Yet in so many ways, what was happening to her felt familiar. Ultimately, others had always made decisions for her and had ever since she'd taken the throne as a child-queen, a terrified little girl trying to stay afloat in a sea of what she didn't understand. *Look at you, weakling, doing the warlord's bidding, pleading for a bath so you can delay the inevitable a little longer. You're still that girl.*

She was supposed to hold absolute and holy power over trillions, but here she was, a plaything for despots. What kind of goddess had no free will, no control over her destiny, no *choices?*

Not this kind of goddess. Her fear and anger transformed into power. She made the decision that one or both of the Drakken leaders were going to die. She'd been a useless figurehead, no more than a breeder, and these men planned to use her in the same way. In that, they were no different than her people. She'd never really mattered, not the way she'd longed to matter, but this was her chance, was it not? Look at the sacrifices Jared had made. She knew he'd not taken his own life. He'd died fighting *her* fight. In his honor she would continue it. *You will finish it.* Yes, even if she died this day, she would have done something to help the galaxy.

That sounded frighteningly altruistic. Perhaps she was finally learning what it meant to be a goddess.

Her breathing quickened as she looked around for an opportunity. *If you look, you will not find it. Let it reveal itself.* That was the voice of her mother! As she opened herself to the power of the goddesses, lost memories seeped out, snatches of lessons, sage sayings.

"In here." The warlord's stick jabbed into her back, steering her into a large suite. She heard voices not too far away. Guards? Attendants? *Let it reveal itself.*

The suite was a typical military man's room. A simple bunk occupied one corner. An entire wall was covered with warlike souvenirs: images of battles, medals, ancient parchments from the age of paper…and a plaque displaying a complete set of daggers with jeweled hilts, just like the ones she had at home. Her mouth curved in a smile as she stepped into the room.

But the warlord grabbed her by the hair, pulling her backward and off her feet. She hated the yelp that escaped her throat.

"Take off your robes." He twisted a fist in her hair and shoved her to her knees. Her insides clenched with fear as she felt her face flush with anger. "Ah, she blushes. My shy mate. Don't be bashful."

He pressed her face to the carpet. She turned her head so she could breathe. Ragged gasps of air hissed in and out. "You promised me a bath," she said. "It is a wedding night tradition. I was told the Drakken are as civilized as the Coalition. Is this not true?"

He shoved her. "Don't take long."

Her scalp stung and throbbed. As she crawled away, he yanked the robe off her and tapped the crop against her bare rear end. "There it is—the holy ass. That's where I plan to start with you, you know."

"And waste your seed?"

"I don't plan to waste anything, least of all my

seed, Goddess." He slapped the stick against her rear, and she suddenly understood what he planned to do with it.

She hid a shudder of dread as she climbed to her feet, backing closer to the wall and the daggers. Poor boy. He would have no idea of her skill with the weapons, no idea that she as a female would have even noticed them on the wall.

His gaze lingered on her body. For a young boy with little or no experience, the sight of a naked woman was fascinating enough, let alone one of a Sakkaran goddess. She smoothed a hand over her belly, drawing his wide eyes to her crotch. She paused there as he waited almost breathlessly to see what she'd do. With a powerful grunt, she kicked her leg up, hitting him square in the balls.

He bellowed, staggering backward. She tore a dagger off the plaque, hefting it in her hands.

"Are you going to kill me, Goddess?" he taunted, raising his stick as a counterthreat. "With my father on this very ship? With a full squadron of imperial guards outside the door? Think again."

"All right." She paused. "I thought about it again." She took aim and flung the dagger.

"Huh!" As she'd intended, it caught the sleeve of his uniform coat, pinning his arm to the wall. She grabbed another knife and nailed his other sleeve.

Now she would change history. The thought exhilarated her, even though she'd likely die before she got off the ship. No one would ever again be able to call Keira, Queen of Sakkara, a useless figurehead.

She grabbed her servant robes, throwing them around her as the warlord struggled to get free. Fabric tore. He'd soon be loose. She tumbled into the corridor. "Help me!"

A group of mean-looking Drakken guards turned to glare at her in disbelief. She must look a sight, her hair wild, her face bruised, her eyes wide with fear. "You must help me. I'm the goddess. The Sakkaran goddess. I was stolen from the Keep and brought here to be raped."

Several of the men swore and made the sign of the goddess. *Thank you.* "Watch your tongue, whore. It is blasphemy what you speak."

Shaking, she turned her hands palm up, revealing the tattoos imprinted on her wrists. "Look, the holy marks of my marriage. The mark of the goddess." She stood still, her heart kicking her ribs so hard she was sure it would break free. The soldiers gathered. Their eyes widened. "She is the goddess...."

"The goddess."

"She is amongst us."

They went down on their knees. She'd taken a wild chance that they'd be believers. It was said that most of the Drakken still were and that only their leadership were not.

"Stop her!" Freed, Rorkk stumbled out of the suite. "She tried to kill me."

"I don't have to," she said. "They will."

She heard his plaintive cries and the snap of his stick as the gang of angry men closed in on him. And then she ran.

CHAPTER TWENTY-TWO

JARED CLAMBERED DOWN the tunnel leading from the docking station. Dressed in his Drakken uniform, he attracted a few curious glances but nothing suspicious. Tibor had told him exactly where to go, but even if the guard hadn't, Jared's gut instinct would have steered him to his mate. It had to be his imagination, but he was picking up her scent. She was here. He fought off images of her being abused at the hands of the warlord. It was her nightmare, he knew, and he would save her from it.

He became aware of some sort of commotion. Guards ran in the direction of the noise. He was almost swept up in the traffic, but he hung back, slipping onto the bridge. The bridge of the Imperial Flagship. If his life had become an episode of *Star Wars,* then this was the Death Star.

"Jared!"

He couldn't name the emotions that exploded inside him at the sight of his wife running toward him. She was dirty and her clothes were torn. But so much love and relief shone in her eyes that it nearly blinded him.

A man in black body armor lunged at her. His cape swirled as he ignited his plasma sword and swung. Keira swerved to avoid him and slipped. Her head hit a console. She crumpled to the floor without a sound.

A raw, hoarse cry exploded out of Jared's chest as the man raised the sword for the killing blow. No time to draw his laser pistol. Jared lunged at the sword, grabbing it by the hilt. His hands closed over the warrior's thick black gloves. They wrestled for control of the weapon. The heat of the blade scorched his knuckles as the sword's blade glanced off a wall.

Muscles straining, they struggled for control of the weapon. They spun, banging into walls and pieces of equipment. Jared would not let go. The man's muffled breaths hissed from behind a black protective helmet. So this was what the four years at Stanford, his military pilot wings and his broker's license had gotten him, Jared thought. A wrestling match on a starship against Darth Vader. As long as the dude didn't say he was his father, everything would be fine.

On the floor behind the warlord's back, Keira stirred. Her slipper-clad feet slid back under her. She was alive! He had to get to her, but he had to get rid of Darth first. *Hang on, Sunshine. Hang on.*

Her moan caught Jared's attention. In that moment of distraction, the man tugged the sword from Jared's grip and swung the blade in a wide circle. Jared flew backward, avoiding involuntary castration by one too-close-for-comfort millimeter. "You must have taken lessons from my wife."

"Huh!" A dagger sailed through the air and sank into Darth's chest. The man staggered backward, clawing at his wound. He crashed into a panel of instruments and fell. His boots gave a couple of twitches and he went still.

Jared swung his focus around to Keira. She stood there, her chest heaving, her wild hair spilling over her determined face. "What a woman," he said.

They crashed together in one hell of a frantic, furious hug. He held her close, burying his face in her hair. He'd never take her for granted again. He'd never let her go. "I'm sorry," he said. "I'm sorry I let you believe I was a prince."

"I didn't care *what* you were, only that you didn't confide in me. But I understand what drove you to do it. I shouldn't have made you choose. It was wrong. You never forced me to choose between my people and you."

"I never will." Stroking her sweet face, he kissed her one last time. "Let's move." They dashed down the corridor to the docking bay. "Was that who I think it was?"

"Yes. Lord-General Rakkuu. You killed him. He's dead."

"Don't rewrite history, baby. You killed him." He threw his head back and laughed as they sprinted to the waiting escape vessel.

WITH THE FORCE OF A BOMB BLAST but with little actual destruction, the revolution of the believers spread from the Drakken flagship to all the worlds of the Horde. Keira accepted their surrender later that week while seated at a meeting table between her husband and Supreme Commander Neppal, who watched Keira with glowing respect as she accepted the Horde's bid to become part of the Coalition. Once more the realm of the goddesses would exist under one flag, within one border. All except Earth.

With Earth's leaders—along with Jana and Cavin—facing them from the original, two-way view screen salvaged from the REEF's ship, Keira finalized the deal to protect defenseless Earth and to keep it from being absorbed into the Coalition. "I declare planet Earth as a holy sanctuary of the goddess, in honor of its being the birthplace of my beloved husband and hero of the realm, Jared Jasper. This holy ground is never to be defiled. It will be defended for all time, but will never have to defend itself. Earth will forever remain under its own, independent rule." She nodded at the planet's leaders. "You have stipulated no visitation and we will respect that."

No unwelcome alien visitation, sure, Jared thought with a private smile, but as soon as Earth became a shrine, it would be showered with gifts from all over the galaxy. Poverty would cease to exist. There would always be wars, but certainly none over oil. Earth would have all the fuel they wanted.

He'd saved his planet. He'd completed his

promise. Now he could finally go about living his life—and he planned on living it to the max with Keira.

As the meeting broke up, Jared saw Keira and Neppal square off against each other to passionately argue a point. Their relationship had changed vastly. It was now built on respect, admiration and trust, and sealed an important alliance necessary for the proper running of what had been a dysfunctional government. Vemekk, apparently a cousin of the late warlord, was in prison awaiting execution for her role in trading Keira to the Drakken, the hiring of assassins to kill Keira's consorts and the murder of two intelligence ministers. Rissallen awaited banishment to a remote farming world for his plan to use Keira as bait to murder the Drakken warlords. He, too, was charged with attempted murder in giving Jared a DNA-specific poison.

Everyone had called for Rissallen's death, but Keira had acted with mercy befitting a goddess, as she had when she'd finally released her rapist from his forced tenure of humiliation at the palace, confiding to Jared she wanted to start fresh. It was a new dawn, a new day. The evil Dr. Parekka was missing, but the best-trained teams were on her trail. As for Tibor, well, his fate had been toughest for everyone to decide.

The man had saved Keira's life, no doubt about that, but the secrets he'd kept had brought the Coalition to the brink of collapse. Keira had chosen the best decision for all, dismissing him as captain of the palace guard and sending him home to his family—and three wives! Jared made a silent snort. Tibor hadn't been a eunuch any more than Jared was sterile. On that note, new blood tests had proved his virility as well as his suspicion that Keira's nanomeds had been tampered with. That had been corrected now.

Suddenly, the huge view screen came on. A military officer appeared. "I have an incoming message for Her Majesty the queen."

Keira strode to the front of the group. "From whom?"

"A group of retired Drakken military men who claim they were once members of the Imperial Wraiths wish to speak with you, my queen."

Keira turned around and caught Jared's surprised gaze. "Assassins?"

She took another step forward even as a terrible sense of dread stole over her. Were these men her family's killers now wanting to ask for her forgiveness for their sin? Would she be able to forgive them? Could she? No one should have to make that choice. "Put them on," she said and pressed a fist to her stomach. *Be strong.*

The men had hard faces of paid killers, but something in their eyes didn't match the hardness of their features. "Blessings, Goddess."

Keira answered with a single, careful nod. Let them say what they'd come here to say. She would not draw it out. She wasn't sure she wanted to hear it.

"We were dispatched to intercept your family's vessel on its way home to Sakka."

Be strong. You're a warrior. Jared moved to her side, took her fist from her stomach and covered her hand with his warm one.

"We didn't realize who we were asked to kill. When we saw it was the goddess and her mate and their child, we took them."

Keira squeezed her eyes shut. "Please," she whispered. She couldn't bear to hear their confession. She couldn't!

"My queen, we did not kill them. We were assassins, but we were believers. We made the decision to keep the Sakkaran blood alive. We brought them to a distant, secret world. We did not tell anyone. We were afraid. We thought the secret of what we did that day would die with us, and if nothing else, we'd thus assure our place in the afterworld."

"You have," Keira whispered, pressing a hand to her mouth. "You have…"

"They didn't learn you were alive until years later. It was because *we* didn't know until later. Forgive us. There are now two goddesses."

"I have sisters." Joy surged in her chest. Joy and disbelief. She was shaking, and so was Jared. He gripped her hand so tightly it hurt.

"You were their one regret. We offered to bring you a message, but they were afraid to do so was to risk your life. Know this, Goddess, they never stopped grieving your loss."

"As I never stopped grieving theirs."

"The hope of reuniting with you lived on in their hearts. But it was something that could not happen without an epic shift in galactic power."

Jared drew her close, kissing her hair as she trembled. "When can I see them?" She turned to Neppal, the new prime minister, and the other leaders. "When can I see my family?"

The screen switched back to the military

officer before she'd thanked the former wraiths. "I did not have the chance to reward them for their bravery and mercy," she protested.

"Let your parents take care of that," a throaty female voice called out as the doors to parliament burst open.

Keira exhaled a sigh of shock and joy as her family—her *family*—strode into the chambers. She shivered, realizing she stood in the exact place where all those years ago she had received news of their deaths.

Jared let go of her hand. "Go to them, Sunshine." His voice was thick with emotion. "Go see your family."

She began to run, haltingly at first, and then faster as she convinced herself they were not an illusion conjured from too many lonely years.

She flew into her mother's arms, drawn into her embrace and the scent that brought her childhood back in a rush of sweet memories. Her father hugged them both to his chest, and soon her new sisters and Narekk, her brother, had joined the huddle of tears and laughter and elation that spread through a war-weary galaxy in a shock wave of joy.

EPILOGUE

"PUSH!" JARED URGED. "Come on, Keira. You're almost there."

Keira gritted her teeth, her breaths hissing, and pushed as hard as she could.

"Come on. Give it all you've got. Push, baby."

"I *am pushing!*" One last time, she shoved muddy gloves against the handlebars of her dirt bike, and with a sucking sound the tires came unglued from the mud.

She walked the motorcycle to where Jared sat astride his and propped it up with the kickstand. Grinning at her, he sat with his goggles pushed into his hair and his gloves tucked under an arm. "Thought you'd never get here."

She pulled off her helmet and shook her hair free. "I told you I could do it."

"You did. And you whooped my butt on that

last trail. Got you stuck in the mud, yeah, but that's because you pushed the limits."

"That's what you taught me to do."

"Come here." She tilted her head and sashayed over to him, throwing her arms over his shoulders. "I didn't teach you to push it to the limit. That, you already knew."

Warm California sunshine spilled down on them. With her family installed back in the palace, she was no longer tied down with the responsibilities of being a queen. Nor was she pressured to continue her bloodline. With so much living to make up for, she and Jared had decided to put off starting a family for a while. They split their time between the palace and the holy shrine of Earth. She turned her face to the blessed sunshine, welcoming it. She adored the primitive pleasures of Jared's ranch. She even sometimes helped cook outside on the contraption called a grill. Mostly, she sat and watched, soaking in the affection his family showered her with. Once, she hadn't had a family. Now she had two.

"What are you thinking about?" he asked tenderly.

"The barbaric pleasures of your provincial home world."

He coughed out a laugh.

"And also how much I love you. Do you love me?"

He flattened his hands behind her rear end and drew her closer. His eyes glowed. "I love you, Keira of Sakka. I love you from your wild hair down to your cute toes. I love your throttles-to-the-max attitude, and how you get mad when you're really scared. I love the way you kiss and those little sounds you do when we're making love. I love your passion and your loyalty to your people, the sacrifices you're willing to make. Most of all, I love that you love me, because all I want is to be a good husband and someday a good father to our children. At the end of our days when you're two hundred and fifty years old, I want you to clasp your feeble hand around mine and tell me you're glad we made the journey." One corner of his mouth tipped up. "Oh, and that I can still rock your world."

"That will suffice," she sniffed. Swinging her helmet, she walked back to her dirt bike.

"Brat."

She stopped, glanced over her shoulder, her smile wicked. Jared sat where she'd left him, his hands in his pockets. "Just because you're the queen doesn't mean you can't get spanked," he said.

"Ooh, we return to the roots of our relationship—corporal punishment. Remind me to get the smart-cuffs out for later. Now, if you don't mind, husband, I've got a trail to conquer."

And a life to live—to the hilt—alongside her favorite Earthling.

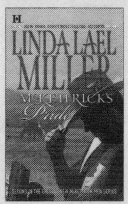

REQUEST YOUR
FREE BOOKS!

2 FREE NOVELS
FROM THE ROMANCE/SUSPENSE
COLLECTION PLUS 2 FREE GIFTS!

YES! Please send me 2 FREE novels from the Romance/Suspense Collection and my 2 FREE gifts. After receiving them, if I don't wish to receive any more books, I can return the shipping statement marked "cancel." If I don't cancel, I will receive 4 brand-new novels every month and be billed just $5.49 per book in the U.S., or $5.99 per book in Canada, plus 25¢ shipping and handling per book plus applicable taxes, if any*. That's a savings of at least 20% off the cover price! I understand that accepting the 2 free books and gifts places me under no obligation to buy anything. I can always return a shipment and cancel at any time. Even if I never buy another book from the Reader Service, the two free books and gifts are mine to keep forever.

185 MDN EF5Y 385 MDN EF6C

Name _____ (PLEASE PRINT) _____

Address _____ Apt. # _____

City _____ State/Prov. _____ Zip/Postal Code _____

Signature (if under 18, a parent or guardian must sign)

Mail to **The Reader Service:**
IN U.S.A.: P.O. Box 1867, Buffalo, NY 14240-1867
IN CANADA: P.O. Box 609, Fort Erie, Ontario L2A 5X3

Not valid to current subscribers to the Romance Collection,
the Suspense Collection or the Romance/Suspense Collection.

Want to try two free books from another line?
Call 1-800-873-8635 or visit www.morefreebooks.com.

* Terms and prices subject to change without notice. NY residents add applicable sales tax. Canadian residents will be charged applicable provincial taxes and GST. This offer is limited to one order per household. All orders subject to approval. Credit or debit balances in a customer's account(s) may be offset by any other outstanding balance owed by or to the customer. Please allow 4 to 6 weeks for delivery.

Your Privacy: Harlequin is committed to protecting your privacy. Our Privacy Policy is available online at www.eHarlequin.com or upon request from the Reader Service. From time to time we make our lists of customers available to reputable firms who may have a product or service of interest to you. If you would prefer we not share your name and address, please check here. ☐

BOB07